The Magic Door

Kerri Edwards

A catalogue record for this book is available from the National Library of Australia

Linellen Press
265 Boomerang Road
Oldbury, Western Australia
www.linellenpress.com.au

Contents

Acknowledgments

Where do you start when so many people play a part in making a book happen? It's a long process, one that takes a lot of patience and time. There are always creative brick walls; no matter how many ideas you throw around in your head, nothing sticks. However, these moments are where you turn to others for inspiration.

So, first and foremost, to Emma, my driving buddy. It was mostly those crazy drives home from work that helped inspire me. We tossed some truly wacky ideas around, and even though they may not have made it into the book, they set me on the right path.

To my dear friend, Bernie, who has always been my champion. Your support and encouragement helped me believe I could do it. You waited so impatiently for the next few chapters to come your way so you could see what happened next. Thank you for believing in me.

Last but never least, to my family. My inspiration, my sounding board, my proofreaders. I know I pretty much ignored most of your ideas, but there were a few gems that snuck through! Clint, Caitlin and Lisa, I appreciate your input and couldn't have finished the book without you. Thank you.

Chapter 1

I couldn't remember when the dream first started, but I knew I'd had the same one for as long as I could remember. I was almost eleven when I told Mum about the dream that kept following me into sleep every night. The same one, night in, night out. It was odd, never dreaming about anything other than that purple door. After I told her, the dream stopped for over a year. I don't know why that happened, but I was grateful it did – until the night the purple door returned to haunt me again.

It was a month ago, the night of my 13th birthday party. Maybe it was something to do with turning thirteen, but I think it was probably more due to Aunt Leah's gift – a snow globe purchased from one of the many countries she was always visiting. Aunt Leah had been to so many places I'd lost count of them. This one, however, was different from all the others she'd given me in the past. It was a small snow globe – you know, the sort with a little scene inside and when you shake it, lots of tiny confetti pieces float around, so it looks like snow. This one was a small cottage in the mountains, with rolling green hills in the background and fluffy clouds suspended in the sky. The amount of detail that had gone into the cottage itself was quite impressive. If you looked close enough, you could see the wood grains of the window frames, and the little curtains looked like they were billowing from a breeze that drifted across the mountains.

But it wasn't that part of the cottage that made me catch my breath when I first opened the gift. It was the cottage door. The purple door. Aunt Leah thought I was speechless because I loved it, but to be honest, it was seeing that door again that stole my breath. Sitting at the table, globe in hand, I could hear the voices behind me.

Oh, look, she loves it so much she's forgotten how to speak. You've done it this time, Leah; I think you've brought back something so beautiful she's astonished into silence. Laughter…

But all my focus was on that door.

To be fair, it wasn't quite the same. The shade was different, and the cottage's door was a lot plainer than the one from my dreams. It didn't matter though, because once I saw that purple door, it triggered something, and the dream returned.

I'd quickly wrapped the globe up again, telling everyone that I didn't want to break it when really, I just didn't want to look at it. I hadn't had the dream for a long time, and I was scared that it would start again now. After the party, I took the globe to my room and put it in the box under my bed. Truthfully,

I tried to forget that I'd ever seen it.

But it was too late. That night the dream returned and it hasn't left me since. Mum told me it didn't mean anything, but I knew better. It always felt so real, like I was wide awake and looking at that door.

I never bothered telling Mum or Dad that I was still having the dream; or that it had started up again. Why would I, when they would dismiss it as nothing – but I knew somehow that it was more than that. They wouldn't understand at all.

The next morning at breakfast, we were all sitting quietly at the table. Dad was reading a newspaper and sipping his coffee while Mum made sure my little sister, Amber, didn't make a mess.

"You okay, hon?" she asked me as she cleaned up around Ambers' plate. "You look tired."

"I'm fine, Mum," I replied.

Dad looked over his paper at me and said, "You do look exhausted, Morgan. Did you sleep okay?"

"No different than normal," I replied again, concentrating on my food.

"Are you still having that dream? The one with the door?" Mum looked closely at me.

I couldn't believe she remembered; I'd told her so long ago, and it hadn't come up again since.

"Yeah," I answered.

Mum's eyes flicked over to Dad's and returned to me so fast I wasn't even sure I'd seen it.

"Every night?" she asked me. She stopped what she was doing and stood very still. Dad did the same, peering at me over his paper. Why were they so interested? Dad held his newspaper so tight I could see the tips of his fingers going white. It was almost like they were afraid of the answer.

"Not every night." I don't know why I lied, but I knew it was the right answer when Dad relaxed his grip on the paper, and Mum started moving again. I didn't want them to worry about me. "Not very often at all," I offered.

Mum smiled at me. "That's good. How boring would that be having the same dream all the time?"

I smiled back but didn't say anything.

"What are you going to do today?" Mum asked me.

"Don't know," I responded. Most of my friends had gone away for the school holiday break. "I might see what Jenny's up to."

"Well," Dad said, closing his paper, "I've got to get to work."

He rose from the table, kissed the top of Amber's head, and winked at me. "Don't do anything I wouldn't do."

"Haha," I replied sarcastically as he left the room.

"We need to go to the shops to sort out shoes for school," Mum added. "Just give me half an hour, and then we can go."

"Hey, squirt," I flicked a Rice Bubble towards Amber, "wanna go play in the treehouse until we have to go?"

Amber poked her tongue out at me. She thought

she was so grown up, but she was still a little kid, and she *loved* that treehouse. "Okay," she answered quickly. "Can I bring my magic stuff?"

Amber had recently been given a magic trick kit from a friend, and she'd been practicing *a lot*.

"Sure," I said. "You can practice on me and show me how awesome you are."

She smiled, her whole face lighting up with happiness. She could be a brat sometimes, but mostly was a pretty good sister, and I loved seeing that grin.

Up in the treehouse, we sat cross-legged on the floor across from each other. Amber had her back turned as she secretly shuffled cards around.

"Just wait," she told me, "while I get this right."

As I sat there waiting, I looked around at the treehouse Dad had built. He'd started it for me when I was about four or five, but I hadn't been in it for a long time. The floorboards were looking a little worn in places, and the rickety old ladder was beginning to splinter. *I should probably tell Dad about that*, I thought, *before Amber hurts herself.* Inside, a bright blue shaggy rug in the middle of the room looked suspiciously like the one that had been in our house awhile back. I'd bet all my money that Mum had happily given it to Amber – I knew she hated that rug and had been trying to get rid of it for years.

"Are you ready yet?" I sighed impatiently.

"Not yet."

I could understand why she loved the treehouse so much. For years the treehouse was the one place I could go to get away from everyone. Mum and Dad used to entertain all the time, and instead of being overwhelmed with adult conversations, I would sneak outside and climb into my treehouse. A few of my favourite teddies and dolls stayed in here as well as the little table and chairs. I would pretend it was my house and would hold tea parties of my own. It really was a special place for me, but I also knew that I should let it be the same for Amber, so I stopped coming up here when she turned seven so that she could have a little bit of magic for herself too. I was getting a little bit big for treehouses anyway.

"Now?" I asked again.

"Okay, I'm ready," Amber announced.

"Good. What are you going to show me?"

"Welcome to Amber's Magical Show!" she exclaimed as she threw an imaginary cape over her shoulder.

I laughed.

"The first trick is a simple one. I will need a volunteer from the audience. Anyone?" Amber looked around the treehouse, speaking to an audience that only she could see and hear.

I smiled and raised my hand. "Pick me! Pick me!"

"Yes," she nodded, "the lovely young lady in the front row. Won't you come on up to the stage?"

I shuffled forward a little. "I'm so excited … I've never been part of a magic show before."

"I'm going to spread these cards out face down, and I would like you to select a card, take a look at it and then put it back in the deck as far away as possible from where you got it."

"Okaaaay …" I selected a card from the deck, the ace of spades. I stared at the card for a minute, a sense of fear coming from nowhere. My stomach started to churn as if I'd eaten something rotten. The longer I sat there holding it, the more I wanted to get rid of it. I quickly put it back in the deck.

Amber gathered the cards back together, unaware of my reaction. "Excellent! Now I'm gonna go through the deck, and I'm gonna tell you which card you picked. Prepare to be amazed!"

I laughed again and watched my little sister fan the cards out. This time the deck was facing her. She wiggled her fingers above, running them over the tops of the cards, trying to draw it out as long as possible. Eyes closed, pretending that she was channelling the energy of the deck, she murmured "Nope, not that one," and continued. Amber looked over the cards at me, her eyes sparkling. She loved this.

"Drumroll please …" Amber stopped at a card and pulled it out of the deck slightly. "Is this your card?" She pulled the card out and turned it around.

The ace of spades!

"OMG, how did you do that?" I squealed. "It's a trick deck of cards! Let me have a look at them!"

I knew it wasn't, but I wanted Amber to think

that I was amazed by her magical talent. I held my hand out, but she refused to give them to me.

"Nope, sorry. A magician never reveals her secrets." Grinning, she hugged me. "You're the best."

"Yes, I am," I agreed.

"Girls! Come down; it's time to go!" Mum yelled from the back door.

"We'll be right there!" I yelled back.

"Let's go, squirt. You'll have to show me the rest another time."

"Okay. That was fun," Amber said.

"Sure was. You did a great job – I have NO idea how you did that."

As we left the treehouse and headed inside, I thought briefly about the ace of spades and how strange I'd felt holding that card. I'd felt fear, but why on earth would I be afraid of the ace of spades? It just didn't make any sense at all.

Curled up in bed later that night reading one of Amber's books – *Operation Hobby Hunt*, which was a little young for me, but I liked that one of the characters went from being a bully that no one liked to a person who'd found a little happiness and friendship – made me feel good, which was why every now and then I would reread it.

"Hey, hon …" Mum's face peered around the door. "Don't read for too long, okay?"

"I won't. I'm nearly finished anyway."

"Okay," she said. "Love you."

"Love you too."

"Good night."

"Night, Mum," I replied, yawning, and feeling more tired than I'd thought, I put the book down on my bedside table and fell asleep in less than a minute.

I am lying there, in my bed, fast asleep. The bedsheets are drawn up to my chin, covering my body except for my left foot hanging off the bed. Silence fills the room, disturbed only by the quiet ticking of the alarm clock on the bedside table. I lay motionless, breathing deeply. My eyes move slowly under my eyelids, and it looks like I am enjoying my dream as a slight smile curves the corners of my mouth.

Across the room, the wall is bare other than the massive poster of Zac Efron, the subject of my latest crush. There's a stillness in the room – as if an audience was holding its breath expectantly. Not even the dust motes dare interrupt the peace.

Slowly, so slowly that you have to look twice or you would miss it, the outline of a door pulses within the wall. First, a faint framework in bold straight lines, holding for a few seconds and then disappearing again. Another pulse, an outline, then the wall begins to bulge out a little before it disappears again. This continues for a couple of minutes, trying to decide whether to make its appearance or not. It finally completes its transition onto the wall and maintains its place next to Zac. Nothing about this door suggests malevolence or a sinister motive. The door stands there, burned into the wall like it was initially built with the house. It begins to glow, determined to cement its place in our world.

Gradually I turn in bed, my sleep disturbed by an unnatural light in the room. I rub my eyes in disbelief as I take in the new door that has suddenly appeared on my wall. I sit up in bed, confused. The door doesn't move, nor does it open or close. I shake myself to check if I am awake or in the middle of a dream. Still, the door stands strong, like it has always been there.

I drag the warm quilt off me as I swing my legs over the side of my bed. Whatever this door is, wherever it has come from, I feel like I need to investigate. I make my way slowly across the room as I study the door. The door is a deep purple. I am distracted by the glow that races around the frame of the door. It keeps my focus on the edge rather than the door itself. I tear my eyes away from the visible glow and try to focus more on the bulk of the door.

As I look closer, I see hundreds of symbols, maybe thousands, racing across the door as if trying to beat the others to an invisible finish line. The marks are faint, almost beyond my line of sight, but still, I know they are there. I reach out and touch the door, hoping to feel the symbols run under my fingertips, but it's as if they aren't there. I try the door handle, but the door is locked. I stand still for what seems like forever, studying everything I see, hoping to find some sort of pattern or purpose to what is in front of me. Frustrated and getting nowhere, I back up until I reach my bed and climb back in. I lay there, head turned toward the purple door, still studying its intricate markings. My eyelids get heavy again and gradually close as I fall back into a deep sleep.

The dream had become such a regular occurrence in my life; it had become familiar to me. It seemed normal to dream of a purple door every night; healthy to dream the same sequence, like a broken record that would catch in the same spot and churn out the same words until you either turned it off or went insane. It had become so common it began to feel more like a memory than a dream.

Why was I the one having these dreams? Why not Amber, or Mum or Dad? What was it about me that meant I was the one who had to see this door every night? I asked Amber once if she ever had any strange dreams, but she just looked at me and shook her head.

I was angry at Aunt Leah for giving me that globe. It didn't matter that it was now tucked away in a box under the bed. What mattered was that once she had given it to me, this dream came back. I knew deep down that the snow globe was the only reason it had started up again. And I didn't think anyone could convince me otherwise. As far as I was concerned, it was all her fault.

There had to be a way to change this endless path I seemed to be following. I grabbed my iPad from my desk and lay down on the bed. Typing in 'recurring dreams', I waited eagerly for the page to load, hoping that somewhere in here would be my answer. I watched the little icon roll around impatiently.

Finally, an article appeared on the screen.

> *"A recurring dream can represent something important that your subconscious mind is desperately trying to convey, but you haven't got the message yet. These dreams serve to remind us of important concerns in our lives."*

I couldn't think of anything that was concerning in my life. I shrugged and continued reading.

> *"A common reason for having a recurring dream is un-interpreted dreams. They are common because people do not know how to interpret the meaning of their dreams, so their subconscious mind will continue to send the message until the dream is understood or the underlying issue is resolved."*

I guess that was certainly true for me, I thought. I didn't know what this door meant, and it sounded like it wouldn't stop until I figured it out.

> *"The best way to end a recurring dream is to resolve the message conveyed by your*

I was right back where I started. A dream, a door and no idea how to make it go away. If doors were supposed to represent transitions in our lives, what was I transitioning to? I was supposed to start high school this year, maybe that was it? The more I thought about it, the more this might have a little truth to it. I hadn't been worried about high school, but maybe deep down I was and just didn't realise it. If that was the case, I wouldn't lose this dream until I started at the new school this year. That was still six weeks away.

I sighed and headed towards the bedroom door.

I spent the rest of the day resigned to the fact that I would continue to have this dream for the next six weeks. I could get through that – it was only a month and a half – a small price to pay, to have a little patience if it meant I would never have it again. Besides, there was nothing terrible in the dream that could hurt me. The dream never changed, and I knew exactly what was going to happen.

That was until the night it did, and it changed my life forever.

Chapter 2

As I looked closer, I saw hundreds of symbols, maybe thousands, racing across the door as if trying to beat the others to an invisible finish line. The marks were faint, almost beyond my line of sight, but still, I knew they were there. I reached out and touched the door, hoping to feel the symbols that ran under my fingertips, but it was as if they weren't there. I tried the door handle, but the door was locked. I stood still for what seemed like forever, studying everything I saw, hoping to find some sort of pattern or purpose to what was in front of me. Frustrated and getting nowhere, I backed up until I reached my bed and climbed back in. I lay there, head turned toward the purple door, still studying its intricate markings.

As I studied the door, my attention was caught by the handle. It had started to turn. My eyes widened as the door slowly opened, hinges working seamlessly to maintain the silence. There was no-one on the other side. The door stood open all the way, welcoming and yet not welcoming at the same time. On the other side of the door, darkness faded as I gradually recognised the attic of my house. My eyes squinted as I tried to make out which section of the *attic I was seeing. The old wooden cupboard in the corner appeared; its doors also opened, inviting me to come in. On the bottom shelf sat an old chest. Suddenly the purple door slammed shut, and the attic was gone from my vision. My eyelids grew heavy again and gradually closed as I fell back into a deep sleep as if I had never woken.*

That night I found myself sitting upright in bed. The room was dark except for the glow of the alarm clock, showing 9:13 pm. Something had woken me from my sleep. And something wasn't the same. I sat for a second rubbing the sleep from my eyes. Looking around the room, I half expected to see the door on the wall. But nothing was there. Then I remembered what had changed.

The attic hadn't been in any of the previous dreams. And for the first time, the door had opened. That had never happened before, and I wondered why it had changed now. Did it have something to do with the attic? Or the cupboard? Or maybe the chest? I hadn't been up in the attic for years; I didn't like the darkness up there or the dust which always made me sneeze.

Still, I felt compelled to have a look. I wondered if the cupboard or the chest was real, and the only way to find out was to go up there and look.

Pulling some socks on so that I could move more quietly, I climbed out of bed and wrapped my robe around me. *Am I really going to do this?* I silently mused. I rechecked the clock – it was 9:17 pm. Mum and Dad would probably still be awake, so I would definitely have to be quiet. They would wonder why I was going up to the attic at this time of night. *I'll pretend to be sleepwalking,* I thought, *if I get caught.*

I tiptoed to the door and opened the handle slowly. Slipping through the gap, I closed it behind me and stood completely still in the hallway, listening. There was a light at the end of the hall, a soft glow, one that would most likely be from the reading lamp in the lounge room. *Dad must still be awake.* Lucky for me, the attic stairs were in the opposite direction. I crept down the hallway and turned the corner toward the attic.

Amber and I had made up a game when we were younger to see who could get up and down the stairs without them creaking. We would spend hours racing and timing each other. I tried to recall where the creaks were, but the information escaped me. Holding onto the railing, I tried to remember which steps would give me away and which ones wouldn't. *What was that little song Amber had made up?* I wondered. Something about a dinosaur roar on four? *There must be a creak on the fourth step; I'll have to avoid that one.* There were only fourteen steps, so it shouldn't take too long to reach the top. The eleventh step had a noisy floorboard, and I knew it well, having stepped on it purposely many times during our games to give Amber the win. I could avoid that one too. I would just have to tread carefully on the other steps and hope I could make it to the top without being heard.

I grasped the wooden knob on top of the first post; could feel underneath my hand the initials I had carved into it as a little girl. It was my best-kept secret with Amber, something that would bond us forever. I smiled knowing full well Mum and Dad would ground us permanently if they ever found out. We would be in so much trouble if they saw it, not just for engraving initials into the handrail, but for using a knife to do it.

I moved my hand up the railing and lightly placed my foot on the edge of the first step, figuring if I kept to the edges or sides, there would be less chance of movement through the boards. On the fifth step, I realised I was holding my breath, so let it out slowly. I continued up the stairs, treading delicately on each level, not bearing any weight down until I was sure it was okay. In this manner, I made it to the top without a sound.

I slipped through the attic door and closed it behind me, letting out a sigh of relief. Leaning back against the door, I waited as my eyes adjusted to the light in the room, or rather the lack of it. I didn't want to move until I could see what was around me, in case I stumbled into something and caused Mum or Dad to come running. Almost immediately, my nose began to twitch as a sneeze made its way out.

Slowly, shapes began to emerge from the darkness. I could make out an old armchair to my right and a pile of boxes along the wall to my left. I looked around the room, trying to find the cupboard.

I could be a bit bolder up here; after all, it was at the opposite end of the house. The chances of being heard were high only if I managed to crash into something. I scanned the walls of the attic and sneezed again. In the dream, the cupboard was in the corner and looked extremely old, like it belonged to a relative hundreds of years ago. *There are only four corners to check.* And there it was, over to the far right, exactly where it was in my dream.

Things are starting to get a little strange now.

The cupboard wasn't wide open this time, but it *was* unlocked. I reached out for the doors but hesitated before opening them. If there was a chest in there, then something I didn't (or couldn't) understand was going on. There was no way I could pass it off as just another dream if the chest was sitting on the shelf. *How could I possibly explain how I could know about the chest and its whereabouts when I haven't been up here in years?* Indeed, I hadn't been up here since before we carved those initials, *and there's no way I would have been more than eight years old.*

If it isn't here, then it is just a silly dream, and I can go back to bed. But I had already starting thinking it was real. It might have been my imagination, but I could almost feel an energy coming from the cupboard, or whatever was in it. Without another thought, I stifled another sneeze and flung the doors wide open.

And there, right in the middle of the bottom shelf, sat the chest.

I sank to the floor, slowly. *What is going on here? How did I know that this was here? What does it mean? Who put it there?* I had so many questions, and I just didn't have the answers. The only way to find out was to pull the chest off the shelf and take a closer look.

The chest wasn't big, but it was heavy, probably because it was solid wood. It had a curved lid about the size of a dinner plate, which was closed with a rusty lock. On the top was a strange carving that I couldn't make out. In the darkness of the attic, I ran my fingers lightly over the engraving to get a sense of what it was. It felt like some sort of symbol or a circle with a tentacle. I tried to count them. I couldn't be sure, but there seemed to be ten branches or arms attached to the ring or symbol or whatever it was.

The lid refused to open for me, but I really didn't expect it to, considering the condition of the lock. Lifting it, I gave it a shake. Something shifted inside the chest, but I couldn't tell what it was. Now my curiosity really spiked – I had to know what was inside. But how was I going to get inside the chest to see what was in there?

I wish I could get inside this thing, I thought.

Suddenly a soft tapping noise came from behind me. *Tap, tap, tap*, it softly went. *Tap, tap, tap.*

I turned, keeping my hand on the chest in case it disappeared. *Tap, tap, tap.* The sound continued. *What* is *that?* I squinted, trying to find the source of the sound, my heart beating faster. Was there someone else up here with me?

"Hello?" I whispered into the dark. "Who's there?"

The only response was: *tap, tap, tap.*

I froze, afraid to move, only my gaze continuing to dart around the room, looking for the origin of the sound. My imagination started to create all sorts of monsters hiding in the attic.

"Amber, are you up here?" I whispered again. "It's not funny."

But again, no answer came.

"Stop scaring yourself," I chided myself. "You're thirteen now, practically an adult, you know there's no such thing as monsters." Of course, I knew this! But before tonight I'd never thought I could dream a chest into existence either. Still, I wasn't going to move a muscle just in case.

Then halfway across the attic, a soft glow appeared in the middle of the floor. What was happening now? I stared at the glowing floor, a mixture of fear and awe chilling, then heating, my skin.

You can't sit here forever.

Bravely, I made my way across the attic floor on hands and knees, keeping my eyes on the glowing light. My next sneeze nearly disguised the tapping.

Tap, tap, tap.

I stopped. It sounded louder here.

Creeping the last metre, I reached out and hesitantly touched the floorboard containing the light – *tap, tap, tap*. I could feel the knocks underneath my hand. Something was under the floorboard.

I found a hole, a knot in the wood, put my finger inside it and lifted the board.

Faster than a bullet, a golden orb flew up, crossed the room and landed straight in the rusty lock of the chest; it sat there as if waiting for further instructions.

I MUST be dreaming. I HAD to be dreaming. Nobody could possibly think a chest into reality, then see a golden orb fly across the room and land straight in the chest that you just created in your head. I pinched my arm.

Ow! That hurt. Now I must be dreaming that I pinched myself. How can this be real? It's not real. It can't be. Yet I could see as plain as day, something golden and glowing, now across the room sitting neatly in the chest's lock.

I wasn't ready to get close to it just yet, so I couldn't quite tell what it was, but it had slotted itself as neatly into the lock as a car parking in its garage. The glow had now begun to fade until it disappeared completely, revealing it was a key. *Could this be the key that will open the chest? Surely it can't be this easy.*

Returning to the cupboard, I knelt next to the

chest, temptation rising for me to reach out and touch the golden key. But what if it burnt me? After all, it *had been* glowing a minute ago.

I smiled in disbelief and shook my head. Yes, I was sure it had been *glowing,* and if I believed that, then I would have to believe that everything else that was happening was real. I *did* dream of a chest. And I *did* sneak up to the attic to find a chest in an actual cupboard that attracted a real, golden, glowing key. I almost laughed out loud – it sounded so bizarre, even inside *my* head.

Past the fear now, and getting more curious about what was in there, my hand hovered close to the key. I could feel no heat, so I bravely touched the end of it.

Nothing. It felt like any other key, although it didn't quite look like the ones that opened the front door or started the car. Firstly, it was very long and had a disc at the end of it. I bent down to take a closer look, noting that the end of the key had the same symbol as the one on the chest. *Now that's interesting.*

Sitting in front of me were two pieces of an unbelievable puzzle that had just found their way back to each other. Like a magnet, the key had gravitated to the chest the second I had released it. I wondered who had put it under the floorboard. It made me wonder if someone in my family knew about this already.

There was no way to keep a secret like this,

although I was going to try my best. Besides, the door had been in *my* dream, so maybe it was only meant for me. Perhaps I was supposed to find this for a particular reason. Until I knew more, I was not telling anyone.

Curiosity winning out, I decided to open it, reached slowly out. Holding the end of the key in my fingers, I drew a deep breath and let it out, then turned the key. It clicked. Then …

BANG!

A giant crack sounded through the attic, so loud it almost shook the windows. I looked around at the walls, half expecting to see massive lines appear. Then came a bright flash of light; it temporarily blinded me. *What was THAT?*

The crack was so loud, I was convinced someone would have heard it and would soon come running, so, without hesitation, I grabbed the chest, tucked it under my arm and raced from the attic as fast as I could. I would shove it under my bed with everything else, but first I had to make it back to my room without getting caught.

My heart beat fiercely as I sprinted down the hallway and back into my room. My stomach tightening, I tucked the chest under the bed, scrambled under the covers and turned off the light. In the darkness beneath the blankets, I prayed the sound was only in the attic, but just to be safe, I closed my eyes, slowed my breathing and waited to see if my parents were on their way.

Chapter 3

Robert

Perching on the edge of the seat, Robert froze, his ears straining to hear the slightest sound. He had fallen asleep reading in the armchair, which was confirmed by the book that was now on the floor, pages bent and buckled, place lost. Something had woken him from his rest, and Robert now had an uneasy feeling in the pit of his stomach. There had been a few break-ins in the area lately, and he'd been considering putting an alarm system in but hadn't yet. Truth be told, he didn't think they would be a target, being so far back from the road. Maybe someone had decided to give it a try after all.

Robert glanced sideways at the clock: 10:01 pm. Thinking about the girls in bed asleep spurred him into action. Courtney had gone off to bed early with a migraine, and both Morgan and Amber were asleep already. He was the only one awake, even at this early hour of the night. If there was a prowler in the house, he needed to find them, and find them fast.

Rising from the armchair, Robert looked around the room for something to take with him. He didn't want to meet an intruder in the dark hallway with just his bare hands. Being a scientist, he was under no illusions that he would be successful if he had to defend himself. There was a fire poker near the fireplace – a very formidable weapon for protection – not that Robert wanted to hurt anyone. He reached down with one hand, keeping an eye on the doorway, and pulled the poker very slowly towards him. The brush fell against the side of the holder with a soft clink, and Robert stopped moving so he could determine if anyone had heard and was making their way towards him.

The place was silent, except for the usual creaks and groans of a 100-year-old house. Amongst the typical sounds, Robert thought for a moment that he had heard a click of a door latch somewhere in the house, but he couldn't tell if that was a genuine sound or just his imagination running wild. Either way, if there was someone else tiptoeing around beyond the door of the library, Robert couldn't hear them. Over at the doorway, he hesitated, arms drawn back with the poker, ready to strike if necessary. He peered around the corner into the hallway, looking both ways like he was about to cross a street. There were no intruders to be seen. Unfortunately, the house was a lot bigger than just the hall, and he would have to investigate room by room until he was sure there was no one here.

Beginning in the kitchen, Robert double-checked the locks on the doors and the windows. If someone had come through this way, he would know by the broken glass on the floor. However, everything was where it ought to be, so far as he could tell. If there was someone in the house, they didn't get in through the kitchen.

He moved through the rooms quickly but quietly. After the fourth room, he was starting to feel a bit silly, creeping around the house in his slippers and tattered dressing-gown; poker raised ready to wreak havoc. Maybe he imagined things; perhaps he had fallen into a deep sleep and had dreamed it all. Still, he would never forgive himself if something happened to the girls because he was too afraid or embarrassed to complete his search. If there was even the tiniest chance that someone was here that shouldn't be, he needed to find them. Robert continued, slowly making his way to the other end of the house, toward the kids' bedrooms.

Reaching Amber's room on the left first, Robert turned the knob slowly and peered in around the door. Curled up fast asleep and turned toward the door, Amber lay with her favourite stuffed toy tucked into her chest. He stood there for a moment, watching her. Amber liked to pretend she was very grown-up, no doubt a result of all the time being around a sister who was mature beyond her years, but you could tell by the way she clung onto that stuffed bear that she was still just a young girl at heart. She adored Morgan, and Morgan adored her little sister, and Robert felt a rush of love for them both as he quietly closed the door again and headed across to Morgan's room.

Morgan was also fast asleep, her back to the door. He could see the rise and fall of the sheets as she breathed in and out. He looked around the room, seeing nowhere for a burglar to hide; not even under the bed with the amount of junk Morgan stored under there. The girls were safe, and he let out a deep breath that he hadn't realised he'd been holding.

He closed the door quietly and returned to the reading room. Picking up his book, he found his page again and settled back into the chair. He wasn't really in the mood for reading now but thought it would be best to stay up for a bit longer and listen quietly just in case he had missed something.

Chapter 4

I knew it! I knew someone would have heard that sound or seen that light. I looked at the clock to see what time it was. 10:14 pm. Was that all? It felt like I'd been up in the attic for hours. Reaching beneath the bed, I touched the chest, making sure it was still there. It was. I wanted to jump straight out of bed and open it up to see what was inside, but restrained myself. What if Dad came back? What if he saw the light coming out from under the door on his way to bed? I couldn't take the chance that he might see me awake; he would just come in and tell me to go back to sleep. I reached over to my alarm clock and set the alarm for midnight. Everyone would be asleep, and I could safely explore the contents then. I turned the volume down and lay back down in bed.

At 11 pm, I couldn't wait any longer. I wanted to know what was in there, and I just couldn't get to sleep. It was an itch that I just couldn't scratch, like the mosquito bites that mum always told us to leave alone or they would just get bigger and more irritating. You knew that eventually, you were going

to succumb, no matter how much you told yourself
not to. The chest was like that. It was calling to me,
a mystery waiting to be explored.

I jumped out of bed and crossed my legs on the
floor, pulling the chest out at the same time. I knew
it was unlocked, having heard it click earlier in the
attic right before the mad dash to my room. I pulled
my flexible bedside lamp down so that it pointed to
the ground, giving me enough light to see
everything, but keeping it low enough to avoid
detection if a nosy parent decided to investigate.

The key was still sitting in the lock of the chest.
Before I opened it, I took another look at the carving
on the lid. In the dark, up in the attic, it had felt like
tentacles and a circle. Now that I could genuinely
investigate, it looked more like a tree, with branches
rather than arms. The branches curved around with
even spacing, and there were ten of them. The circle
I had felt seemed to represent the bulk of the leaves
of the tree. The trunk of the tree reached down the
lid and wrapped around the lock itself. Studying the
carving, it didn't look like any tree I had ever seen.

I noticed one of the branches looked different to
the others and began to rub the dust off the top as I
leaned in for a better look. It looked like the third
branch from the outside was darker than the others,
which was harder to see. I wasn't wrong though,
because on closer inspection I could see the branch
had been painted black.

What was the reason for that? I wondered. Either

way, what *was* important was what was *in* the chest, not on the outside of it. I wrapped my fingers around the key, prepared myself, and opened the chest.

What looked like a hundred keys, maybe more, were nestled inside against the purple velvet lining. What would be the purpose of locking away hundreds of keys where no-one could ever find them? I reached in and took one out. It didn't look any different to the one that had unlocked the chest, except this one was black, not gold. I held it under the light to get a better look at it. It was the same long skinny key with the disc on the top. I peered into the chest and realised that all the keys were black. Every single one of them. A little strange, I thought. I'd never seen a black key before, only silver and gold ones. I pulled a handful out and laid them on the floor, under the light.

That was when I realised that every key I lined up had a different picture on the disc at the end. A fox, a tree, a diamond, a car, a cloud – every one of them showed something different. I reached into the chest and pulled out a few more. A fish on this one, on the next one, two squiggly lines. I kept pulling them out of the chest, one by one, realising not one of them had the same picture on it.

Eventually, I removed every key from the chest. In piles of ten, I counted them: one hundred and thirty-seven keys. Sitting back against the bedside table, I looked at the fourteen collections in front of me. I couldn't for the life of me figure out what they would open. They were the same as the ones next to it, other than the picture on the top. Why would you need 137 keys the same? I had only ever seen two identical keys, like the ones Mum and Dad had for the house, and I'm pretty sure they just had them copied. But the ones out of the chest were much more old-fashioned. The key's stem was round, not flat, and I couldn't picture how you would go about recreating that. I would have to do some research in the morning to determine what use those types of keys had.

Yawning, I looked up at my alarm clock to check the time. 11:56 pm, no wonder I was tired! I packed all the keys carefully back into the chest and pushed it back under the bed. My spare pillow, which I usually threw on the floor when I went to sleep, went under the bed in front of the chest so no-one would be able to see it. I followed that with my quilt, to complete the hideaway. It was warm enough tonight that I wouldn't need it anyway.

Back in bed, my mind raced over everything that had happened tonight: the dream that had been haunting me every night for years; the attic; the flying golden key and the chest hidden away in a cupboard. And one hundred and thirty-seven keys with no idea what locks they would fit.

At the start of the night, I was convinced I had still been dreaming, but now I was 100% sure that it was real. I don't know how it was possible, but it was all real. It was like being inside a movie, and I was the main character.

But in every good book I'd ever read, the hero always had a sidekick. Did I need my very own partner in crime for this adventure? Was I going to tell Amber? I didn't like to keep secrets from her, but this was a pretty big one. If I told her, she would probably sneak into my room to play with the keys – even the thought of that alarmed me. She wasn't the sort of person who would go through my stuff, but I didn't think she'd be able to help herself with this. This secret was way too big, and the curiosity of an eight-year-old would override any concerns she would have about invading my privacy. No, it was safer not to tell her for now. Besides, I still didn't know what it all meant.

What was there to tell really? I had a whole bunch of keys and no idea what they opened. It wasn't that exciting when you looked at it that way—just a heap of keys in a box. Besides, I would know for sure in the morning, because either the chest was there, or it wasn't. If it wasn't, then it was all just a crazy dream. But if it was, well … then, I was looking at the biggest mystery I had ever encountered. Either way, I hoped I was ready for whatever was to come.

Chapter 5

It was still there.

I had woken up early, despite being up until close to midnight – something to do with the magical chest underneath my bed, most likely. I awoke before 6 am and frantically ripped the quilt and pillow from under the bed to check. When my hand touched the chest, I sighed out loud and smiled inwardly. It was all real.

A feeling overcame me at that moment, an intense need to make sure that this chest was hidden away where no one else could find it. I could feel the panic rising through my rib cage as I pictured the chest in someone else's hands. It was mine; it wasn't supposed to belong to anyone else. I looked around for a suitable place. There was no way it was leaving my room; I couldn't risk someone else finding it. I had to keep it safe.

I settled on the old air vent on the wall. The screws holding the mesh on the front were old and easy to take out. I was eight or nine when I figured out how to remove the screws with a 5-cent piece, and it had become a great hiding spot for many treasures over the years. Once the mesh was down, I reached in and pulled out a well-worn shoebox, the edges soft and falling apart. Full of special items to me, they didn't compare to the mystery chest I now had in my possession, and I didn't hesitate to replace the shoebox with the chest. Putting the screws back in place, I breathed a sigh of relief as the knot inside me released – the chest was safe for now.

I dressed and made my way to the kitchen for breakfast, but each step I took away from that chest became heavier and heavier, and I began to waver before reaching the kitchen. Was it safe enough, hidden away in the vent? Did I put those screws back on tightly?

I began to doubt myself; stopped in the doorway, not even seeing Amber at the table, smiling at me. I felt like I needed to go back and guard the chest, or at least double-check it, just to be sure.

A nudge from behind snapped me out of it as Dad pushed me into the kitchen. "It's going to be hard to eat breakfast if you're standing in the doorway," he said.

"Oh, yeah," I replied absently, pulling out a chair and sitting down.

"Morning, Morgan," Amber smiled brightly at me. "Mum made waffles today. Yum!" The happiness in her voice brought me back into the room.

"That's great, Amber; we haven't had waffles for ages."

"I want all the maple syrup," Amber sang as she reached for the bottle.

"Save some for everyone else," Mum replied.

"I seem to have lost my keys," Dad said, darting around the kitchen, picking up and shifting things around. "And I need to get to work early."

All background noise disappeared as my ears locked onto that one word. *Keys. Does he know about the chest? Why would he be after my keys? How did he figure it out? It must have been when he came to my room to check on me last night.* I thought I had managed to fool him into thinking I was asleep, but maybe I hadn't after all. *Why suddenly is he looking for my keys?* I needed to get back to my room to guard them.

My hand was on the back of my chair, ready to push back and get up when Dad exclaimed, "Ah ha! What on earth are they doing in the fruit bowl?" He pocketed his keys and waved to the rest of us as he backed out the door. "Gotta go, love you all!" he threw out as he slammed the door.

I felt a little sheepish as I realised he had been looking for his car keys and nothing else. What was wrong with me? Why did I have such a furious need to protect the chest? I lifted my head and resolved not to let it ruin my entire day. It was safe.

I needed to act as normal as possible, although I felt anything but ordinary. Amber and I spent a lot of time together; she would know if I kept something from her. I had to force myself to engage in conversation. "Hey Amber, what trick are you working on at the moment?"

Her face lit up with a smile. "There's this cool trick I found the other day on the internet to make a coin disappear. I keep trying and trying, but I haven't got it right yet. I will though," she added.

"I know you will," I encouraged her. "Just keep practising."

"When I get it right, I'll show you, but not before then. Us professional magicians don't want to give away our tricks," she smiled again and winked at me.

"Did you see that, Mum?" I said incredulously. "She WINKED at me! Winked! I think she's eight going on eighty."

Mum laughed as she poured more batter into the waffle maker. "Didn't I tell you she was born a hundred years ago and she's actually your older sister?"

"That would make you and dad ancient," I said.

"Hey! Let's leave my age out of it!" Mum pretended to be insulted, but I could see her smile.

"So, you're 100, huh?" I looked at Amber, who giggled. "I guess you can start driving me to school then?"

"Sure," Amber said, playing along. "I don't see why not."

"Great!" Mum said happily. "I can sleep in then?"

"You still need to make us breakfast, Mum," Amber replied.

"So I do, and it's one of my favourite parts of the day."

"So, what does your car look like, Amber?" I asked.

"It's red and big and has wings."

"OMG! So, we can fly to school?"

"No silly, they're just pretend ones. Have you ever heard of a flying car?"

"You're right, sorry," I said. "But the car is real?"

"Yeah, I just keep it at the neighbour's house normally."

"What do you mean, normally?" I asked.

"It's getting fixed at the moment; otherwise, I could show you."

Wow, this kid has a great imagination.

"What's wrong with it?" I had to ask.

"The flux capacitor isn't working properly."

I covered my mouth with my hand to stifle a laugh. We had watched *Back to the Future* a couple of weeks ago. "The flux capacitor, huh? I hear those things are a real problem."

The three of us looked at each other and started laughing.

"Any big plans today, girls?" Mum asked.

"Magic practice," Amber announced.

"I'll probably just read," I added, providing a reason to stay in my room and guard the chest.

"Exciting," Mum replied.

We finished the rest of our meal in silence.

"Thanks for breakfast," I said as I got up, ready to go back to my room; I wanted to see what I could find out about the keys and where they might have originated. I put my plate on the bench next to the sink and turned to leave the room.

"Forgotten something, hon?" Mum asked me.

I looked around. "I don't think so?" I replied. Now that I was thinking about the chest and the keys again, I was very anxious to get back to my room.

Mum looked at me and nodded her head toward the sink. "Is that what we do with our dishes?"

"Oh yeah, right. Sorry." I returned to the sink and rinsed out my plate then put it in the dishwasher.

"Thank you," Mum said as I walked out the kitchen door.

I didn't bother replying – I barely heard what she'd said. Back in my room, I pulled out my iPad again, wanting to search for the keys and see if I could find any information. As I searched, I couldn't stop thinking about what could be behind that door. I wondered if I would dream of the door tonight and if it would open to show me the attic again. There had to be more to it. I couldn't wait to see what would happen tonight. Maybe it would open to show me a different room or a different house. A different world even! Now that would be exciting!

Scrolling through the articles on keys, I came across a picture that showed a similar key to the many I had stashed away. It was called a 'skeleton key'. The only difference that I could see was on the top of the keys. Mine were flat discs with symbols on them, and the one I saw online was just an open circle. *OMG, the symbols on the keys!* Did they have anything to do with the symbols that raced across the door? How was I going to check this when the door was only in my dreams? I wished there was a way to hold the real keys that I had against the door in my dream to see if any of the symbols matched.

For the first time, I found myself wanting to have the dream again. I promised myself that if I did, I would try my best to remember some of the symbols running across the door to see if I could find them in the chest.

It was interesting to read that the skeleton key symbolised uncovering secrets or gaining entry to fortified areas; secret knowledge – all similar to the locked door meanings. I felt like I was onto something, that these things were all tied together in some way. But how? Other than the obvious, I had a feeling there was much more to be discovered. I don't know how I knew this, but I did, just as I knew that the sun would rise each morning and set each night. I just couldn't figure out how I was going to make my dream and reality come together, but I was determined to find a way.

Chapter 6

The rest of the day went by so slowly it felt like time stood still. Each minute stretched into hours; each hour felt like a day. I tried to read, but focus was as far away from me as touching that door seemed to be. I wished wholeheartedly for the night to come quickly, but those wishes went unheard. I tried to find things to do in my room, so I could keep the chest safe. I killed time just staring at the walls, willing the door to show itself, although of course it never did. Nothing stopped me from thinking about the dream and the door – I was curious what would happen when I dreamed of it again tonight, as I knew I would.

The rest of the day passed with a disturbing lack of speed. After dinner, I excused myself, citing a headache and went straight back to my room. Amber came and sat with me for a little while, trying to get me to play a game with her, but I didn't want the chest or the keys to make themselves known to her, as they had with me. I wasn't ready to share it with anyone yet, not even Amber.

Sleep eluded me that night, keeping its distance

as if coming closer would mean catching something contagious. Restless, I tossed and turned and shifted in my bed, convinced that keeping my eyes closed would mean my body would eventually give in and relax and finally let me go to sleep.

Frustrated, I sighed and sat up in bed. Looking over at the clock, I watched as the last digit flipped over to 9:58 pm. This whole situation was crazy. I was never going to get to sleep, never going to dream of this purple door. Disappointment coursed through me, moving me from frustration to immense sadness. I don't think I ever went through more feelings in one day than I did today.

I sighed and thought about what was going to happen once I dreamed of the door again. How was I going to make it a reality? How could I take it from my dream and bring it into my world? I needed to get the keys to the door somehow, so I could see if any of them would fit the lock and open it. Maybe if I went to sleep with a key in my hand? Perhaps that might make it appear in my hand in the dream too. It was worth a try.

I slipped my legs over the edge of the bed and tiptoed across the room to the hidden chest. It took less than a minute to get the chest out and open it. Now, how to decide which key. It was an impossible choice, so I reached in and grabbed the first one I touched. This one would do; it would have to. Even if it didn't open the door, I would know in the morning whether it allowed me to bring the key into the dream. I quickly pushed the chest back into the vent and put the screws back in place, albeit loosely.

Turning around, key in hand, I was about to step forward and return to the bed when I suddenly froze. Almost losing my balance, my foot hovered mid-air as I lost the capacity to move. Every muscle in my body had locked into place; I forgot to put my foot down, I forgot how to walk. I could not believe what I was seeing. The door was on the wall. The door was there. On the wall.

It can't have taken more than a minute or two to retrieve the key. I glanced over at the clock to see just how long it had taken me. 10 pm, it said – two minutes at most. Expecting the door to vanish again, I shifted my gaze back to the wall, afraid that it had disappeared in those few seconds I had looked away. It was right where it had been in my dreams, and I was sure that at this moment, I was very much awake. Willing my body to move again, I shuffled across the room toward the purple door, which was now as real as the curiosity that filled me.

Reaching out hesitantly, I wondered, not for the first time, if it was dangerous to touch. There were so many reasons to fear what was in front of me, yet I couldn't help but feel amazement at this incredible door that had magically appeared, literally while my back was turned. I wasn't sure if it was unsafe, but I had to see if I could open the door and see what was behind it. I had to see what was on the other side.

Stepping forward, I put my hand on the door.

Just like my dream, symbols ran under my hand, the light glowing a little brighter as it brushed against my skin. They didn't give away their secrets though, they just continued to run past my hand to the edge of the door and off into nowhere. I stood there in my pyjamas leaning against the door, touching it lightly.

I needed to see what was behind it. It was time to try to open it.

The handle was plain silver, one of those long skinny ones that you pushed down. I closed my hand around the doorknob and lowered it. The door popped open quickly enough without a creak or a sound, again just like my dream. As I swung it outwards, I stood in the doorway and peered curiously into the room on the other side.

Ahead of me, a very dark, long narrow corridor seemed to go on forever. The downlights that provided only limited visibility seemed not to care about the hallway as much as the white doors that lined the walls.

I held onto the purple frame and tried to lean in to see further, worried that if I took a step into this place, I might not be able to come back. What if I got stuck in there? I had to be smart about this. What I needed was an anchor of some sort – something that could tie me back to the room, so that I could return safely.

I turned back, scanning for something suitable. Searching my cupboards, my drawers, I tried frantically to find something I could hold onto – something that could serve as a base for me to come back.

Remembering a movie I had watched a while back, I wondered if I could also knot the sheets together to make a rope. It had worked in the film, and the girl had escaped out of her second-storey window and ran away. While I didn't want to run away, the idea of the rope made of sheets might just work.

Using both bedsheets and the quilt cover, I might be able to make something long enough to go through the door. I measured the distance between my dresser – a suitable place to tie it to – and the door, I paced it out to see if it was long enough.

But when I turned around again, the door was gone.

I stood in disbelief: how could it be there one second and gone the next? Rechecking the clock, I noticed it had only been on the wall for five minutes before it had disappeared. Disappointment filled me as I realised I had missed my chance to explore.

Sitting down slowly on the bed, I wondered if it would come back again. I thought of all those white doors on the other side, which hopefully opened as easily as this purple one had. If they were locked, then I was out of luck. Locks, keys – the chest!! Frantically I looked around for the key I had taken from the chest only a few minutes before and exhaled when I realised it was still in my hand.

The indentation in my palm was deep, having held this piece of the puzzle tightly without even realizing it. I tucked it into my sock drawer, underneath my old unicorn socks – no one would even think to look there. The excitement started to brew when I began to understand that I just may be able to use the key to open one of those doors on the other side.

I contemplated the next problem: how to get into the corridor, find the right door for the key, and then explore – all within five minutes.

Stifling a yawn, I crawled under the covers, my mind racing. How fast could I be? How many keys could I take with me? I needed to set an alarm somehow, so I could be back before the door disappeared. What was behind the white doors? Would the purple one come back at all, or was that the last time I would ever see it?

Sheet line forgotten, I planned my adventure, fully assuming the door would reappear for me again. It would be incredibly unfair to dangle something so exciting in front of me and then take it away. I wasn't sure how or why it had appeared, but I didn't care anymore. All I knew was the next time it came, I would be ready.

Satisfied, I eventually drifted off to sleep.

Chapter 7

The following night I was ready. My mini backpack held the ten keys I had carefully selected and taken out of the chest during the day. The watch around my wrist was one of Dad's old ones, with an alarm, which hopefully he wouldn't notice was missing before I could sneak it back. I set it for four and a half minutes, which I hoped would give me enough time to get back to my room before it was too late. I had dressed in an old, comfortable pair of jeans, to be ready for anything.

A knock on the door interrupted my thoughts.

"Just a second!" I yelled out. I raced across the room, dropping the backpack on the floor as I leapt into bed and pulled the covers over me, grabbing the book on the bedside table as I did. "Okay, you can come in."

Just as the door began to open, I realised the book was upside down and quickly spun it around then looked towards the door just as Mum peeked her head through the opening.

"I knew you were still awake." She smiled at me as she sat on the edge of the bed.

"Just reading," I replied.

"I wanted to check in on you, hon. You've been a bit quiet the last couple of days. I'm worried you're spending too much time in your room. You need to get outside into the fresh air."

"I'm fine, Mum." I said, rolling my eyes.

"I know," she said, tucking a piece of hair behind my ear. "I just wanted to be sure."

"It's not against the law to want to hang out in my room," I replied.

"It might be," she teased. "I'll have to look up the local government laws and see if it's there."

"Funny," I replied.

"I try," she grinned.

I focused back on the book, hoping she would leave me alone. I didn't want the door to appear with Mum in the room, not when I hadn't even had a chance to explore it yet. Glancing over the top of the book, I asked, "Is that all?"

"You're growing up way too fast … where has my little girl gone?"

I groaned quietly – she would never leave at this rate.

"I'm right here, Mum, but I want to finish this chapter and go to sleep. I'm tired."

I wasn't sure if she would believe me or not. Sleep was the furthest thing from my mind right now, and to be honest, I was jumping out of my skin in anticipation. I hoped Mum didn't notice.

"Okay, then."

She stood. "But you will always be my little girl. Doesn't matter how old you are."

She started to turn away but then said to me, "Are you still having that dream?"

"What dream?" I answered carefully.

"The one with the door," she replied, just as carefully.

It felt like we were tiptoeing around a glass room, cautious not to run into anything.

"Oh, that one? I haven't had that in forever,"

Mum beamed. "Well, that's good news, isn't it?"

"I guess so."

"Well, I'll let you get back to your book then. In the morning you need to spend some time to clean up this room, it's a mess."

"There's barely anything messy!"

"This doesn't belong here on the floor." Mum picked up my backpack.

I held my breath, hoping she wouldn't hear the keys moving around inside. She placed the bag on my desk and said, "Put it away properly tomorrow."

"Okay." I was so relieved I would have agreed to anything.

"Don't read for too long, okay? It's after 9:30; you should be asleep."

Faking a yawn, I replied, "Don't worry, I'll be asleep soon. I just want to finish the chapter, and there are only three pages left."

"Good night. Love you."

"Love you too, Mum. Night."

She closed the door softly behind her as I continued to look at the book. When I knew she was gone, I jumped out of bed and quickly moved to check on my backpack. If she'd heard the keys rattle against each other and asked what was in there, I would've been in trouble. I pulled the chair out from my desk and spun it around so I'd be able to see the wall while seated. My plan tonight was to make sure I didn't miss the door if and when it appeared. I was going to sit and watch all night if I had to.

Backpack on my lap, I waited for something to happen. I'd already decided I would take the opportunity to explore as soon as it appeared – I had a bunch of keys ready to go, hoping to match a key and a door on the other side. Apart from that, I had no idea what to expect, but I was ready, and there was nothing else to do now but wait, and wait.

I sat fidgeting, checking my watch every couple of minutes. *It's true: time goes so slowly when your biggest wish is for it to pass quickly.* And this clock had never moved slower.

I stared blankly into space, watching nothing, thinking of nothing, fighting my eyelids which were growing heavy.

Then the door appeared on the wall. Immediately, I snapped back awake and jumped up so fast the backpack fell to the floor. Picking it up, I caught sight of the watch. It was again 10 pm. *That's interesting,* I noted.

I didn't have time to ponder more than that as I

only had five minutes to explore. I threw the backpack over my shoulder, raced forward and, without any hesitation, grabbed the handle and reefed to door open. Danger never entered my mind, the excitement of this adventure overriding everything.

The corridor lined up in front of me, just as it had last night, door after door on both sides highlighted with downlights that focused on the doors themselves. It made the corridor seem darker in the middle, with all the lights concentrated on the walls instead. *It's time.* Gripping the strap of my backpack a little tighter, I inhaled deeply, and stepped through the magic doorway.

Chapter 8

Courtney

"She's just reading at the moment," Courtney told Robert as she walked into the kitchen.

"Good, and she seems okay?"

"I think so. A little quiet maybe but otherwise same as usual."

"So maybe it's just typical teenage stuff going on then. I'm glad you checked in on her. At least that way she knows we are worried about her, or rather, thinking about her."

"Very true, love." She smiled at him. "You always know the right things to say to put me at ease."

"I don't know about that," he replied.

"I asked her about the dream as well, while I was there."

"And …?"

"Not for a long time, she said."

Robert beamed at her. "Excellent! It looks like we dodged a bullet then."

"I agree … unless she's lying."

"No, that's not like Morgan. Why would she lie? She doesn't know that we know about the door and that it could be more real than she realises. To her, it's just a dream that has stopped now. That's it." He handed Courtney a cup of coffee.

Sitting down on the chair next to him, the cup in her hands, she said, "I'm so relieved. I never want her to go through what happened to me. Imagine if she found out about …."

"Stop!" Robert interrupted. "Stop beating yourself up over what happened thirty years ago. It wasn't your fault then, and it isn't your fault now. What happened was tragic, but you can't spend your whole life living in what-if's."

"I know," Courtney sighed. "I can't help but wonder though if I had done something differently …"

"Stop!" Robert said again, this time a little more sharply. "You were what, thirteen or fourteen? What could you have possibly done?"

"Thirteen. Maybe if I'd tried a little harder, just a little, or ran a little faster or held on a little tighter …"

"Enough. Look at me." Robert turned her face towards his. "You're worrying about nothing. One, she's not dreaming of the door anymore. Two, we locked it up, and the chest and key are both hidden where no-one will ever find them. Three, *she's not dreaming about the door*. Relax, it's over."

"Do you think so?" she pleaded with him.

"Yes, love, I do," he smiled gently and kissed her cheek.

Courtney slumped back into the chair. It was easy for Rob to say, but he wasn't there when it had happened. He would never know just how it felt in that last moment when so many lives were drastically changed forever. Robert wasn't there to see the look in her eyes. He wasn't there to see the horror of what was behind her. He wasn't there, so he couldn't feel the ache and the terror that welled up inside during those last moments – moments that Courtney had wished a million times over that she could have back so she could do things differently.

Chapter 9

The first thing I noticed was the silence. A deep, almost unnatural silence that made me want to speak aloud to break it. A faint staleness exuded, as if this was a room that hadn't been opened and aired out for years. On either side, the white doors stood to attention like well-trained soldiers, each guarding its place and highlighted by a downlight on the ceiling.

Turning around, I checked to make sure I could still see into my bedroom from where I was, so at least I would know how to get back. It was still there.

Now I was through the purple door in the corridor beyond the wall; the next logical step was to take a good look at the doors. Maybe the keys I had brought with me would open one of them. I stepped carefully and quietly, now wanting to maintain the silence rather than break it. The first door was only ten metres away. I headed towards it and stopped, staring. I was standing in front of a large white door that no-one knew existed, in a corridor I had found behind a purple door that I had dreamed of for years, which only appeared at 10 pm for five short minutes. My dream had become a reality.

The door in front of me seemed like a typical house door, but contained an ancient locking system attached, unlike the purple door, which had none. This lock, I noticed, was rectangular, dark silver with a keyhole at the bottom, the doorknob round. The door was indeed locked, and I wondered if any of the keys I had would fit this lock. I pulled the keys out of the backpack, and one by one, tried to insert them into the key lock.

But none opened that door. So I moved across the hall to the next one, once again trying all the keys without luck. I continued down the corridor, testing every door I came to. *Surely one's going to fit.* I huffed a sigh out, my enthusiasm diminishing. *Surely my adventure won't start and end with a corridor full of doors I can't access.* The next door, however, the fifth one on the left, made a resounding click with the third key I tried. This key had a tree symbol, and for the first time, I noticed the same picture at the top of the door. The downlight seemed to highlight the symbol, and it suddenly dawned that the sign on the key must match the one on the door. *How did I miss that?* I wondered briefly.

I tried the doorknob again and felt it turning. This door was going to open for me.

At that very moment, the alarm went off on the watch. I stood there, my hand on the doorknob, knowing I must leave, but strongly drawn to stay. An internal struggle of logic versus magic raged. My head urged me to rush back to the bedroom before it disappeared, but my heart insisted I stay and explore whatever was behind the 'tree' door. The longer I stood there debating, the less time I would have to get back to my room. I just couldn't make my feet move away from that door.

Everything is magic, I fathomed, *surely it wouldn't lock me in here. I have to go through that tree door and see what's in there. What will happen if the purple door never appears again? This might be my only chance to explore this other world?*

I watched the second hand on the watch tick towards the five-minute mark, and continued to stand with my hand on the doorknob. I wouldn't make it back to my room now and had little choice but to continue standing and watching what would happen when the hand reached the five-minute mark. With more curiosity than fear, I stared at the opening to my room, wondering if it would just disappear or shrink or if something else would happen.

The second hand ticked over.

Nothing.

That's what happened: absolutely nothing. I was apparently wrong about the door disappearing after five minutes because we were past that now and it was still there. *Perfect! Now I can explore for as long as I want.* A small part of me questioned just how long it would remain open, but I fought back on that and squashed it down and ignored it. I had to discover what was behind this tree door, and no one was going to stop me.

Before I could change my mind, I swung the door open, stepping into a world nothing in my thirteen years could have prepared me for.

Chapter 10

My eyes widened as I stepped into a world of white – a soft white that felt welcoming and pure. White to my left. White to my right. White above and behind me too. I stood, turning slowly on the spot, the disappearance of the purple door all but forgotten.

There seemed no beginning and no end to the room I was in – if that's even what it was. All five senses became muted. There was nothing to see or smell, and it was silent. Even my footsteps made no noise, as if the ground swallowed them up intentionally.

"Who are you?"

A voice floated from nowhere. I looked around to see who had spoken to me.

"You shouldn't be here."

The voice was melodic, calm and worldly; it made me feel welcomed – almost expected - even though the words spoken didn't relay the same sentiment. I continued to look around, trying to locate the source of the voice.

"Who are you, child?" the voice asked again.

Child? They must be able to see me, I thought. I looked around again, and finally saw a shimmer of something move in the distance.

"My name is Morgan," I said, staring intently at the movement I had seen, trying to make out a shape and a face as it came toward me. I peered intently.

Wearing a white robe, the person came toward me sedately, gliding rather than walking, giving me the impression they did nothing in a hurry. Hands clasped in front of her body, she approached serenely, studying me as I stared back at her.

"Morgan," she repeated. Her face was young, but her aura gave away her age. I had the immediate feeling she had been around forever. "Morgan," she said again.

I waited for her to speak again, or even just smile at me. Her violet eyes stared right through me, absorbing me, reading me like a book. She nodded almost invisibly.

"Where am I?" I asked.

Ignoring my question, she turned away and said, "Come." And she floated away, leaving me no choice but to follow. I trailed behind her through the maze of white nothingness, wondering where we were going. Whiteness still surrounded us.

"Come," she said again, turning to check I was indeed still following her. "There is much to see, much to understand."

Understand? What is she talking about? I didn't understand anything, but I followed her anyway, rather than be left in the middle of nowhere by myself. I couldn't see the door anymore, only a small light that seemed to hover where the door had been.

She stopped suddenly and pointed to the most beautiful tree I had ever seen. The trunk wound tightly around itself in thousands of strands that reminded me of licorice twists. Around they went, making their way up the tree trunk until eventually, they became branches. Millions of leaves graced the branches and continued so high up I could barely see them. I had never seen a tree so big before, and I had the most definite feeling that what I could see wasn't even a tiny per cent of its total size.

"What is it?" I asked.

"Dream tree," she replied.

"What does it do? Who are you? And where am I?" All these questions came pouring out before I could stop them. "Why isn't there anyone else around?"

"Shhhh," she whispered as she put her finger to her lips. "You will disturb them."

"Disturb who?" I asked before it even registered that I'd just done what she had told me not to do.

"The dream fairies," she said, pointing to the tree.

Dream fairies? What is she talking about? I didn't see any … *oh, wait.* Concentrating a little harder, I stared closely at the dream tree. They were so small I hadn't seen them at first, but she was right. Fairies fluttered around the tree – they were everywhere. I couldn't believe I'd missed them in the first place. What seemed like hundreds, even thousands, of tiny fairies raced around the leaves and the branches.

"What are they doing?" I whispered.

"Fixing the dreams. Watch closely."

I stared at the tree once again, trying to understand. What was I seeing? Hundreds of leaves were continually falling from the tree to the ground, disappearing before they reached their destination while hundreds of fairies raced around, too small for me to focus on. I could see the movement in the air, but not what they were doing. *And what else?*

Most of the leaves were a vibrant green, like an emerald from the Wizard of Oz. However, scattered throughout the beautiful greenery were dark grey leaves. As I watched, I noticed some grey leaves changing colour back to emerald green before they fell from the tree.

"Why are the leaves changing colour?" I asked quietly.

"It is the fairies' job," she explained, making absolutely no sense at all.

"It's their job to change the colour of the leaves?" I questioned.

"Yes."

"Why?"

"They are bad, horrible," she answered.

"The fairies are bad?" I felt bewildered. Why were the fairies bad, and what did that have to do with the leaves changing?

"The leaves."

"The leaves are bad?" I frowned, wishing she would talk in longer sentences.

"The leaves," she sighed.

"So why are the grey leaves bad? Or are all the leaves bad?" I asked, confused but curious.

"Leaves are dreams. Dreams are leaves."

She continued to talk in riddles, which I had trouble deciphering. How can leaves and dreams be the same thing? One is a leaf, and one is a dream. They can't be the same thing. One is attached to a tree, and the other is something your brain does while you're sleeping.

"I don't understand," I said a little sadly.

"Grey is bad. Leaves are dreams," she repeated.

Then it suddenly dawned on me: she wasn't talking in riddles at all – she was telling me precisely what was going on. This was a dream tree, and the fairies were fixing the dreams.

"Does that mean …" my voice trailed off.

"Yes," she smiled at me. "Leaves are dreams."

"So, each leaf represents someone's dream?" I felt I was on the right track.

"Yes." She smiled at me again.

"I don't understand the grey and green leaves, though. What do they mean?"

"Good and bad. Evil and pure. Right and wrong."

"So the green dreams are the good ones? Or the bad ones?"

"Green is good."

Wow. The more I started to understand, the more amazing it felt to be standing here. To be here in front of this tree that held millions of dreams from around the world – every boy and girl, every man and woman that lay asleep at this very moment might have a leaf on this tree.

"Why are they falling?" I asked.

"It is the end," she replied.

"The end of the dream? Where do the leaves go?" As hard as I stared, I couldn't see them landing on the ground. They seemed to disappear into thin air.

My thoughts drifted back to the grey leaves again. The last one I saw had changed back to green before it fell from the tree. These grey leaves seemed different, and I remembered the lady's comment about the fairies fixing them, and I wondered how they did it.

"Fairy dust," she said.

How did she know what I was thinking? Suddenly I felt overwhelmed by what was going on.

"Sit." She pointed to a white garden seat next to me, a seat I hadn't noticed when we arrived at the tree. Whether that was because I was focused on the tree itself or because she had conjured it out of thin air, I couldn't tell. Nevertheless, I gratefully sat down on the soft cushion and heaved in a deep breath as I summed up what I was seeing. A dream tree, with fairies fixing the coloured leaves that were good or bad dreams with fairy dust. Falling leaves were the end of a dream. I guessed new leaves would sprout as a person fell asleep and started a vision of their own. I looked around in awe.

"Why me?" I muttered, not entirely understanding why I was able to visit this world. No one could ever imagine something like this, let alone actually come here.

"It is in your blood."

I looked at the lady and frowned.

"It is in your blood," she repeated.

"What do you mean?"

"It is in your blood."

She smiled suddenly. "Would you like to meet a fairy?"

Would I like to meet a fairy? That's a silly question — of course, I would! I imagined telling Amber that I had met a real-life fairy — she would die of jealousy.

I tried one more time. "What do you mean about my blood?" But she wouldn't answer. Instead, she moved toward the tree and pulled something out of her pocket. Bringing it up to her mouth, she blew very softly into it. The sweetest melody I'd ever heard drifted around me; filled my ears with music so beautiful it nearly brought me to tears.

The music stirred up the tree, several leaves swaying as if the music had become a wind with the ability to create movement. The whole tree seemed to move at once, although it was more of a feeling rather than anything visual. The white lady stood, as the whirlwind that was the tree slowly settled again. She held her hand out.

Turning toward me with her hand still stretched out, she said, "Come closer. Quietly."

I held my breath as I stepped forward. Was I about to see a fairy?

The lady held up her other hand in a stopping motion, indicating I should stand still. I did so immediately. She lifted her hand slowly towards me.

On the back of her hand stood a tiny fairy about three inches tall, yet every beautiful feature was apparent. Her brown hair was braided at the back of her head; I assumed so it wouldn't get caught in her stunning wings. The wings on her back were as broad as she was tall. Like a rainbow, they shone with distinct colours, finding the light at different angles, and creating the most amazing blues and greens. She wore a white dress and no shoes. She stood looking up at me, smiling silently.

The lady in white stood looking at her adoringly. Then she leaned forward and whispered something to the fairy.

"What is her name?" I asked softly.

"Flora."

"She's amazing," I said, keeping my distance, afraid that if I spoke too close, I might blow her right off the lady's hand.

"She says you are beautiful," the lady said, looking at me.

"Oh, wow, she is just incredible." I couldn't pull my eyes away from her. "Where is her fairy dust?"

The lady whispered to Flora again. Flora lifted her

hands and made a sprinkling motion in front of her. I could faintly see the twinkle of the fairy dust motes scattering in the air before they fell away.

"Where does the dust come from?" I asked. She hadn't been holding anything, yet the fairy dust had magically fallen from her fingers.

"Secret," the lady frowned at me.

"Sorry," I said quickly. I didn't want her to send Flora away just yet.

"Do you think ... do you think she would sit on my hand?" I asked timidly.

Smiling again, the lady whispered to Flora.

"Hold out your hand," she said to me.

I lifted my hand slowly, and before I could blink, Flora stood there, gazing up at me. This experience was beyond amazing. Here I was, standing in a strange world holding a fairy in my hand. This tiny fairy had put her life in a stranger's hand without hesitation or fear. *In my hand.* Her wings had fluttered so fast I had missed her flying altogether. No wonder I couldn't see them flying around the tree – they were way too quick!

"Ready?" the lady in white asked me.

"For what?"

"Time to go back."

Immediately, I was disappointed.

"I want to stay." I sounded like a whining child, but I couldn't help it.

"Must return," she replied.

I looked down at my hand for one last glance at

Flora, but she had already left.

"Come." The lady was already walking away.

I started to follow but hesitated. I looked back at the tree, wanting to burn the picture of it in my memory forever. *What a wonderful place*. I turned around and followed the lady until we reached a glowing portal suspended in the middle of the air.

"Through the light, home you will be," she said.

"Thank you. I will never forget this place."

She smiled back at me. Even though I wanted to stay longer, I wasn't going to have a chance to do that. I returned her smile, ready now to step into the portal and into whatever was behind it.

Suddenly a hand gripped my arm.

"Tell her!" she whispered fiercely to me. "All is not lost!" Her firm grip was unexpected and rough compared to the lady with whom I'd just spent my time.

"Tell who?" I asked quickly.

"All is not lost, she is not lost, all is not lost, she is not lost ..." She loosened her grip on me. "Tell her!" she almost yelled as she pushed me into the light.

Before I could react, I was back in the corridor of doors. To my right was the opening to my bedroom, and I let out a sigh of relief. I hadn't even thought about the real world while I'd been exploring but now that I could see it again, I thought I'd better get back there before the purple door disappeared and I would be stuck in here until it opened again; Mum and Dad would worry where I was, and I didn't want to scare them.

Turning, I headed toward my bedroom, thinking more about what I'd just seen rather than where I was going. The lady's last words to me were very confusing: who was I supposed to tell? All is not lost; she is not lost … what did that mean? How was I supposed to deliver a message that I didn't understand to a person I couldn't identify?

I stepped back into my bedroom and placed my backpack on the floor. Collapsing onto the bed, I turned and noticed the door was no longer there.

Wondering just how long I had been in there, I glanced at the clock. 10:05, it said. *That's not right. It can't be right – there's no way I've only been gone five minutes.* I picked up the alarm clock and gave it a shake. I could still hear it ticking away. I could swear I had spent at least an hour inside that dream door, maybe even more.

Slipping into my pyjamas, I crawled into bed, already yawning furiously. There were so many things I didn't understand. Why did the door appear at 10 pm every night? How was it possible for five minutes to pass in my world while I spent an hour in the other? Why me? What did the lady mean when she kept chanting 'all is not lost … she is not lost?' I was still puzzled over these things when exhaustion overrode my curiosity, and I drifted off to sleep.

Chapter 11

I woke just after 9 am the next day, which was much later than usual. Thankfully, everyone had let me sleep. Any other day, Amber would've woken me by jumping all over the bed to get me up.

Stretching out as far as I could, my mind filled with last night's adventure – the purple door, the white doors, the lady, the dream tree, and Flora. I had never met a fairy before – well honestly, where would I? – which remained the most incredible part of last night.

"Wakey, wakey!" Amber sang as she burst into my room.

I grinned: I had a feeling she'd be coming in any minute. "Haha, you didn't wake me because I'm already awake."

"Oh, poo!" she pouted.

I laughed. "You are so dramatic."

Amber crawled onto my bed and lay down next to me. "You missed breakfast this morning, sleepyhead."

"Did I?" I yawned. "I must've been tired. I was up late reading."

A tiny flash of guilt swept over me as I told a little white lie.

"Yeah, Mum said. What were you reading?"

"Operation Hobby Hunt," I replied.

"Hey!" Amber sat up. "That's my book!"

Reaching over to my side table, I grabbed the book and handed it to her. "I know, and I finished it last night so you can have it back."

"It's one of my favourites," she said as she hugged the book to her chest.

"Which is why I always take such good care of it," I replied. "Now get up so I can get out of bed and get dressed. I'm hungry."

She scooted over to the edge and jumped off the bed. "Mum's put everything away already."

"Well, I'll just have to have cereal then, won't I?"

"Okay," said Amber. "I have to keep practicing my coin trick. I'll be in the treehouse if you want to come and play."

"Maybe later, squirt," I said. "I want breakfast, and then I have to clean my room."

Amber looked around. "It doesn't look messy to me."

"I know, but Mum said it was, so I better tidy up." I looked around and saw the backpack I'd dropped on the floor last night when I returned. I needed to get those keys away and safe in the chest before anyone found them. I realised as I put them away that I was fortunate to have matched a key and a door. I had no clue how many doors there were, but I knew how many keys I had, and was glad I had chosen those keys to take with me. But how would I decide which ones to take next? There was no guarantee I'd be able to find a matching door, and there was no way I could take all the keys with me. It would take me forever to go through them all to match them to a door. What I needed was a list of the symbols on the white doors so I could find the right keys and take them with me next time.

I decided to take a pad and pen with me to draw the symbols from the doors on my next visit, that way I'd be more prepared next time. Happy with my plan, I dressed and made my way to the kitchen for breakfast.

"Aunt Leah is coming over today," Mum announced as I ate.

I wasn't sure I wanted to see Aunt Leah. At first, I'd been angry at her for giving me that globe, but now that I'd seen what was behind the door, I didn't know how I felt.

"Where's Dad?" I asked.

"He had to go to work early."

"Don't worry," she added, "You don't need to be here; she's just dropping off some flowers for me."

"What are the flowers for?" I asked.

"Mrs Montgomery at the hospital. She doesn't have any family here, so I wanted to brighten up her day a little." Mum volunteered in the senior's wing of the hospital once a week and spent the day just visiting the older adults there. It was a pretty nice thing to do, and she was always coming home with interesting stories.

"Is that the one who can't remember who she is?"

"No, that's Mrs Donahue. Mrs Montgomery is the lady who was in a car accident and didn't have any family in the country. Remember, she's the one who told me about rescuing all those kittens when she was a little girl."

She was only my age when she found a heap of kittens dumped in a drain. She tried to get them out by herself, and when she couldn't, she called the fire brigade and the police and made *them* rescue the kittens. It made the news and everything.

From the front of the house came the sound of tyres crunching on the gravel.

"That must be Leah now," Mum said.

"I'm done," I said. "I'll be in my room listening to music." I hurried from the room before Aunt Leah walked in and saw me.

Chapter 12

Courtney

As usual, with breakfast complete, Courtney started by wiping down the table. *Always a mess for me to clean up*, she thought as Leah breezed into the kitchen. Sometimes Courtney envied her sister, who travelled the world meeting new people. Courtney was too busy to jet-set the globe – she couldn't even consider it with two daughters, a husband and a household to run. Too many people depended on her. Leah, however, had no commitments and no family except Courtney's, so time was her friend.

She swept into the room, as she always did, and fell flamboyantly into one of the chairs at the table.

Courtney looked at her, one eyebrow raised, waiting for whatever drama concerned her at this moment.

"Would you believe the police pulled me over for a breathalyzer? At 9:30 in the morning? That's just crazy. Can't they see that I am NOT the type to drink and drive?" She pointed to herself as if that explained it all.

"They're just doing their job," Courtney told her, taking the sensible road as always.

"But for me?" Leah held her hands up in a confused gesture.

"You did get up to a bit of mischief when you were younger." Courtney smiled. "Remember when you painted the side of the shed in those logos you were into at the time? You spent all day, or most of it, meticulously painting that wall. And then when you realised Ma and Pa were due home in an hour you tried to wipe them all off ..."

"... only to find out that I'd used the wrong paint and water wouldn't remove it," Leah added, and then laughed. "I still remember watching you on your bike, pedalling furiously down to the local shop to get some scourers and methylated spirits."

"Yeah, well it took all our pocket money to buy that stuff, and you never paid me back either. Besides, you couldn't have gone yourself; you wouldn't have been able to get to the shop and back in that time without collapsing," Courtney said, looking sideways at her.

"I was sick a lot," Leah agreed.

"We tiptoed around you for a long time, making sure you didn't exert yourself and end up in the hospital. Imagine how much trouble I would have been in if that had happened."

"That's why you went to the shops, and not me?" Leah suddenly realised.

"Yes. We were always protecting you. Coffee?"

"Darling, I'd love one," Leah smiled at her sister and nodded. "It'll help with my hangover."

They looked at each other and laughed.

"What flowers did you bring me?" Courtney said, changing the subject.

"Oh yes, they're in the car. I'll get them out in a minute. A beautiful mix of yellows and whites. Roses, carnations, and a few orchids for good measure. Beautiful flowers that say Get well soon."

"Sounds lovely. Thanks, Leah."

"You, my dear, are most welcome. Anything for my big sister."

Courtney loved Leah's flower arrangements. You could see so much of her personality and flair in each collection. It was no wonder she owned the largest chain of florists in the state.

"So where is the next holiday?" she asked. Leah was never around for long. She was one of those people that needed to keep moving, both figuratively and literally.

"Well, I read about this fissure underwater where you can swim between two continents. It's in Iceland, and the water is so clear and in some places the spaces are so narrow you can touch both continents at the same time."

"Wow, that does sound interesting," Courtney said.

"Or the Marble Caves in Chile are supposed to be beautiful too."

"Take me with you …" Courtney joked.

"Dear Courtney, when your girls are out of school, I will take you on the trip of a lifetime," Leah promised. "Where are the girls by the way?"

"Morgan's in her room listening to music, and Amber's most likely in the treehouse. They didn't seem keen to hang around today."

"Did Morgan love that snow globe I got for her? It was from the Swiss Alps that one."

"Hmmm …" Courtney frowned. "I don't recall seeing it in her room. I wonder where she put it?"

"I just had to get it for her."

"Another useless trinket …"

"It's no worse than that silly rock you have on the mantlepiece in the lounge."

"Hey!" Courtney quipped. "It's a beautiful rock. Lots of colours."

Leah sat silent for a moment.

"I have a confession," she began but didn't elaborate.

Courtney waited patiently for her sister to reveal her big secret.

"I bought that specific globe for a reason," she said.

"What do you mean?" Courtney asked her.

"Did you take a look at it?"

"Well, no. She wrapped it up that day and put it back in the box."

"The door is purple."

As soon as Leah finished her sentence, Courtney

felt time stop. The birds stopped singing. The clock stopped chiming.

Courtney stopped breathing. "Oh, Leah, what have you done?"

Chapter 13

Leah

Okay, Leah knew her sister wasn't going to be happy when she finally told her, but she didn't understand why it was such an issue. The way Courtney acted now though, you would have thought Leah had stolen one of her children. She watched Courtney as she paced the room, left, right, left, right, arms wildly swinging as she gestured away. She looked furious, so much so she could see the redness creep from her face down past her neckline. Leah almost admired how she was able to go from a pale white to an angry red in seconds.

Focus, she told herself. *Wait until she calms down and then have a rational conversation.*

That door was one of the most beautiful things that had ever happened to Leah. What kid wouldn't love a secret like that to explore? The lure of magical worlds; wonders of the kind you would never see in the real world. Leah had spent many years travelling all the continents and countries, seeking out something, anything that was half as beautiful as some of those places she'd seen behind that magic door. She felt lucky Courtney had taken her in there at all. For some reason, Courtney was the only one who could go through it, and the only way Leah could go was if they were holding hands. Leah was never able to go by herself – she'd snuck into Courtney's room too many times to count when she wasn't there, but she couldn't even find the door.

Courtney had been her ticket in, and they'd had a lot of fun experiences in there. She was pretty sure Courtney even took Robert in there once or twice after they'd met. Even though it was wondrous, adventurous and amazing, Courtney had stopped exploring those worlds the summer her best friend, Tiana, went missing. She was about thirteen or fourteen at the time. Leah assumed she didn't have the heart to enjoy anything again after that. But that had also meant Leah couldn't go back there either, and that had devastated her.

She looked up and noticed Courtney was crying, and lowering herself slowly to a chair opposite her. Alarmed, Leah leaned forward. "What's wrong?"

"Haven't you been listening to anything I've said?" Courtney cried. For the first time, Leah noticed real fear in her sister's eyes.

Oh crap, I think I'm in real trouble here, Leah thought. She hadn't expected this reaction at all. Anger, yes. But fear? Not at all. Leah moved around the table and sat down next to her sister, and wrapped her arms around Courtney's shoulders.

The moment Courtney felt her there, she wept even harder, and Leah's eyes welled up too. What had she done?

Chapter 14

Courtney

Anger, sadness, confusion all flowed through Courtney, but most of all she felt a terrible ache in her heart she thought she'd gotten past a long time ago. Misery reverberated through her whole body, making its way slowly through her extremities, simultaneously freezing and heating her. Alongside that came an almost incapacitating fear, becoming more prominent by the second, for Morgan, her beautiful daughter, who may be in danger of finding the magic door.

"Court?" Leah whispered as she squeezed Courtney's shoulders.

Courtney wasn't ready to talk to her yet. She wasn't prepared to make nice with her. Leah had brought that globe into her home, intending to start something. Gathering all her strength, Courtney sat up and said, "I think you should leave."

Leah looked at her, her jaw dropping open. "You don't mean that."

"I do. Please go. Now."

"But Courtney ..."

"Now!" Courtney spoke a bit sharper than she intended.

Leah moved slowly, a little shocked, and hesitantly headed toward the door. Courtney could feel Leah looking back at her, but she refused to engage, knowing she might lose her resolve and tell her to stay. Leah walked out the door and returned a moment later with the flowers. Placing them on the table, she lingered for a moment, hoping for an invitation to stay but it wasn't coming. Resigned, she left the house, and when Courtney heard the car start her tears flowed again.

In the late afternoon, while Courtney was preparing dinner, Robert walked through the door.

"Hi, hon," Courtney said, giving him a peck on the cheek.

Robert smiled at her and put his briefcase on the chair. She caught his eye and stared at the case.

"Oops," he said, "sorry."

Picking up the briefcase again, he walked out of the room and put it in his study before returning to the kitchen.

"Nice flowers," he said, nodding towards the flowers in the middle of the table. "Leah's?"

She nodded. "For Mrs Montgomery at the hospital."

"Ah," Robert replied. "That's right. You didn't take them to her today?"

"No." Courtney sighed.

"That doesn't sound good."

"No. We need to talk."

Robert looked at her. "What have I done now?"

She smiled and said, "You haven't done anything. It's Leah."

"Has she got herself in some sort of trouble? We can't help her out financially."

Courtney laughed. Like Leah would ever need money. "No, it's nothing like that. It's something she said to me today that's got me worried."

Robert picked up the peeling knife. "Can I help with something?"

Without replying, she handed him the carrots and potatoes. They'd done this process so many times there was no need for instructions.

Passing a bowl to him, Courtney said, "Do you remember that snow globe Leah got Morgan for her birthday?"

"Not really," he replied. "Can't say I paid that much attention."

"Well, she bought her a snow globe – a little cottage in the mountains."

"Cute."

"Turns out it had a purple door on it."

Robert stopped his peeling mid-air. "She did what?"

"I know." Courtney sighed and put the knife on the bench. Turning to him, she said, "Robby, she did it on purpose. She wanted Morgan to see that door hoping it might trigger something. At first, I was shocked. Then angry, and then all the memories of Tiana came flooding back."

"Oh, Courtney, I'm so sorry. I know how much you still miss her."

"I didn't realise how much. More importantly, though, is Morgan. What if she finds the door?"

"She can't. We locked the door, remember … when she was having those dreams a year or two ago?"

"I know, but what if she can? We don't know exactly how everything works. What if she finds it?"

"Then we'll deal with it when it happens." Robert hugged her. "Besides, she's not having that dream anymore, is she?"

"I don't think so," she admitted. "I asked her only last night if she was still dreaming it, remember? She said she hadn't had it in forever. And those were her words. We know it will only show once she has it every night. I think we're safe for now."

"Well then …" He smiled. "… no need to worry. But I think you need to tell Leah the truth about Tiana."

"That's not a good idea."

"Why not?"

Courtney couldn't think of one. "It's just not."

"There's no reason not to. I know you wanted to protect Leah because she looked up to Tiana when she was little. But Courtney, she's an adult now, she'll understand. Besides, if she knew what happened to Tiana, maybe she wouldn't have brought that snow globe back."

"So, it's my fault now?" Courtney retorted.

"That's not what I'm saying." Robert's voice stayed calm and soothing. "But you know I'm right. You need to tell her, and soon." He picked up the peeler and kept working on the vegetables.

They stood side by side in silence while contemplating what would happen if she told Leah about Tiana. Would she blame her? It's possible, considering Courtney was the reason she went missing.

"Do you think she will blame me?" she asked softly.

"It wasn't your fault, Courtney. There is no way you could have done any more to find her. You must let it go, or it'll eat you up inside. Leah will understand."

"I'm not sure. Besides, I asked her to leave the house. She probably won't come back in a hurry anyway."

"She would if you asked her." He smiled. "So you told her to get out, huh?"

"I did," Courtney said sheepishly.

"I wish I was there to see that. I bet Leah doesn't get too many people brave enough to turf her out of anywhere."

She laughed out loud. "Probably not."

Chapter 15

This time I was prepared. My backpack was ready to go. Nestled inside it was everything I needed for tonight's exploration, including the notepad and pen. I had carefully selected ten keys this time, hoping I would get a chance to see what was behind another one of those doors. With thoughts of dream trees and fairies swirling around in my head, I was eager to get going and discover more worlds like the last one.

The clock showed a quarter to ten as I waited impatiently. The day had gone by slowly, but not quite as slow as yesterday had. Deep down, I knew the door wouldn't appear until 10 pm, so there was no need to tie myself up in knots wondering. I understood a little better now the magic of the door and how it worked.

Amber and I had played most of the day up in the treehouse, only coming down for food. It was a good day and a great distraction for me. She almost had that coin trick down, although she still wouldn't tell me how it worked or let me help her perfect it. At least it wasn't the cards this time – the strange feeling the Ace of Spades had given me now stuck in my memory. Playing cards would probably never be the same for me again.

Dinner had been unusually quiet. Mum was usually very chatty and always cracking jokes and trying to make us all laugh. Not tonight. Tonight, she was reticent and barely spoke at all. I wondered if it had anything to do with Aunt Leah's visit this morning, but because I had been in my room, I could only assume. On the other hand, Dad spoke way too much, like he was trying to fill in the silence. It was a bizarre meal, and I couldn't wait to get out of there.

Amber and I had sat in the lounge room afterwards talking about it, trying to figure out what was going on.

"Did you see Mum tonight?" she had whispered to me.

"Yeah."

"She was weird, wasn't she?"

"Yeah," I repeated.

"And Dad too."

"Yep. I know, I saw."

"What do you think is wrong?" Amber had asked, looking a little worried.

"I'm sure it's nothing serious." I hugged her. "Honestly. Probably just a bad day or something."

Whatever it was, it wasn't our business. I could tell it wasn't Mum and Dad fighting with each other, and that was all that mattered. "Parents are allowed to have off days as well," I told her. "Maybe she's just tired? I know I don't talk much when I'm tired." Amber had seemed to be okay with that answer, and we spent the rest of the night playing board games until bedtime.

So here I was now, sitting at my desk waiting impatiently for the door to appear. I had mixed feelings about everything that had happened lately. It was beyond exciting – never in my wildest dreams could I have imagined something like this. Yet at the same time, I felt I should keep it a secret. But what was the use of having all of these worlds accessible to me if I couldn't share it with anyone?

At precisely ten o'clock, the door pulsed its way onto my wall, as it had done the last few nights. I stood and made my way to it, throwing my backpack over my shoulder. The door opened as smoothly and quietly as it had the previous night, and I made my way into the corridor with more confidence than before. Stopping for a second, I pulled the pad and pen out of my backpack's side pocket and prepared to make notes.

Wandering down the corridor, I studied the symbols on each door, taking my time now I knew the door wasn't closing in five minutes. As I passed each one, I sketched a picture and wrote a description of what I saw on my notepad for later inspection. Just like the keys, each one was different. I must've gone past at least fifteen doors before I came to one I thought I recognised.

Putting my bag down, I reached in for the ten keys I had brought with me. I pulled out the black key with the rectangle around an oval and, holding it up, smiled that it was a perfect match for the symbol on the door. The rest of the keys I tossed haphazardly back in the bag as I focused on entering a new door for a new adventure. Without hesitation, I placed the key in the lock, opened the door and stepped inside.

Chapter 16

I almost walked into someone rushing past at the exact moment I entered and I reeled backward. Unlike the last world, this one filled my ears with hundreds of different sounds at once, with smells both good and bad, and sights I had never seen before. I tried to keep to the side out of everyone's way and looked around to take in my surroundings.

I stood in a city, a city in the middle of its busiest hour. People were everywhere, although I couldn't see them clearly through the falling snow. Most of them hid beneath beanies or oversized ski jackets and furry hoods. It made me wonder how cold I would get here; the jeans and t-shirt I had on obviously wasn't going to be enough. I looked down at my arms while considering what I was going to do and noticed I wasn't wearing my own clothes anymore.

I held my arms out in front of me: I now had on a grey ski jacket with a fur-lined hood that was pulled up over my head. *Strange.* Not only did I walk into this world but somehow managed to change my outfit on the way. At least I wasn't going to be cold.

I looked around again, now enthralled by the layers of falling snow. I had never seen snow before, except in that little snow globe Aunt Leah had given me. I'd seen it on TV of course, but that wasn't the same as standing in it. I held out my hands in wonder and turned circles on the sidewalk. *I am standing in snow!* I held my hand out again as if waiting for Flora to arrive and instead watched as the tiniest of snowflakes landed on me. *Incredible!*

Masses of people hurried past on the sidewalk, taking me with them, sweeping me along like seaweed flowing with the tide. Growing up in a large house with a huge backyard, the quick steps of the crowd and the frantic feel of the city had me a little overwhelmed. Head down, I followed the heels of the person in front, searching for a gap. I didn't know where I was anymore, nor what was around me and could feel panic start to settle in. I needed to get out, away from the crowd, so I started trying to push my way through.

"Excuse me," I mumbled. "Pardon me, can I get through? Excuse me ..."

It made no difference: they flanked me on both sides like soldiers deliberately marching me towards an Evil Queen. They weren't letting me go anywhere except for where they wanted me to go. The panic began to rise as I felt completely stuck inside this mob of people. We reached an intersection with traffic lights and came to a standstill. Each person around me stood in silence as they waited for the lights to change.

Finally, the lights turned green for the pedestrians to cross, and without delay, the crowd that had surrounded me moved in three different directions. I found myself standing on the corner, now alone. I sighed with deep relief, realising my overactive imagination had probably attributed more evil intentions than was warranted. I wasn't expecting a city when I'd gone through the rectangle door. Being swept up in that group had scared me a lot more than I realised, and now I just wanted to go back. Back to my bed, back to safety, back to the home that I knew. The trouble was that while I was stuck in the crowd, we had taken so many turns I had no idea where I was now.

The city continued its busy pace while I tried to work out where I was. My best bet was to retrace my steps, so I turned around and started walking back the way I thought I had come. Trying to remember anything from those moments when I'd first stepped through the door, I only succeeded in getting more frustrated as I realised I'd been too busy looking at my clothes and the snowfall to notice where I was. By then, I had been swept away by a human wave, and it was too late.

What was I going to do? Could I ask someone where the glowing light that led back to the corridor was? Presumably, laughter would follow. *Think!* I told myself. *I must've seen something.* Nothing came to mind, however, and I was just about ready to burst into tears.

"Are you lost?" a small voice came from below.

Looking down, I found myself standing in front of a young girl, maybe five years old or less, but certainly way too young to be out here by herself. She had a tiny scar on her left cheek and looked familiar, though I was sure I didn't know her.

"A little," I replied with a forced smile. "Are you lost too?"

"No, I'm here with my sister," she said proudly.

"Where's your sister now?" I asked. The little girl pointed at a small park a little further down, where an older girl sat under a tree on a bench, head down, hoodie over her face to stay warm.

"Why would you come outside in this weather?" I asked.

"I wanted to play on the swing," the girl replied.

"Maybe you should get back to your sister before she starts to worry," I said to her.

The girl ignored me. "Come meet my sister; she can help you. What's your name? You're pretty just like her."

Before I could say anything else, she grabbed my hand and started dragging me over to the park. I wondered for a moment whether this was a safe thing to do, considering all the stranger danger talks Mum had with Amber and I … but how dangerous could a five-year-old and her sister be? As we drew closer, I wondered whether the sister would appreciate a stranger dragged over to her for help.

It's a little late; I thought as we approached her.

"Hey Morgan, this girl is lost and needs help. She's pretty like you."

Morgan? The girl sitting under the tree is also called Morgan?

I didn't know any other Morgans, so it was weird to meet another one.

"Please will you help her? She's lost," the little girl persisted, not unlike Amber.

The girl under the tree stood up. She was about my height and had my colour hair. She lifted the hood away from her face and stared at me.

"Are you lost?" she finally asked.

I couldn't respond. I couldn't even breathe. The girl in front of me *was* me. She had my hair, eyes, nose, and mouth, even down to the little scar on my left cheek where I had hurt myself at three years old. Her skin tone was the same as mine, and she even spoke the same way.

"Are you lost?" she repeated.

Still, I couldn't respond. I looked around in disbelief, wondering if anyone else was seeing what I was seeing. No wonder the girl kept saying I was pretty like her sister; we were identical.

"Um, yes I am," I replied. "The little girl, your sister ..."

"Morgan," Morgan interrupted.

"Yes?" I answered, confused.

"No ... Morgan." She pointed to her sister who had run over to the swing. "My sister's name is

Morgan."

What were the odds of meeting two other Morgans, especially from the same family? It was more than a little strange, but I needed someone's help to get back, so I ignored the niggling feeling and asked, "Your sister said you might be able to help me find my way back home. Is that true?"

"Not me," she replied, and my heart dropped into my stomach. "Mum might be able to though."

"Where is she?" I looked around.

"She's not here. She's at work. But she'll be home in the next hour or so if you want to come and wait for her."

"Um, where is home? Is it far away?"

"Nah, just around the corner. Come on, Morgan, time to go," she yelled out.

I wasn't sure if I should follow her or not. I didn't know these people, but I also didn't know where I was or where I needed to go. These two Morgans were the only option I had at the moment to find my way back.

"Okay," I agreed.

"But it's just stopped snowing!" little Morgan complained.

"C'mon, squirt, you know we need to get home."

I called Amber 'squirt' all the time.

Little Morgan ran ahead of us but always seemed to keep the same distance. Morgan and I walked along the sidewalk and talked.

"So where are you from?" Morgan asked me.

I didn't know how to answer that, so I asked her a question instead. "How old is Morgan?"

"Six, but she thinks she's way older," she smiled. "Do you have a sister or brother?"

"I have a younger sister too, but she's eight."

"Do they get less annoying?"

"Nah, she's great. I love spending time with her," I replied. "Have you lived in the city forever?" I couldn't imagine growing up here at all. Morgan started to respond, but her voice faded as I began to notice the people around me. Now that it had stopped snowing, they had pulled their hoods from their faces, and I could see them much better. The lady coming toward me on the left looked like a mix of my Mum and me. She moved quite close to me, allowing me to see the scar on her left cheek also.

Morgan continued talking beside me, but I wasn't listening. I was watching. Another teenager walked past; a scar on the left cheek: another teenager, and another – all the same. An older lady about twenty-five, also looking like me – a scar on her cheek. That one pushed a pram with a baby, and the baby looked just like my baby pictures that Mum kept on the wall. An older lady nudging a walking frame came by next. She had a lot more wrinkles, but I could still see the faint lines of that scar on her cheek too.

What is going on?

"I can't handle this," I said, my voice trembling.

"It's okay; we're here anyway." Morgan had reached a small set of steps leading up to a plain brown door. She followed her sister up the stairs and unlocked the entrance to the house. "Do you want something to drink?" she asked as she held the door open for me.

I wasn't sure about a drink, but I needed to sit down. "Just water, thanks."

We moved into the kitchen, which was small and cosy, and poured me a glass of water. Little Morgan raced off to another room, and I heard the TV set click on.

"How did you get that scar on your cheek?" I asked suddenly. I had to know how it happened. Mine was an accident when I was three. I had inadvertently pulled some trinkets off a shelf when I had tried to climb up it, and one of them had cut me as it fell. I don't remember it myself, but Mum had told me the story a couple of times.

Morgan laughed. "Just a silly accident. I was only three, and I was climbing everything at the time. There was a statue of a fairy on top of a shelf that I just had to have. I somehow moved a chair over to the shelf and tried to get the fairy. Mum says I grabbed the shelf when trying to climb it and the whole thing came down on top of me. I think I may have even broken the fairy after all of that."

"And Morgan?" I said faintly. "How did she get hers?" I didn't dare breathe.

"Hers was just a silly accident. She was only three, and she was climbing everything at the time. There was a statue on top of a shelf that she just had to have. She somehow moved a chair over to the shelf and tried to get it. Mum says she grabbed the shelf when trying to climb it and the whole thing came down on top of her." Morgan laughed. "Like I said, a silly accident."

My heart thumped heavily. Morgan didn't even seem to realise that she'd given me the same story for both of them. These people were me. Little Morgan was me at six years old. Older Morgan was me as I was now. All those people on the street had looked like me, or different versions of me. Some were old, some were young, but they were all the same. They were me.

"So," Morgan said to me, "you never said where you live. Do you stay in the city as well?"

I stared at Morgan. Every time I looked at her, it was like looking into a mirror. I kept waiting for her to copy my movements as a reflection would, but it never happened. "No, just visiting." *And not for long,* I prayed.

Morgan frowned like she didn't understand what I had said. "So, you don't live in the city? That's weird."

"What time will your Mum be here? I'd like to get home."

"Should be any minute. She's probably been at the hospital with some of the patients."

"Is she a doctor or a nurse?"

"No, she just volunteers once a week. She's just nice like that." I dropped my glass onto the table, the water splashing onto my hand. Morgan looked at me suddenly. "Are you okay?"

"Sorry," I mumbled. "It must've slipped." She was me, living my life in this other world. But then what about little Morgan? Was she living my life too, just years behind me and this other Morgan? I was thoroughly confused, or confuzzled as Amber liked to say. This world was making my head spin, and it was all I could do not to stare at her.

The sound of a key in the lock broke the silence as Morgan's mother came into the house. Walking into the kitchen, she carried two bags of groceries, handing them over to myself and Morgan.

"Morgan," she said, handing one bag to her daughter.

"Take this bag, will you?" she said again as she gave the second one to me.

I couldn't take my eyes off her as she moved around the kitchen. This lady was me, but older. Always warm and smiling, she looked like one of those who regularly took care of others. She spoke warmly and fondly to me even though she didn't know me. She seemed to be around forty-five-ish, but I couldn't see the scar on her cheek on closer inspection. Maybe she wasn't me? Was this the first person I had seen that wasn't Morgan?

"You don't have the scar on your cheek," I blurted out before I could stop myself.

She laughed and said, "Well, of course, I do. But the wonders of makeup these days means I can cover it up. Now hurry up and bring that bag over here before the ice cream melts. It's my favourite - mint choc chip." Then she winked at me. Mint choc chip was my favourite too.

"How did she know who I was?" I whispered to Morgan after I'd handed the bag over.

"She's got the Instinct," she whispered back.

"What's the Instinct?"

"She just knows. She knows everything before it happens. It's kind of cool."

I stared at her Mum again. Does she know everything because she has already lived forty-five years of her life? She therefore must know what will happen and when.

"I need to get home, but I don't know how to get there. Can you please help me?" I couldn't stop the pleading in my voice.

"Oh, of course, Morgan." She hugged me and smiled. "That's why I came home early. I knew you'd be here and that you'd need my help."

"Thank you, Mrs ..." I hesitated, not knowing their last name.

"Please, just call me Morgan," she finished.

Of course.

"Thank you, ... Morgan." Never had I said my name so many times in one day.

"Morgan, leave us now. Morgan, come sit at the table with me."

She patted the seat next to her as she stared straight at me.

"Was nice to meet you," Morgan said as she left the room.

"You too. Thank you for everything," I added.

"Now, we need to get you back to the door. Can I have one strand of your hair?"

Like a puppet, I plucked a single strand of hair from my head. *Maybe she does know everything.*

"You know where the door is?" I asked excitedly.

"Pffft," she laughed. "Of course not. But I know how to help you find it. Morgan is always finding strays around the place. She seems to have a sense for them. Always a door they are trying to find. I've never seen one myself, but I can feel them around me."

"How do you find them if you don't know where they are?"

"As I said, I can feel them. It's like a magnet when you put the same sides against each other. Remember? Like in year five, when we had them in science with Mr Edwards? We were making them shoot off the table with Jenny."

Lost for words now, I listened to her talk as if we were one person.

"The last one flew off the table and landed on Christian's foot. Don't you remember how much we laughed and laughed until we were told to be quiet?"

I couldn't speak, so I just nodded.

"Just like those magnets, the doors push me away. That's how I know they are there. That's how I know they aren't for me, only for those strays that

Morgan finds. I know you're not a stray, I'm sorry if that offends, but that's what we call them … you."

"How do you know all this?" It came out as a whisper.

"Haven't you worked it out yet? I am you. You are me. We are the same."

"But so is Morgan and Morgan."

"All you. Every one of us carries the story of you."

"You know what happens to me in my future." I wasn't speaking to her so much as myself.

"Well, yes, but don't ask me to tell you because I won't."

She cupped her hands into a ball. "Now place your hands over mine, close your eyes and think of whatever is behind the door that you want to get back to."

My eyes closed, and straight away I pictured myself curled up in bed.

"Good," Mrs Morgan said. "Now tell me, what is your favourite colour?"

"Huh?"

"Keep your eyes closed," she warned, "or you'll break it before we've finished making it."

Obediently I kept my eyes closed and replied, "Aqua."

"Aqua it is! I love that colour too. Well, I did when I was younger, my tastes have changed a little now." She shifted in her seat. "Are you ready?"

I nodded.

"Okay, you can open your eyes now."

Eagerly I opened my eyes and focused. Mrs Morgan was holding the end of an aqua thread. It didn't look real to me; it didn't seem substantial enough to do anything with it like tie a knot or knit a jumper. What I did see though was a translucent glow around the thread itself that shimmered in the light like a ray of sunshine bouncing off a lake. It was pretty – I couldn't stop staring at it.

"Now you need to hold onto this thread very carefully. Follow it back to your door. Its power comes from the strand of hair and the images of home you gave it. No one else can see it except you, but you can't drop it, or it will disappear. If you drop it, it's likely you won't find your way back here either." She held out her hand for me to take the thread.

I grasped it between my fingers but could feel nothing. It was visible to me, and I couldn't feel anything between my fingertips at all. To make sure I didn't lose it, I wrapped the thread around my finger a couple of times and tried to hold on tight to the end.

"Good luck," she smiled as she opened the front door and hugged me before I left.

Looking out the doorway, I could see the thread as it floated down the street to the end of the road and turned right. Double-checking to make sure I still had hold of it, I started down the steps. "Thank you again."

Mrs Morgan just smiled and closed the door behind her, like she had done this a dozen times before. I headed down the street, eyes glued to the thread that would take me home. When I was nearly halfway to the first corner, I heard my name called out.

"Morgan! Morgan!" I turned to see little Morgan running after me. She came sliding to a stop on the snow-covered sidewalk and beckoned at me with her finger to come closer. I leaned down as she put her hand up to her mouth and whispered into my ear.

"Don't forget to tell her. She is not lost. Two must become one! Don't forget to tell her!"

Before I could say anything, she turned and started running back.

"Wait!" I yelled out. "What does that mean? Who am I supposed to tell? Wait!"

But of course, she didn't wait; she ran back to her house and closed the door.

That was the second time I had heard similar words, and I still wasn't any closer to figuring out what it meant. I turned and continued to follow the thread through the city. How was I going to find out what they meant? I didn't know who I was supposed to tell. Even if I did, those words wouldn't mean anything to anyone I knew.

I'd had enough of this 'world of me'. Everywhere I turned it was like looking into a mirror. I was definitely more than ready to go home. Continuing to walk through the streets of the city, I kept the thread secured to my fingers. Several turns had come and gone, and I had started wondering if she was sending me in the wrong direction, but I had no choice but to trust her Instinct. I was getting close to panicking when I noticed the thread disappear up ahead on the left. Hopeful, I raced up ahead to the point where it stopped.

There it was: the door I had come through. Without pausing to see who was watching, I jumped straight through, back into the black corridor. On this side of the light, I noticed my clothes had changed again. I was back in the black passage, looking at the magic door at the end of the corridor that led straight back to my room. Without hesitation, I ran back through the door and flopped down on my bed, glad to be back home. I swear I fell asleep smiling.

Chapter 17

The next morning, I slept in again, except this time the smell of pancakes wafting through the house woke me. My stomach rumbled in hunger. No way was I missing out on my favourite breakfast, so I jumped out of bed and headed to the kitchen without even bothering to change.

"I smell pancakes," I announced as I entered the kitchen.

Mum laughed at me. "You should be a sniffer dog at the airport."

"Well, I know I would find the pancakes," I replied. I grabbed the syrup from the bench and put it on the table. "Where is everyone else?"

"Your sister is still asleep, believe it or not. Maybe you can go and wake her up for me?"

"Sure," I said. In my head, I was already planning revenge on her for trying to wake me up yesterday.

"Be nice."

It was like she could read my mind. I blinked innocently and said, "I don't know what you're talking about."

"You know exactly what I'm talking about." Her

words were stern, but she was smiling. "Go get your sister."

When I peeked into her room, Amber was still fast asleep. I tiptoed in so that she wouldn't hear me and spoil all my fun. Looking around her room, I spotted a bird toy made of feathers. The tail would be perfect for my plan.

Holding the fake bird by the head and crouching down beside the bed, I brushed its tail softly against Amber's cheeks and nose. Absently, she reached up and scratched her nose, then returned her arm to her side. I brushed her face again. This time her hand shot up to her face and she rubbed it more forcefully. Giggling, I brushed it over her nose again.

She nearly smacked herself in the face trying to brush it away. I couldn't help laughing out loud. Amber's eyes opened, slowly letting the world in but not expecting me to be inches from her face. She let out a scream when she saw me right in front of her. That was all it took for me to fall on the floor, tears rolling down my face.

Frowning, Amber threw her pillow at me. "That's just mean," she said.

I was so busy trying to catch my breath and wipe the tears from my eyes I couldn't reply. Then, "So … funny …" I managed to get out.

Amber started laughing with me. "I guess it was a little bit funny."

I'd finally managed to control my laughter. "A lot funny," I replied, starting to laugh again. "Come on, squirt, out of bed – Mum's making pancakes for breakfast."

"Yum!" Amber smiled and stretched. "We haven't had pancakes for ages."

"Well let's go then before they get cold."

"K."

Amber followed me down the hall back to the kitchen.

"That smells so good," she commented as she sat down at her usual seat at the table.

"It does, doesn't it?" Mum replied as she placed a stack in the middle of the table. "Go for it girls, I've got to do some work on the computer."

"Thanks, Mum. Pass me the syrup?" I asked Amber.

She handed it across, and we sat in silence as we tucked into our pancakes. Today I was planning to figure out what keys I could find for the symbols I had written down on my notepad the previous night. Proud of myself for thinking ahead, I could now check the keys I had and hopefully walk into the corridor tonight with a key that would match one of the doors there. The harder choice would be deciding which door to go through first.

Still puzzled over the message given to me, both by the lady in white and little Morgan, I struggled to figure out what it meant. *All is not lost. She is not lost. Two must become one.* Now that I'd been given similar messages by two different people in two other worlds, I realised it had to be something important, maybe more critical than I realised. There had to be more to it, something I didn't know or didn't understand yet.

"Hello? Hello? Earth to Morgan?"

I looked up to see Amber waving her fork at me.

"What?"

"You weren't even listening to me!" she complained.

"I'm sorry, squirt. I'm listening to you now. What were you saying?"

"Nothing," Amber pouted.

"Don't be like that," I said. "Tell me. Please."

"Well … okay. I was just saying that I need another trick to do now that I can do the coin one. You need to help me find another trick. Maybe I should do a scarf one or a magic ring one …"

I drifted off again, my thoughts drawn back to the puzzle handed to me through the magic door. Why would the message have come from two different people? They weren't aware of each other from what I could see, although I didn't know that for sure. How can a six-year-old be so wise and seem so old? What a strange gift to have, to be able to collect 'strays', as Mrs Morgan put it. What did that mean? She had spoken about other doors and other strays, like she had done the same thing for many different people. Did that mean other people could go through those doors? I didn't see anyone who looked out of place, but then again, every person I had seen had been me.

"Morgan!!" Now she was yelling at me. "You're not listening AGAIN!'

"I'm so sorry, Amber," I apologised.

"No, you're not."

"I am, honest."

"You are not. You haven't listened to me all morning. You don't care about what I'm saying at all."

"That's not true, squirt." I think I'd upset her this time.

"Don't call me that!"

She shot up from the table and stormed out of the kitchen. Sighing, I rose and put all the dishes in the sink, including Amber's. I would have to go after her in a minute, but Mum would kill us if we left a mess in there.

Making my way down the hall a few minutes later, I knocked quietly on Amber's door.

"Amber?" I said through the door frame. "I'm sorry."

But I was met with silence.

"Amber?" I said again, opening the door just a fraction so I could peek in. She wasn't in her room after all, which meant she was most likely in the treehouse. I couldn't let her stay angry with me, so I headed straight out there.

At the top of the ladder, I was able to see over the edge of the flooring. Amber sat in the corner of the treehouse, playing with a deck of cards. Instantly remembering the Ace of Spades, I paused before climbing onto the planks. Then I pushed my thoughts aside and sat down next to Amber.

"I'm sowwy …" I sang to her in my best baby voice. "Pwease forgive me?" The best way to fix this was humour. "I wuv yooooooo!"

A tiny smile floated across her face, stayed for a second then disappeared.

"Amboor … I wuv yooooo, pwease don't be mad."

It was working, as she now tried to hide her face from me; she was trying not to smile. Stepping it up a notch, I reached over and started tickling her. For as long as I can remember, Amber had been ticklish everywhere – and I mean everywhere. Any time I wanted to make her laugh, all I had to do was tickle her. Down her sides, behind her knees, even her shoulders and neck could elicit a laugh.

Listening carefully for forgiveness's first sounds, it didn't take long for her to concede defeat and start laughing aloud.

"Stop it!" she giggled. "I'm going to pee myself!"

I gave her a big hug and said, "Truly, I'm sorry. I just have a lot on my mind at the moment. Forgive me?"

Glaring at me, she tried to stay angry but couldn't make it stick. She hugged me back.

"Okay. Can I show you my new trick?"

"Of course! What is it?"

For the next half hour, we sat together while Amber tried to perform magic for me. She hadn't perfected this one yet, and after several attempts she gave up and moved onto another trick, hoping to dazzle me with that one instead. Sitting there watching her, it always amazed me how vibrant and full of life she was. Okay, yes, she had gotten mad at me earlier, but it didn't take her long to get over it and back to her bubbly self. It never did. She always impressed me with the amount of energy she had – *pretty cool for a little sister*, I thought.

Later that afternoon, I finally stole some time alone to go through the keys and the symbols. I'd drawn thirteen symbols from the doors I had passed in the corridor the previous night. Some of the drawings were a bit rough, and it was difficult to make out what they were supposed to be. Admittedly I wasn't exactly good at drawing – I wasn't very creative – but at least I could make out some of them. I just had to hope a key in my chest resembled something close to the rest.

It was very time consuming going through all the keys because of the sheer volume. One at a time, I pulled them out and checked them against the drawings on my page. When I found a key that matched, I circled the picture and put the key aside. After going through every key, I only had three matches, two of which I'd already been in, and a third one that seemed to have some sort of tent picture on it.

Only three? What about all the other doors? How can I

have 137 keys and only three matches? Does that mean there are more keys somewhere that I don't have? I'd drawn thirteen pictures in my notepad, surely that meant there were at least another ten keys that weren't in my stash. *Interesting. So there must be more than 137 doors then.* If that's how many keys I had and missing ten of them that I knew of, there had to be at least 147 doors.

I sat back astonished. This magic door continued to amaze me. There were *so* many doors to explore, and I had access to 137 of them. That would keep me busy for quite a while! Then I would have to figure out whether to search for more keys in the house or start counting all the doors in the corridor. My curiosity grew as to just how many doors there were.

My thoughts drifted back to the matching key I did have. It had a tent symbol, kind of like a circus tent, not a camping tent. Of course, I could have been wrong about that too, but I didn't think so. A circus would be exciting to see, considering I had only ever seen them on TV.

I separated the key from the rest and hid it in a book on my desk. I would explore this one tonight.

Mum opened the door and came in with a pile of washing for me.

"Thanks, Mum."

She just smiled and put it down on the edge of the bed.

"All is not lost … she is not lost … what does

that mean?" Mum asked me as she looked over my shoulder.

I looked down in horror – I hadn't even realised I'd been doodling on my notepad. I'd written the same thing all over the page, written it again and again. "It's nothing."

"And what about this one?" Mum asked, pointing to the other words on the page. "Two must become one. It's a weird thing to write, isn't it?"

"Yeah, I guess so," I replied, trying to think of something fast. I said, "I'm thinking of writing a story for Amber. I was just playing around with ideas."

"What a great idea!" Mum said. "She would love that. What's it about?"

I nearly opened my mouth and started saying a magic door, but shut it quickly. I wasn't giving away my secrets – whether she believed me or not didn't matter. No one was going to find out about my magic door. "I was thinking a girl who was lost in the woods, maybe. She has to find her way out again."

"It sounds a little like Red Riding Hood to me."

"Oh yeah, it does too. I'll just have to keep thinking."

"I'm sure you'll come up with something," Mum said as she started walking out the door.

Once she had left, I put the notepad in my backpack, ready for tonight. The notebook would stay there; I might need it if I got a chance to look at more doors. The keys I packed away in the chest and stored it back behind the vent. *Tonight, I will need only one key because I know which door I'm going to explore.*

Later that night, I stood in front of the door, key in hand, symbols matching. I'd half expected the doors to move around and change positions, but they had stayed as they were last night, making it easy to find this one again. The first door had been fantastic, the second door a little scary. What would this one bring? Taking a deep breath, I unlocked the door and stepped through.

Chapter 18

The first thing that hit me was the sights and the smells. Popcorn, fairy floss and hotdogs invaded my nostrils all at once. Cinnamon doughnuts, toffee apples and hot chips soon followed. Hundreds of people surrounded me, all busy chatting with each other and having a great time. Some carried giant stuffed teddy bears while others busily ate ice-creams and other delicious-looking food. I worried about my sudden appearance, but no one paid any attention to me as I slipped unnoticed into the crowd.

The road I stood on appeared to be very long. On each side were game stands enveloped by colourful tents that had music blasting from hidden speakers and flashing neon lights that fought for my attention. Each stand looked more outlandish than the last, and was operated by men and women, some with microphones, others just using loud voices to make them stand out to the crowd. If they caught someone's eye, they would try and convince them to spend their money with them and not at the next stall.

Above me, a bright yellow sign mounted on poles reached high above the crowds. SIDESHOW ALLEY, it said in bold red writing. In smaller text underneath, the sign promised so much fun one would never want to leave. I could certainly understand why; it looked like a big party – this was every kid's dream: food, rides, games, toys, bright lights and sounds all within one's reach. Amber would have loved this: a sideshow alley fit her personality perfectly. She was probably a human version. Bright, bubbly and always bringing joy to others.

As I continued wandering, I heard faint screams echoing through the alley. No one else around me seemed to be worried, so I figured it wasn't what I thought it was. The further down the road I went, the louder they got. Eventually, the game stands started to thin out, and the spaces began to offer rides instead. Fast rides, slow rides and even rides that went upside down – which is where the screams came from – peppered the sides of the alley. Gradually, the games disappeared altogether, replaced with rides designed to take your money. *I'm glad I didn't bring any*, I thought, *or I would spend it all!*

Reaching the end of the road, I could only go left, and continued around a ninety-degree angled corner. I could now see stands selling items with hefty price tags, the sort of stuff Amber would like, things you didn't need and would probably never use again. A person walked by on stilts, standing at least two metres higher than me. He leaned down, shoved a flyer in my hand and continued on his way. It was a flyer for the midday show, and it promised to be the best show I'd ever seen, boasting a special guest appearance that would make it worth my time.

Deciding to take a look, I followed the signs for the midday show. The tent, made from sections of red and white canvas, sat in the middle of the carnival, as a centerpiece. People started to turn up and headed inside to get the best seats, carrying armfuls of popcorn from the food stand outside. Moving closer to the giant sign on the stand out the front, I tried to read the details of the guest appearance.

"Oh my gosh, there you are darling ... where have you been? We don't have much time." A lady around fifty years old rushed up to me. "Your entrance is around the back." She grabbed my arm and pulled me around to the other side of the tent, seeming a little frazzled. Her hair stuck out every which way, and she had a pencil stuck in her hair. Pushing people out the way, she hurried to get there.

"I think you have the wrong person ..." I started to say, but she ignored me and continued to pull me around to wherever this back entrance was.

"Francine! Francine!" she yelled as we entered the tent. "Francine! Where are you? She's here!" She gawped around the tent frantically. "Francine!!!" she screeched.

A young girl, no older than twenty, hurried in from my left.

"There you are," the girl said, visibly sighing with relief. "We didn't think you would make it."

"I think you have the wrong person ..." I said again.

Francine laughed out loud. "You are so funny." She steered me to a seat in front of a dressing table.

"George, Candy, Jules ... quickly, we don't have much time for you to work your magic." Francine clapped her hands together and people around her instantly responded, unlike the other lady.

"Now," she said, stopping for a second to lean toward me. "Is there anything I can get you?"

Dumbfounded, I just stared at her. *What's going on?* These people all seemed to know and expect me; I had no idea why. I sat on the chair – more a stool than a chair – and tried to make sense of everything.

"I know you like to have water in your dressing room when you are getting ready, and I am so very sorry that we don't have any here for you now. We can get some brought over straight away. Julian!" she yelled to a young boy who looked about ten years old. "Here, quickly."

Am I getting ready? What am I getting ready for?

Julian raced over and stood looking at Francine expectantly.

"What water would you like? Still? Sparkling? Tap? Hydrolyte? Flavoured? Julian can get you whatever you like."

Julian stood staring at me like I was some sort of celebrity. The other three that had been summoned fluttered around me, panicked but very efficient. George stood behind me and had pulled out my ponytail and was doing something with my hair. One of the girls, I didn't know which one, tested makeup colours on the back of her hand while the other girl riffled through a rack of clothes.

"I ... I don't ..." I stammered, completely lost for words.

"Just get one of everything, Julian. Be quick now." Francine pushed him towards the door. "You don't want to keep her waiting." Julian nodded as he raced out of the tent; he did not look back.

"Zis hair is just so bootiful," George gushed behind me. "Zis is a privilege for me to do zis for you." He twisted my hair into some weird do at the back.

"Green. No, maybe red, or a shade of red. Orange? No. Blue! It should be blue," the makeup lady muttered. She looked over to the rack of clothing and said, "Jules, what costume colour?"

Now I knew Jules was with the clothes, which meant this must be Candy in front of me now.

"What's going on?" I asked Candy as she leaned forward with the brush.

"Burgundy," Jules said from across the room.

"Burgundy," Candy muttered again. "Why must she always make things so difficult for me?" She changed brushes.

"What's going on?" I asked again.

"Shhh," Candy said. "I need you to stay still for a

moment."

I sat quietly and watched everyone in the mirror. This world was even stranger than the last. When I'd first come in through the door, I'd thought this was a relatively normal world – ordinary people that didn't look like me, having fun and enjoying the carnival. Ten minutes later, I was in a tent being treated like a celebrity and getting a makeover.

George behind me frowned as he tried to capture a rogue strand of hair that kept escaping. Candy busily painted my face while Jules had laid an outfit over a chair and now raced around trying to match shoes to the dress.

Despite my attempts to find out what was going on, they all stayed focused on whatever they were doing, none answering my questions. Francine had disappeared behind Julian, and I hadn't seen either of them since. It reminded me a little of the times Amber and I would play when we were younger, dragging out Mum's clothes and shoes when she wasn't looking. We never had makeup though and had to make do with pretending the lip gloss was the real thing. Today, however, felt very real.

"Zis is perfection," George announced as he stepped back. "Zis is my best work yet." I had to admit it did look pretty good.

"Done!" Candy declared. "Amazing!" She stood up and backed away. I looked in the mirror to see someone staring back at me that looked much older than my thirteen years. There was a striking resemblance to Mrs Morgan from the last world, who had helped me find my way back home. It was quite scary seeing myself as I would look in another twenty years. There was no time to study myself in the mirror though as Francine returned at that moment.

"You look lovely," she said when she saw me. "Now quickly, into the dress. It's time."

Jules held out the dress for me to change into it. Embarrassed, I hid behind a dressing frame and slipped it on. It fit perfectly, as if it were made for me, and it was my second favourite colour. For a brief second, I wondered again what it was 'time' for. Where were they going to take me?

"No time now," Francine said, looking over at Julian, who must've returned when I changed. He stood eagerly; arms full of bottles of water. "Put them over there."

"I'm a big fan, miss," he said shyly, looking my way.

I smiled at him, although I didn't understand why he was a fan, or how he knew me at all.

Francine steered me towards a big black curtain and stood me in front of it. "Thank you for coming today," she whispered. "Knock 'em dead."

That was the moment everything clicked into place for me: the clothes, hair and makeup, the tent, the celebrity status. I was the special guest at the show!

"No," I said, my face draining of colour.

"No, no, no, no, no ..." I kept repeating, but it was too late.

Everything happened at once. Someone with a microphone on the other side of the curtain announced my name and the curtain opened. The crowd cheered, and I was shoved onto the stage. *Now, what am I going to do?* The curtain closed behind me, and I now stood alone on a stage in front of hundreds of people.

The crowd and I stared at each other in silence. Heaviness in the air felt full of excitement, awe and expectation, which made it difficult to breathe. Or maybe that was just my fear of public speaking or the dress that suddenly felt too tight. Time came to a grinding halt as I looked out at the crowd who had all paid good money to see a special guest ... Me.

They waited patiently and impatiently; some with hands paused above their buckets of popcorn, others with toffee apples halfway to their mouths. My hands crossed in front of me, glued together as a million thoughts ran through my mind.

What was I going to do for them? I wasn't a performer. What did they expect from me? I couldn't sing. I couldn't dance. And the only poems I could recite were nursery rhymes. I thought briefly about turning around and leaving, but all those expectant faces staring back at me stopped that thought in its tracks. My mind ran wild, but no ideas came. I had to find something to do, and fast.

I opened my mouth, and the only thing that came

out was, "I'm not sure what I'm supposed to do."

The audience stared at me, and for a second, a pin dropping would have sounded loud. I watched as the crowd's expressions slowly changed. Suddenly, they erupted in cheers and whistles. The roar grew louder and louder as every person stood and clapped furiously. *A standing ovation?* Cameras flashed from every corner, and several people hugged those they'd arrived with as they struggled to stop the tears of joy flowing down their faces.

Stunned, I wasn't sure what to do next – I certainly hadn't expected this. With the clapping not slowing down, I decided it was time to get out of there. Bowing slightly, which I felt was expected, I stepped backward, my right hand was frantically trying to find the gap in the curtain so I could get off the stage. The audience erupted again, the cheers following me as I saw the opening and slipped through it.

"Oh my gosh, you were amazing!!" the lady who had grabbed me from outside the tent wailed excitedly. Her hair was still doing its own thing, except now her eyes looked a little crazy too. *I need to get out of here.* Julian still stood where he'd been when I'd gone out on stage. I caught his eye again, and he seemed to understand what I was thinking. He nodded towards a dark corner. I followed him quickly as he showed me a secret exit out of the tent.

We stood outside, and I breathed in the fresh air with relief. Glad to be out, I looked around, immediately thinking about getting out of there.

"How do I get back?" I asked before I realised he would have no idea.

"This way, miss," he replied.

We rounded the corner to find most of the crowd milling around, still talking about the show. When they saw me, they rushed to me, many of them thrusting pen and paper under my nose.

"Great show."

"You are amazing."

"Can I have your autograph?"

"Please can we take a picture with you?"

"I've seen all your shows."

The compliments continued as I was mobbed by people wanting to get close to me. Hands reached out just to touch me, and I started getting crushed by them in their eagerness.

"Julian!" I called out. "Help!"

He appeared from nowhere and grabbed my hand; yanked me out from the middle. We walked fast towards the games and rides. He seemed to know where I needed to go and walked briskly in that direction. Most of the crowd went their way, but quite a few diehard fans decided to follow us.

Back through the sales stands and the rides we went until we reached a game stand where Julian stopped.

"Miss?" he said, looking at me. We were almost back at the door; I could see the glow from where I stood.

"Yeah?"

"This is my family's stand. Will you please play a game? Just one," he begged.

"I don't have any money," I said a little sadly. I wanted to do this for Julian because he had helped me, but I didn't know how I could.

His face dropped. "Are you sure? It would mean a lot to me."

Out of habit, I tucked my hands into the dress's pockets and pulled out a coin. Staring at it, I asked Julian, "Will this be enough?"

His eyes lit up as he nodded.

Over at the stand, I watched the plastic fish bobbing in the water. Each fish had a metal loop on its back which I assumed I had to get with the rod that Julian handed me. The fans that had followed me stood around watching and waiting.

"How many do I get?" I asked as I watched the fish bob past.

"Three," he explained. "The two lowest numbers are deducted from the highest number and whatever number is left is the prize you get."

I frowned: it seemed like a weird way to do it, and I wasn't sure the math would work, but I could see his father nodding behind him. *Oh well, what do I have to lose?* I fished out three fish and handed them to Julian. He did the math and whispered the number into his father's ear.

"What number did I get?" I asked, curious. My fans had also moved in closer to see what I had won.

"It's number ten," Julian announced, and everyone gasped. I looked around, once again puzzled. What was so special about the number ten?

Julian's dad held out his hand and my prize.

It was my turn to gasp as I recognised what he was holding – a black key. A black skeleton key, just like the 137 other black keys in my chest.

Julian's dad released the key into my hand and said, "All is not lost. This is the key to everything. To her."

My head snapped up as I heard those familiar words.

"Julian, take her to her door."

Without another word, Julian pulled me further down the road to the door, the key firmly locked in my hand – there was no way I was letting it go.

"Thank you," I said to him.

"You're welcome, miss. I'm your biggest fan." He smiled at me. "Thank you for playing our game. Now everyone will know that it was the only game you played, and everyone will come to play the same game as you."

"I'm glad I could help," I replied, even though I still didn't understand how I was so popular here, for doing absolutely nothing. I looked up from Julian's face and finally noticed the crowd hadn't followed me. He was right; they were all at his family stand trying to give Julian's dad money to play. Smiling, I turned and stepped through the door back to the magic corridor.

On the other side, I checked myself over. I was back in my clothes, the backpack still on my back, even though it hadn't been there while I was wearing the dress. My hair was back in its ponytail and if I had to guess I would have said all the makeup was gone too. My hand still wrapped firmly around the key, I held it tight as I made my way back to my room. I would investigate more in the morning.

Chapter 19

Courtney

With breakfast over, Courtney sat nervously, phone in hand, trying to work up the courage to call Leah. Their fight the other day wouldn't leave her mind. Taking a sip of her coffee, she tried to figure out what she would say. Leah had already attempted calling her several times, but Courtney had let the phone ring out each time.

They had always been more than sisters – they had been best friends growing up. Just like Amber and Morgan, they never felt they had to hang out just because they were family; they *wanted* to be together. When Leah got sick, Courtney never hesitated to look after her – there was never a question whether she would or wouldn't. She had loved hanging out with Leah, and if they had to spend their time in her room or the lounge room while she sat under a blanket, then that was what they did. She had plenty of good days, and on those days, they would go outside and play in the sunshine.

Courtney's heart burst watching Morgan with Amber and seeing the same love and devotion to each other that Leah and she shared. Something that unique didn't come along very often.

That connection was what had led her to this moment - sitting, phone in hand, while an internal struggle ensued.

Yet she still couldn't bring herself to press that button. What would she say? The last time they'd spoken, Courtney had told her to leave, and that now left her more than a little embarrassed and unsure how to proceed. Courtney wasn't sure how honest to be with Leah regarding what had happened all those years ago. In all honesty, she was uncertain how much she wanted to admit to herself.

She had worked hard to get past the guilt that had threatened to consume her. To speak of it now would only bring back all those memories that were deeply buried.

Sighing, Courtney realised that she didn't want to lose her sister. She had to make the call.

With her finger hovering over Leah's name on the contact list, she felt the phone vibrate in her hand. It was Leah.

"Hello," she said quietly.

"Courtney!" Leah sounded upset. "Please, don't hang up. I'm sorry, I'm so very sorry. I should have asked you first. I should have spoken to you before giving her that gift. I'm so sorry! I can't stand fighting with you."

"Leah," Courtney's voice was soothing. "It's done. But I think I owe you an explanation. It's time you know the truth."

Silence from the other end.

"The truth?" Leah queried.

"Yes," Courtney replied. "The truth. Not over the phone though."

"I can be there first thing in the morning," Leah said quickly.

"Okay," Courtney conceded. "I'll be here."

"See you tomorrow," Leah said and hung up.

Courtney leant back in her chair and felt a weight lift from her shoulders. They had made the first steps to reconciliation. The next question would be if Leah would ever speak to her again once she knew what had happened.

Chapter 20

When I returned last night, it had been just after 10 pm, and I was more tired than I realised. Exhausted from all the exploring over the previous few nights, I could barely keep my eyes open long enough to put my pyjamas on.

At breakfast the next morning, everyone had been quiet.

"You okay, squirt?" I had asked Amber after she hadn't said anything for a few minutes.

"Yeah," she'd replied, "just tired."

"You're very quiet," I'd commented.

"Didn't sleep well. Had a bad dream."

Mum had looked up from her seat. "What about?" she asked, looking closely at Amber.

Amber had gone on to talk about dinosaurs and fires and all sorts of weird things. She was the queen of creativity, that one.

Finishing up, I ruffled Amber's hair and kissed Mum on the cheek, leaving her with her coffee and phone in hand as I left the kitchen.

Back in my bedroom, I found the key tucked in the corner of my sock drawer, exactly where I'd put it last night on my return. Armed with my notepad, I sat cross-legged on the bed to take a closer look.

It was the same type of key – that had been obvious the previous night when I'd received it. The only difference was the symbol on the key itself. Turning it over, I couldn't pull my eyes away from the mark.

An uneasiness gripped me as I stared at the spade icon. Dropping the key quickly, it fell to the bed and lay there. I couldn't bring myself to pick it back up.

I knew I didn't have this symbol in my notepad; there was no way I would have forgotten if I had seen it on those doors. But the presence of that key meant there was a matching door somewhere. I immediately promised myself I would avoid that door at all costs if I should ever come across it.

But Julian's Dad had said that this was the key to everything. *What did he mean by that?* If it was the key to everything, then it might be critical. But to what? If it was important, could it really be so bad?

I didn't understand why it made me feel this way.

If I was going to continue exploring, I would have to go further than the first thirteen doors. Tonight would be about looking at as many as I could. That way, I could work out which keys I needed to take in with me the following night.

My backpack sat in the corner of the room; I wouldn't need it tonight. This journey was going to be about matching the symbols on the doors with the keys.

Once again, I found myself waiting for ten o'clock to arrive so I could go and explore. Thinking briefly about why it appeared at the same time each night, I promptly forgot about it as the outline of the door started to pulse on the wall. *Here we go*, I thought, as it got brighter and brighter.

Standing up, I grabbed my notepad and pen, ready to go. The door handle opened quietly, as it had every other night, and I swung it open and was about to step through when I heard the click of my bedroom door open.

Chapter 21

Amber

Tossing and turning in bed, Amber couldn't get back to sleep. She'd just had another dream about a dragon that kept chasing her. No matter where she went, it kept finding her, even when she was sure she was well hidden. It had a dog's face, and wings, and water – not fire – kept spurting from its mouth, trying to drown her. Amber had tried to hide behind a tree, but it found her again, and this time it had grabbed her. She hung from its claws, ready to be dropped into its mouth. She could clearly see the rows of sharp teeth. That's when she woke up.

What she'd told Morgan at breakfast earlier that morning had been true. She *was* tired because of this stupid dream she kept having, and the previous night she'd had it three times. Every time she'd drifted back to sleep, the same dream came back to her. She'd had it again tonight, and would probably go straight back into it if she fell asleep now. *If Morgan is awake, I could talk to her, she thought. She might be able to make it go away. Morgan's awesome at cheering me up when I'm sad.*

She looked at the time: it was nearly ten o'clock. *Maybe it's too late to see her. She probably won't be awake*, but she decided to go and peek anyway. If Morgan was awake, she could help her think of other things so she could get some sleep.

Tiptoeing down the hallway, Amber reached Morgan's door without making a noise. Super impressed with herself; she looked around to make sure her Mum or Dad weren't watching. It would be just her luck to get there and turn around to see Dad watching her creep down the hall. It would be exactly the sort of thing he would do – letting her think she'd snuck around without getting noticed until the last second.

Amber pressed her ear to the door, listening for any signs of movement. With her fingers crossed that Morgan would still be awake, all she heard was silence. *Just a quick peek through the door will be enough.* If Morgan was asleep, then she would sneak back to her room. No one would ever know.

Amber turned the handle as quietly as possible. The door slowly opened inward and she squeezed her head through the small gap created. It wasn't dark, which surprised her. *Maybe Morgan is awake after all.*

Her sister's bed was empty, so she poked her head around the edge of the door. There stood Morgan holding onto a strange purple door on the opposite side of the room. Amber froze.

Chapter 22

My head twisted around so fast I nearly gave myself whiplash. Amber was at the door, peering into my room. *What is she doing here at this time of night?* Guilt flashed through me instantly for keeping this secret, followed by shame for being caught out. Then disappointment reigned that now I would have to share, until relief overrode it that I would not have to hide it anymore.

"Get in here," I hissed. "And shut that door!"

She quickly obeyed. "What are you doing?"

"Exploring. It's a magic door," I explained.

Amber laughed uncertainly. "A magic door. Yeah, sure."

"It's true," I said. "You can see it, right?"

"The glowing purple door? Yeah. But how did you do it? It's some sort of magic trick, isn't it?"

"I didn't. It's a long story, but we have to get inside quickly."

Amber let out another nervous laugh. "Stop playing tricks on me. You're making fun of me."

"No, I'm not, I promise."

"If I step in there, you'll shut me in and leave me

there."

"Amber, you know I'd never do that. We're running out of time."

Amber looked at the purple door, then back to me. "Really? Truly? A magic door?"

"Yes!" My impatience grew: the door would close in five minutes. I had to get Amber to step through before it disappeared for the night.

"You're not joking?"

"No, Amber. I AM NOT JOKING. Please, we must go through now, or it will be too late." I looked at her standing by the bedroom door then knelt beside her and said as sincerely as I could, "This is not a trick, it's a real magic door. I can prove it to you, and I can explain everything, but we have to get to the other side of it NOW."

She still looked unsure, so I said, "I'll go in first. Watch me. Then you'll know it's okay."

Without waiting, I opened the door and stepped straight through. From the corridor side, I could see her standing there, her eyes wide open. I waved to her.

"See? It's okay. You just need to walk through, like any other door."

"What if you can't come back?" Amber asked.

"You can," I said, stepping back into the bedroom. "See?"

"Um ... okay. If you say so."

"I promise you'll be fine," I laughed. "Just follow behind me." I stepped through the doorway again.

Amber hesitated, then walked towards the door.

"You can do it," I encouraged from the corridor.

She moved closer.

"That's it."

She looked into my eyes with total trust as she approached the door and took a giant step forward. Amber immediately bounced off an invisible barrier and landed on her butt on the floor. I wanted to laugh, but the look on her face stopped me instantly.

"It's not funny!" she almost yelled at me.

"Shhhhh," I whispered back. "You can't wake Mum or Dad."

She stood up and said, "You've had your fun. I don't know how you did it, but it's a bad joke. It's not funny at all."

"Amber, please," I begged. "It's not a joke. I promise you, there are things here you could never imagine in a million years. A zillion years even." I moved back into my room.

"You saw me go through; it's real. Look, we'll go through together." I grabbed her hand and looked directly at her. "Trust me."

This time when she nodded at me, I didn't wait. I pulled her straight through into the corridor behind me.

On the other side, I tried to let go of Amber's hand, but she clung to me tightly. She looked around with amazement, taking in the white doors and the long black corridor. Her face reflected the surprise and wonder I had initially felt, along with a bit of disbelief.

"Where are we?" she whispered.

"You don't have to whisper here. I don't think Mum and Dad will hear us."

"Where are we?" she asked again, this time louder.

"This is a corridor with lots of doors," I explained.

"Well, duh," she said.

"Sorry, squirt. What I've figured out is that each of these doors goes to other worlds that we can explore."

"Other worlds?"

"Yeah, a little hard to believe I know, but I can show you." Then I realised I didn't have any keys with me. "... but not tonight."

"Why did we have to get in here quickly?" It was a good question.

"Well, it seems the door only stays there for five minutes ..."

"Then we have to go back now!"

"If you let me finish ... it stays there for five minutes in our world. On this side, it's like time stands still. I can be in here for hours and when I get back to my room only five minutes have passed."

"That is so cool! So how do we get into these doors?"

We'd started walking down the corridor, Amber looking around in awe while I inspected the symbols.

"With a key of course."

"Well, where are the keys then?"

"I left them in my room."

"Why? I want to go into the doors."

"It's not that easy," I explained. "Each of these doors has a symbol up the top, see? The symbol matches the picture on the key. That's how you know which door and key fit together. I've only managed to match three of them up so far."

"You've been through three doors?" Amber gushed.

"Well, yes."

"What was in them?"

"I'll tell you later. Right now, I have to see what other symbols are on the doors. That's why we have the notepad. You have to help me."

Straight away, Amber accepted the job, like an eager detective on her first case. "What do you want me to do?"

"Well, I guess we need to draw the symbols from the doors. Maybe you should do that because you're much better at drawing than I am." I handed the pad and paper over.

"Sure," Amber said keenly.

I made my way down the corridor a little further until we reached the thirteenth door.

"This is where I got to last time. We need to draw from this door onwards." I looked at the next door, explaining the symbols as she tried to draw them. Door after door we passed, and still, the corridor continued.

"Geez, there are lots of doors here."

"I know. A lot more than I thought there were."

"My legs are getting tired."

"Okay, just a little further. How many have we done?"

"Amber looked at the notepad and flicked some pages over. "Four pages."

"I must have some keys that match some of those."

"Can we go back now?"

"Just a little further. I need to get a few more done."

Amber handed the pen and paper to me. "You go then. I'll wait here."

"Are you sure?"

"Yeah. Just don't go too far away."

"I can't, it's just one long corridor, and I can't go through any doors because I don't have the keys."

"Where are the keys?"

"As I said, in my room," I answered. "Give me five minutes."

Amber sat on the floor against the wall as I worked my way further down. So many symbols to draw, so many doors. Finally, I decided I'd had enough and headed back. Amber was right where I'd left her.

"You ready?" I asked.

"Yep." She jumped up. "Where did you get the keys from? How many keys have you got? There are heaps of doors. Where did the purple door come from? How come you didn't tell me about it? How long has it been here for?"

Laughing, I replied, "I promise I'll tell you everything tomorrow. Right now, we have to get back home and get some sleep."

"I don't want to go to sleep. I want to see more."

"I know, and I promise I'll tell you everything. Pinky swear." That showed Amber I meant business. "Tomorrow."

"Okay." She sighed.

"You can't tell anyone, though. I mean it – it's our secret now. You can't let Mum and Dad know."

"But why?" Amber asked.

"Do you think they would let us go exploring strange places at night? That's assuming they believe you of course. They would probably think it's part of your crazy imagination. I don't want them to find out. You're not allowed to say ANYTHING, okay?"

"Geez, okay! I'm a little confuzzled right now."

"You can be whatever as long as you don't say a word to anyone."

"Okay, okay! I won't tell anyone. You're right, no one would believe me anyway."

"There it is." I pointed out the door to my room. "We're back."

Amber yawned. "I am getting a little tired."

"Hold my hand, just in case the same thing happens going this way too." I didn't want her bouncing off an invisible door again.

Hand in hand, we walked out of the corridor back to the real world.

Amber looked back and gasped. "Where is the door?"

"Gone. I told you, it's only here for five minutes. Look at the clock; it's 10:05."

"Wow, this is so cool! You had better tell me everything tomorrow …"

Hugging her, I promised. "Now you'd better get back into bed before anyone notices you aren't there. Good night."

"Night, Morgan."

"Night, squirt."

She slipped through the door and closed it quietly behind her, muttering something about a magic door. I laughed inwardly, picturing her face earlier that night when she'd caught me. As much fun as it had been discovering things by myself, I was glad she knew. It would be twice as much fun exploring it together.

Chapter 23

A sleep-in wasn't going to happen once my little sister knew my biggest secret. I didn't hear her come in but felt her jump on the bed. Groaning, I rolled over and tried to pull the covers over my head.

"What are you doing in here? It's …" I peeked at the clock. "6 am! Amber, it's way too early!"

"I wanna know, I wanna know, I wanna know…"

Despite the early hour, I couldn't help but smile. I should've known she'd be too eager to wait.

"C'mon then." I lifted the covers. "Come curl up with me. It's way too early to get up just yet."

Amber scooted under the cover and curled into a ball. We lay there facing each other and sharing my pillow.

"What do you want to know, squirt?"

"Everything! Don't you dare leave anything out!"

"Hmmm, where do I start?" I teased.

"Start with the door on your wall. Where did it come from?"

"Okay, the purple door. It just appeared one night."

"Just like that? How come it didn't appear to me

then?”

“I don’t know. I’ve seen it in my dreams hundreds of times, and then one night it just appeared.”

“Where did you get the keys from? Can I see the keys?”

“I’ll show you later. I found them in the attic.”

“No way!” Amber’s eyes grew wide. “How many?”

“There’s 137. No, hang on, 138,” I corrected, remembering the key I had won at the carnival.

“Wow!” Amber looked impressed. “That’s a lot of doors.”

“It sure is,” I agreed. “The only problem is that I have to match them up, and there are a LOT of doors. More doors than keys, I think.”

“What was behind the doors you went in?” Her eyes shone bright in anticipation.

“Oh, Amber, you should see it! Every door takes you somewhere different. Well, it has so far.”

“Tell me!” she insisted. “Don’t leave anything out!”

I told her about the first door, the dream tree, the lady in white and Flora.

“A fairy?!” Amber held her breath. “A real live fairy?”

Smiling, I answered, “A real one. She even stood on my hand.”

“What did she look like?”

“She was so pretty, Amber. She was tiny, and her

wings were all the beautiful colours of the rainbow. She had on a white dress and her hair was in a bun."

"I want to see her! Take me there so I can see her."

"Maybe one day. There are so many other places to see, other doors to go through. We can always go back to that one later."

Disappointed, Amber frowned. "It's not fair. I want to meet a fairy too."

"I promise you can come with me to the next one. Maybe we won't see a fairy, maybe we will. Maybe we will find something better. Who knows?"

"What about the other doors you went through?"

"The second one was full of people that were me."

"What do you mean? I don't get it."

"Well, every person I came across was me, just different ages. I met a family, and the little girl was six, and she was me. Her sister was a bit older than me, but still me. The mum was me, but at forty-five years old. It was weird."

"Sounds creepy."

"Nah, not really. Just strange seeing my face on every person I passed."

"What about the last door?"

"Yep. The last one was a carnival, with games and rides and shows and all sorts of food."

"That sounds like fun."

"It was, except in there I was a celebrity."

"Cool!" Amber grinned.

"Yes, but then I ended up on stage with everyone waiting for me to perform."

Amber laughed at that. "But you can't sing or anything."

"I know." I pulled a face at her and changed the subject. "I got another key in there too."

"So, what happens now?"

"Now," I replied, "we look at all the pictures we drew last night and see if we have any of the matching keys."

"Can I help?"

"Sure can," I replied. "After breakfast."

"Let's do it now," Amber begged.

"Nope, can't risk Mum or Dad walking in to see why we aren't at breakfast. I promise we'll do it straight after."

Sighing, Amber agreed. We lay there in silence for a few minutes, both lost in our thoughts. We'd drawn a lot of symbols last night; surely I'd have a key that would match one of those. I watched Amber as she lay next to me. She was staring into nowhere, no doubt thinking about these places that I had visited, or maybe Flora and how she could meet her. It would be a lot for her to take in, but it wouldn't take her long to see the possibilities.

"C'mon, squirt. Let's go." I threw the covers back and pushed her toward the edge of the bed.

"Promise you won't do it without me?"

"Of course."

"Say it."

Rolling my eyes, I said, "I promise."

Happy, Amber scrambled out of my bed and headed for the kitchen.

After what felt like the fastest breakfast in history, we were back in my room within fifteen minutes. We sat on the floor, the chest between us. Amber looked at me expectantly, waiting for me to open it.

"We have to be quiet," I said.

"Hurry up and open it!" Amber ignored me.

"I mean it. We can't have Mum and Dad in here. You need to put the keys close to the bed where we can hide them quickly if we need to."

"Okay! Just open the thing up already."

"Alright. Remember what I said. Where's the notebook?" Looking around, I spotted it on the desk. "Grab it for me?"

Amber collected the notebook and laid it on the floor beside us. I turned to the first pages we had filled. "Ready?"

She nodded impatiently and I put my hand on the wooden box that contained all the keys. When I'd brought it out, she had stared at it then reached out to touch the carving of the tree just as I had when I first found it. Now that I had explored the doors a little, the tree carving reminded me of the dream tree.

"This was up in the attic?" Amber asked.

"Yeah, sitting in a cupboard on the bottom shelf."

"Wonder why we never noticed it before?"

"Haven't been up there in years." I was barely listening, more intent on getting all the keys out.

Amber held one up and looked at it. "What a weird key." She focused on the symbol at the end. "Is this what you were talking about?"

"Yeah. Check the notebook and see if we drew that symbol." I placed the rest of the keys on the floor, except for the three I had already used. They were now in a separate bag.

We cross-checked the book and the keys and placed the unmatched ones in a pile. The pile got bigger and bigger as we continued unsuccessfully. Frowning, I started to worry that we wouldn't find another match after all.

"How many pictures do we have? Maybe twenty or thirty? There *has* to be a key in here somewhere." I grew frustrated. There had to be thousands of doors for which I didn't have keys. The thought became a little overwhelming.

"Got one!" Amber yelled excitedly.

"Shhhh!" I replied. "Let me see."

Sure enough, Amber had found a key with three rectangles on it. It matched the picture. We looked at each other and smiled.

"Guess where we're going tonight …" I sang.

"Me too?" Amber waited for my response.

"Of course! You found the key. No way would I leave you behind."

Amber leapt forward and hugged me. "Yay!"

"Let's check out the rest of these keys," I said, but we were unable to find any more.

"Oh well," Amber said. "At least we have this one."

She was right, but I still couldn't help feeling disappointed that we didn't find more. It was overwhelming to think about the number of doors there must be. Considering we had only matched four so far, and with all the keys I possessed, the maths alone meant there must be thousands of doors. The thought made my head spin.

"True," I said. "We'll have to look at some more before we go into this one. There have to be more matches in there."

"Or we could explore this one first and do it after?" She looked at me, pleading.

"We'll be too tired afterwards. It has to be before."

"Fine." Amber folded her arms across her chest.

"How exciting!" I smiled. "I get to take you through your first door."

Ambers' face lit up again. "I can't wait! How soon can we go?"

"The door doesn't appear until 10 pm. You going to be able to stay awake that long?" I asked.

"Probably not," Amber admitted. "But I'm gonna try really hard!"

"I'll come and wake you if I have to."

"You're the best sister ever!"

"I know, right? Should we go out to the treehouse

for a while?"

"Yeah! I'll get my magic stuff, and we can play outside. I'm working on a new trick too."

I collected all the keys and put them back in the chest, all except the match that Amber had found. We needed that one to explore tonight. I placed it very carefully into the zip pocket of my backpack. While Amber collected her magic tricks, I locked the chest away. *It's going to be so much fun exploring with Amber*, I thought. I too could hardly wait.

Chapter 24

Leah

Leah pulled up behind the house, turned off the car and sat in silence. The last conversation she'd had with Courtney resulted in them not speaking. She now wasn't sure what greeting she might get when she walked through that door. Hopefully, they could put everything behind them, but she wasn't sure. Courtney had said on the phone that Leah needed to know the truth. She had no idea what Courtney was talking about, but she would do just about anything to get their relationship back to where it was.

Taking a deep breath, she pulled the key from the ignition and stepped out of the car.

Just before she reached the kitchen door, it flew open and both girls rushed out of the house.

"Whoa!" Leah said. "What's the hurry, girls?"

"Treehouse," Amber said as she raced past.

"Hang on! Where's my hug from my two favourite nieces?" Leah stood with her hands on her hips, pretending to be offended.

Both girls stopped and ran back to her, gave her a quick squeeze before continuing on their way.

"Hi, Aunt Leah," Amber said.

"Bye Aunt Leah," Morgan yelled over her shoulder, already halfway to the treehouse. Amber giggled.

Shaking her head, Leah smiled, walked into the house and closed the door behind her.

Courtney sat at the table, reading a magazine. A second cup of coffee sat there for Leah. She took a seat next to Courtney and pulled the cup towards her. They sat in silence for the next few minutes, neither sure of how nor where to start.

"I am sorry." Leah thought it best to break the silence first.

"I'm sorry I reacted the way I did."

"No, I should've been more considerate," although Leah still didn't understand what she'd done that was so bad.

"Why did you give that snow globe to her?"

Leah sat, considering the best way to answer then said, "Because that was the most magical part of growing up for me. I wanted her to experience it too."

"I don't want her to ever know it exists."

Leah looked up, surprised. "Why?"

Courtney shook her head. So Leah continued. "That door, and the moments I got to experience with you were the highlight of my world. So much of my time was spent sick in bed. The door was an escape for me that made me forget for a while that I was so unwell. When we explored those worlds full of the most amazing things I had ever seen, it felt like that was the person I was supposed to be – not the person stuck in bed watching the world go by."

"I guess I never really thought of it that way," Courtney replied.

"I just don't understand why you would want to hide it from Morgan."

"It's not just me. Robert doesn't want her there either."

"But why?" Leah asked again.

"When you told me that you had given her the snow globe because of the purple door, all I could think of was that it might destroy the barrier we had put in place."

"You put a barrier in place? Wow, you did want to hide it!" Leah said.

"I told you about the dreams I had all those years ago, and how the door one day just appeared out of thin air. I've been watching Morgan closely, wondering if she was having the same dream too. She was for a while, but it seemed like it had finally gone, and then you brought that gift. I was worried that it would trigger something again."

"Did it?" Leah asked.

"No, I don't think so. Morgan said she's not having the dream anymore."

"Well, that's good then, right?"

"For now. But I couldn't bear it if Morgan went through the same thing I did." Courtney lowered her gaze, and Leah put her hand on Courtney's arm.

"What happened, Court? You can tell me."

"Do you remember my friend, Tiana?" Courtney changed the subject.

"Of course," she smiled. "Your best friend in early high school."

"She was amazing. I still miss her, even today."

"You will always miss her, Courtney. She was one of your dearest friends, and she was a beautiful soul."

Courtney smiled at Leah when she said that. "You loved her too, didn't you?"

"Always. Tiana was so nice to me. I remember that she let me hang out with you guys, even when you didn't want me to. She always included me."

"That was because she was a foster kid. She didn't have a real family of her own, so I think she loved being a part of ours."

"I don't know anything about that. All I know is she was a lovely person. That's what I remember. So why are we talking about Tiana? I know she went missing when she was only fourteen, and that was truly one of the saddest things we've ever dealt with. Why are you bringing this up again?"

"It was the single saddest moment of my life, Leah. Tiana was my world. She was my closest friend and the only person with whom I could share my deepest darkest secrets. The day she went missing was the day I wanted to curl into a ball and never get up again." Courtney's eyes welled up with tears. "She was everything to me, and it was my fault she disappeared."

Chapter 25

Up in the treehouse, Amber and I tried to keep busy. Amber had her deck of cards and her coins and was trying to show me a trick with a set of rings. It was a new trick for her, and she hadn't perfected it yet. Eventually she got so tangled, we tossed it on the floor and she decided to give up for a while.

"That's a bit harder than I thought," she said. We grinned. "But I will keep working on it."

"Good idea," I replied.

"Hey, tell me more about the purple door and how you first saw it."

"More? What do you want to know?" I asked.

"Tell me about your dream."

"Okay, well it was the same dream every time. I'd wake up and see a glow on the wall, then the door would appear. I'd walk over to it and put my hand on it, and then I'd go back to bed and back to sleep."

"So how did it become real?"

"I don't know. One night in the dream, the door was open, and I could see into a room. It was the attic."

"How can you look out of your room and see the

attic?" Amber's brow creased with confusion.

"I don't know. But that's what happened."

"Then what did you do?"

"Well, then I woke up and decided to go look in the attic. I snuck up there and found the cupboard exactly where it was in the dream."

"And the chest was there …" Amber prompted.

"Yep, the chest was there. Right where I saw it in the dream. Oh, and then I heard tapping, and it was a magical key under a floorboard."

"A magic key?"

"Uh-huh. When I lifted the floorboard, it flew out and went straight to the chest."

"It flew out?"

"It did. Then when I tried to open the chest, I heard this huge bang, so I grabbed the chest and ran back to my room."

"A big bang?"

"Stop copying me!" I exclaimed.

"Sorry," Amber said. "What do you mean the key flew?"

"Like it had wings. It went by me so fast I could feel the wind."

"I'm so jealous; I wish I got to see the magic flying key too."

"That's okay, squirt; you'll get to see something amazing tonight. I'm sure of it."

"Do you think we'll get to see more fairies?" she asked, hopefully.

"I don't know. Every door has been different so

far. I have no idea what we'll come across."

"Do the pictures on the keys give you an idea of what's behind the door?"

I hadn't thought of that. "Maybe. … I guess so because the first key was a tree, and the dream tree was there. The second one was a rectangle with an oval, not sure how that fits in. The carnival was a tent though, so yeah, maybe it does."

Amber looked pleased with herself. "What do you think three rectangles mean?"

"No idea. Maybe three doors? Or three pieces of paper? Three remote controls? Who knows?"

"Three playing cards," Amber added. "Three scarves. Three wands."

"Three plates?"

"Three books."

"Three notes."

"Notes?" Amber raised her eyebrows.

"As in money. Maybe there's a money tree in there."

"That would be cool. Imagine what you could get with that."

"Anything at all, I would think." I smiled. "We'll just have to wait for tonight to find out."

"What if I don't wake up in time?"

"I promised I would come and get you, and I will."

"And then what?"

"Then we go back to my room and wait for ten o'clock. As soon as the door is there, we go through and explore the door with three rectangles."

"Don't you dare forget me."

"I won't. Honest."

She would never forgive me if I left her behind.

Chapter 26

Courtney

Courtney searched Leah's eyes for signs of how she felt now she'd confessed it was her fault Tiana had disappeared. She fully expected Leah to draw away, but instead, Leah leaned closer.

"What do you mean, it's your fault? How on earth does this come back to you? She didn't come home one night, remember? Her backpack was gone; her foster family said she'd run away."

Looking up, Courtney could barely see through her tears. "She didn't run away."

"She didn't?"

Courtney shook her head.

"What happened to her?" Leah asked warily.

"I took her into one of the doors – she was so excited to see what was there. When we tried to leave, we ran into some trouble, and somehow, I made it out, and she didn't." Courtney bowed her head. "I couldn't get her out."

Leah sat back and considered what she'd heard.

They sat quietly, their eyes locked on each other for what seemed like forever.

"What sort of trouble?" Leah finally asked.

"I couldn't get her out," Courtney repeated, lost in her past. "I tried; I tried so hard, but I failed! It's my fault."

"Why didn't you go back in and get her?"

"The key was gone. The second I was thrown out, I turned around and tried to get back in, but somehow the door was locked, and the key was gone. I couldn't get back in."

"Which door was it? Maybe we can break it down and try to find her."

"Don't you think I tried that?" Courtney raised her voice. "I did everything I could. I even took Rob in there to see if I could get through. I tried for months."

"So you just left her there," Leah said flatly.

"There wasn't anything else I could do. The door wasn't going to open for anything. Not without that key."

"We have to try again. We can't just leave her there."

"Leah, it's been over twenty-five years. She's gone."

"She can't be gone. God, it's like losing her all over again."

"That's why I don't want Morgan to go in there. It's not all fluffy puppies and roses. Some doors don't lead to nice places. She should never go through what I went through."

"Tell me what happened," Leah demanded.

"It's in the past now," Courtney said sadly. "I don't want to re-live it again. I've spent years trying to make peace with it."

"Well, at least I understand now why you got so upset about the snow globe." Leah stared at her sister. "I would never have bought it if I'd known what had happened."

"I know. I probably should've told you sooner, but I didn't want you to hate me for letting Tiana down. I know you loved her too."

"I did, and I believe you when you say you did everything you could." Leah looked straight at Courtney. "You've carried this secret with you for a long time."

Nodding, Courtney wept silently, years of guilt finding its way out.

Leah wrapped her arms around her sister. "I'm so sorry you had to go through this alone."

"I had Robert."

"Still," Leah replied. "I wish you'd told me. What happened after that?"

"Her foster family didn't care. They assumed that she ran away, as so many of the foster kids do. I guess they just thought she'd come back one day."

"What about the purple door?"

"I never went in there again. Tiana was gone. I didn't have the will to go back through another door. I tried to forget all about it."

"You said before that you hid the door. What did you mean by that?"

"Morgan was starting to have the dream. I had to stop it from happening. Robert helped me get rid of it."

"Just like that."

"Pretty much. As soon as we locked up the chest and hid it away, the door stopped appearing. To be honest, it was a horrible time for me. On the one hand, I was saving my child from going through something terrible, and on the other hand, I was giving up on my best friend."

"It wasn't all terrible," Leah said gently.

"Yes, I know. We had some great times. The bad outweighs the good though; I couldn't risk it. I can't risk it."

Leah nodded in acceptance. "Fair enough. I guess if it were my daughter and friend, I would have done the same thing."

Chapter 27

As promised, later that night, I crept down the hallway in the dark, heading for Amber's room. I would never tell her this, but I was glad she was coming with me. She was great company, and she was so happy all the time; she made things more fun. I certainly looked forward to this.

Reaching her door, I twisted the handle and pushed. Amber was sitting on the bed, waiting for me.

"Hey," I whispered. "You ready?"

She nodded, her eyes wide and excited.

"You have to be quiet."

She nodded again.

"I don't just mean with your mouth. With your feet too."

Amber rolled her eyes and nodded at me again. "Okaaaaay."

Following me out the door, she tiptoed back to my room and shut the door quietly behind us.

"Now what?" she asked.

"Now we wait for the door."

Amber sat on my bed. "How long will that take?"

"Ten o'clock."

Amber looked at the clock. "That's ages away!"

Looking over, I said, "it's only four minutes."

"Do we need to take anything?"

"I've got it all in my backpack. Notepad, pen, and key. That's all we need."

We sat silent for a few minutes, waiting for our next adventure to appear. Finally, after what seemed like forever, I whispered to Amber, "Look," and nodded towards the wall.

Amber watched the door appear, and I watched Amber.

Eyes darting left to right, from top to bottom, she took in everything as it grew brighter. Sitting on the edge of the bed, almost falling off in anticipation, Amber watched the symbols race across the door. I knew that she hadn't seen this before; after all, the door had been open the first time she came in.

Once the process had been completed, she looked over at me, full of wonder.

"Can we go in now?" she prodded excitedly.

"Sure, let's go." I grabbed my backpack and slung it over my shoulder. We walked to the door, opened it, and walked through, hand in hand.

"It looks the same," Amber said softly, as we entered the corridor.

"It is the same."

"Let's go!" Amber ran ahead as I started to check the doors for the three-rectangle symbol. It didn't take too long, and knowing where it was made it much quicker to find. I dropped my pack in front of the door and continued down the corridor to find Amber. *Trust her to keep going until I can't see her anymore.*

We were in unexplored territory now, and I remembered that we were supposed to check more doors before going into the other. I'd left the notepad in the bag, and just made a mental note of some of the others I saw. I stood in front of one door, trying to work out what the symbol was when Amber came flying back.

"Guess what I found?" she said a little breathlessly.

"What?" I asked, half listening.

"A door that will match one of the keys."

Turning to her, I said, "Which one? How do you know?"

"I saw the key today when we went through them all. I know where we can go tomorrow night."

"That's great. Which key?"

"The ace of spades."

"The ace of spades …" I repeated.

"Yeah! It's like it's meant to be because I'm always doing magic and it's part of a deck of cards which I use for my magic tricks."

I stayed silent.

"Can we please?" Amber begged. "Do you think the world is full of magic tricks? I bet it is."

"No. Not that one." I was thinking about the promise I'd made to myself earlier.

"What do you mean, no?" Amber pouted. "It's the only other door we can go in."

"I don't think it's a good idea," I said uncertainly.

"It might be all magic. You don't know for sure it's not."

It wasn't very likely.

"I guess I'll think about it," I replied, not wanting to disappoint her.

"Yay! I'm so excited!"

I instantly regretted my decision.

"Let's go back to the three rectangles and explore that one. We can worry about the other one tomorrow."

To say I wasn't excited about the prospect of going through the door with the ace of spades would be an understatement. The thought of it brought back that peculiar feeling almost instantly. Worried about what we would find there, I was in no hurry to see it or take Amber through it.

Standing in front of the white door with three rectangles, I smiled and turned to Amber.

"Are you ready to do this?" I asked.

Amber nodded swiftly. "Let's go."

I inserted the key and turned it, listening to the lock disengage smoothly. I reached for Amber's hand. "Let's do this."

The door swung open, and we stepped through onto a green grassy field. Rolling hills surrounded us, the smell of spring tickling my nostrils. The sun shared the bright blue sky with hundreds of butterflies, each different from the next. I checked on Amber, but she was too busy leaping after them as they fluttered by close enough to touch.

The sun was warm on my face, and I closed my eyes for just a second to enjoy it. A tug on my sleeve interrupted me.

"Look over there." Amber pointed off to our left, to a sign that looked totally out of place in the green grassy fields. Beside it stood a wooden ramp that led to nowhere. Next to the ramp sat a pack of dogs, a goat, and a donkey, all seemingly oblivious to the two strangers who had just appeared.

Why would all these animals be out in the middle of nowhere? I wondered.

"I love dogs," Amber said, smiling. "Let's go see them." Before I could stop her, she started running down the hill.

"Amber wait!" I yelled. "Don't run at them!"

I imagined the pack going wild and attacking her. She didn't hear me and kept going. When she drew closer, I saw the tails stop. The dogs stood up and focused on Amber coming their way at full speed.

"Hi, doggies!" she greeted them as she reached them. Straight away their tails started wagging again.

The bright red sign above the pack showed the words Cat Stop. *What is a cat stop, and why are there animals at a cat stop?* Frowning, I caught up with Amber at the sign, where she was surrounded by several canines begging for her attention.

"Thanks for waiting for me," I said crossly.

"She's fine," came the reply, but it wasn't out of Amber's mouth.

"Who said that?" Amber's eyes flew wide open.

"I did."

Amber and I looked around, looked everywhere, but could not see another person anywhere nearby. We stood scratching our heads.

"Down here," I heard from the voice again.

"Who said that?" I asked aloud.

"Me," the voice replied, full of patience.

I looked at the dogs again and noticed the brown one staring at me. I stared back at it, its gaze so strong it made me feel uncomfortable.

"Stop staring at me, dog," I said to him.

"I'm sorry," he replied. "But how else can I let you know it's me?" His tail wagged, and I swear he almost smiled at me.

"Whaaaat?" Amber shrieked. "Look Morgan – it's the dog talking! No way!"

"Hello, my name is Rover. I've never seen you before."

"Ummmm …" *What do you say to a dog?* I said, "Hi?"

"Hi, Rover. I've never met a talking dog before. Is this your family? Where did you come from? Where are you all going?" Questions spilled out of Amber's mouth.

"Amber!" I scolded.

"It's okay …" Rover grinned. "… we are taking Grandpa Duke to the rejuvenation tree today."

"What's a reju…rejuvranation tree?" Amber struggled.

Rover howled with laughter. "It's an extraordinary tree."

"Which one is Grandpa Duke?" Amber asked.

"That would be me," replied a brown and white pooch at the back of the pack, a Jack Russell type, but bigger. His gruff voice matched his coat. His tail moved furiously from side to side as the attention turned to him.

"Can we go see it too, Morgan?" Amber asked. "Please?"

"We shouldn't bother them," I replied.

"But I want to go with Grandpa Duke to the special tree."

"You should come." This came from one of the other dogs, a poodle type. "I'm Fifi, and you and your puppy should come too. It's something special to see."

Laughing, I said, "She's not my puppy; she's my sister."

"Still, you should come."

"I don't know …" I trailed off, wondering if we should bother this family – this talking dog family.

"You should decide quickly – the cat is coming now."

Expecting to see a cat coming over the hill, I turned with interest, wondering how the cat and the dogs would get along. I soon noticed two sticks appearing over the crest; little balls on the stick ends waving frantically in the air. It didn't look like a cat, and moved way too slow. Confused now, I turned to Rover with a million questions. Amber got there first.

"Are you going to chase the cat?"

Rover howled again. "You are a very funny puppy. Why would I chase it? It will stop here for us."

The cat continued coming over the hill at a sedate pace, except it wasn't a cat at all. As it climbed over the peak and started its descent, I could see all of its what seemed like hundreds of segments following one another. On and on it came. But it was no cat – this was a caterpillar!

Pulling up next to the ramp where we stood, the caterpillar came to a halt. Each segment of its body had a seat strapped to it, many of the seats full of creatures. Birds sat next to lions; frogs sat next to camels. I even saw an elephant sitting next to a mouse! I turned to make sure Amber saw all this.

She did, her mouth hanging wide open at the sight.

"C'mon, Amber, let's see what the rejuvenation tree is all about."

I grabbed her hand and followed the dogs up the ramp. The caterpillar must have been at least three metres high, and the ramp only just came to the bottom of the seat. The dogs jumped up onto one segment, and Amber and I sat behind them.

"We're sitting on a caterpillar," Amber

whispered.

"I know. Pretty amazing, huh," I whispered back.

Rover turned and faced us from his seat in front. "Now hold on, puppies – it's express straight to the tree from here and goes pretty fast!"

I didn't believe the caterpillar would be able to go that fast – it certainly hadn't been travelling at all fast when it had come over the hill.

"Hold on to the handles if you need to," Rover added.

Handles? What handles? All I could see was fur around the seats except where my feet were, where it was trampled flat. Grandpa Duke in front of me grabbed hold of some of the hair next to him with his teeth. Was that the handle? All the other animals seemed to be hanging onto the fur, so I did the same.

"Hold on, Amber …" I pointed to the fur. "… just in case."

"It's not gonna go fast," she said, but she held on anyway.

We started moving slowly, and I wondered if the dogs were playing a trick on us. But once we drew away from the ramp, we began to move quickly. Faster and faster, we went until my hair flew behind me as the wind rushed past.

"Look at the legs! Look at the legs!" Amber giggled and pointed.

The legs indeed moved fast; so fast they were just a blur of motion.

"It looks legless," she giggled again.

Rover's family ahead of us enjoyed the ride. With their tongues hanging out the side of their mouths, they stretched over, leaning into the wind. As quickly as we had picked up the pace, we began to slow again.

"Is it over already?" Amber said, disappointed.

Not sure what was going on, I tried to see at the front, but it was impossible; we were too far back.

"I don't know. I think so."

We pulled up to another ramp with the caterpillar crawling slowly forward to disembark each of the animals.

"Looks like we're here," I said.

"I want to see!" Amber tried to see what was going on, but there were too many animals around.

"Let's just get off and see what's here once we're on the ground."

We followed the crowd as they ambled down the ramp, and all started heading in the same direction.

"Where are they all going?" Amber asked me.

"To the trees, of course," said a scratchy voice from behind us.

It was an emu. She stood up tall, taller than me, and stretched one sleek wing out to the side.

"What trees?" I asked.

"The twin trees. This is the stop for the twin trees."

"What are the twin trees?" I asked.

"One tree is a rejuvenation tree," the emu explained. "You enter the tree and come out the other side rejuvenated – as someone young and new."

"Really?" Amber said with a touch of disbelief. "Can you pick what you want to be?"

The emu fell into line beside us. "No, the gatekeepers decide."

"Gatekeepers?" I asked.

"The centaurs. They make sure you go to the right tree. They decide what you become in your next life. They keep everything running smoothly."

"What's the other tree then?" Amber queried again.

"That's where I'm going. That's the healing tree."

"A healing tree? Does it fix you up?"

"It does," the emu nodded. "The centaurs make sure you go to the tree that you need most. I need my wing fixed, so I'll go there."

"What happens if you go to the wrong tree?" I asked, curious.

"That doesn't happen. The centaurs will send you where you need to be. They never get it wrong." The emu hurried on ahead. "I have to go now."

Amber and I looked at each other.

"This is so amazing!" she said. "I can't believe we're here. Look at all the animals together. No-one's fighting or trying to eat each other."

Indeed, they were all getting along fine.

Eventually, the line came to a stop. I pulled Amber out of the line and stepped to the side.

"We don't need to be in line," I told her. "Let's

see if we can get a bit closer to the front."

We slowly made our way forward.

"Look for Rover and the others," I told Amber.

She scanned the line and found them straight away. "Over there," she pointed.

Grandpa Duke was still in line, but Rover and the others had stepped aside just as we had. We caught up with them as the line was about to round the corner.

"Hi, Rover," Amber grinned.

Rover wagged his tail and said, "hello again."

"Where are the twin trees?" Amber asked immediately.

"Just around the corner. You can wait with us if you like."

"You're not going?" I asked.

He grinned and replied, "I don't need them. We are here for Grandpa Duke. We want to see what Grandpa becomes."

"What he becomes?" I repeated.

"Oh yes," he said, tail swinging excitedly from side to side. "It's exhilarating."

"Why aren't the animals trying to eat any of the others?" I asked.

"You'll see."

Chapter 28

As he spoke those words, we turned the corner to see three massive purple doors, similar to the one in my room. Guarding them were the most magnificent creatures I have ever seen. I'd always imagined centaurs to be giant scary creatures with big hooves that chased down people with bows and arrows. At least that's the sort of thing I'd read in books. But these? These looked like angels.

The back half of the body of both centaurs was sleek and shiny. Black hair covered each of them, and long flowing tails sparkled in the sunlight. Black hooves shone visibly in the distance. The human torso of each centaur was tanned and muscled. Both had a sash of cloth across the shoulders, and they radiated kindness. Both were incredibly large, standing at least four metres tall. They were awesome.

The doors behind them were even taller and did not have handles. Animals stood in single file until they reached the centaurs. We watched as a little rabbit hopped up to the centaurs on three feet. They spoke briefly, quietly, then let the rabbit pass as one of the doors swung open.

"O.M.G."

"I know. Aren't they beautiful?" I said. "I've never seen anything like them."

"They are special," Rover admitted.

"What's the third door for?" I asked.

"For those that don't need the trees."

"What do you mean?" Why would someone line up for the trees but not need them?

"Mostly it's for the rejuvenation tree. Those that aren't quite ready to move on to the next life can't go through. The door takes them back to the cat stop."

As I continued to watch the line, I spotted the emu we had spoken to earlier going through one of the doors.

"Oh look, Grandpa Duke's going in now!" Amber jumped up and down.

"We must wait to see which door he goes into." Rover stood to attention, waiting anxiously as he watched Grandpa slowly walk forward. The door on the right swung open, and Grandpa Duke walked through.

"Now, we must hurry." Rover jumped up. Fifi and the others joined him as he raced off.

"Let's follow!" Amber raced after them, while I tried to stay close behind.

We turned yet another corner and found ourselves in front of a huge tree. Not as big as the dream tree, but it was still a decent size. Rover and his family stood and waited at a door set in the trunk base.

"What happens here?" I asked.

"You ask a lot of questions," Rover said.

"Don't mind him," Fifi spoke up. "He's waiting for Grandpa Duke to come out."

"He's gonna come out of here?" Amber squealed.

Fifi's tail wagged, and she nodded.

We waited in silence for Grandpa Duke to appear, wondering what was happening to him inside that tree. Would he come bounding out again? How different would he be? Would he look the same but maybe younger?

I didn't have to wait for long to find out. A shape started to appear from the darkness of the tree trunk, and I could see Rover's tail begin to move lightly.

"What is he? What is he?" Rover muttered quietly.

Not a muscle moved, not a sound was heard amongst the group as the anticipation built.

Out of the base of the tree came a black and white horse.

"Where's Grandpa Duke?" Amber frowned and looked at me.

"Duke? Is that you?' Rover's tail wagged furiously.

Duke tossed his mane and nodded.

"A horse!" Rover and Fifi jumped about, excited. "A horse!" he repeated.

Amber and I stood confused.

"I'm confuzzled," she said to me.

"Me too."

"How come you went in as a dog and came out as a horse?" Amber demanded.

"Amber! Don't be rude!" I scolded her, although secretly I also wanted to know.

"It's okay," Grandpa Duke replied. He tossed his mane again. "This is my new life."

"So you're a horse now?" I asked uncertainly.

"Yes. And a handsome one too," the horse said, prancing on the spot.

"Yes, you are," I replied. "Can I pat you?"

"Sure," he said. I ran my hand down his neck, and he pushed gently into it.

"I'm very happy for you," said Rover. "But we need to head back."

"On the cat?" Amber asked.

"Yes."

"Cool!" she replied through a yawn.

"You're getting tired," I said. "I'd better get you home."

"Not yet," Amber complained through another yawn.

"Yes, now. Rover, do you mind showing us the way back?"

"Would you like a ride back to the cat stop?" Grandpa Duke offered.

"Really? Can I? Can I?" Amber begged me. "I've never been on a horse."

"That's not true," I replied, "you've had pony

rides before."

"Yeah, but not on a real horse. Just ponies."

"As long as Grandpa Duke promises to look after you."

"I promise," he said sincerely.

"Okay, I'll give you a leg up." I helped her climb onboard. "Hold onto his mane."

Amber obediently gripped a piece of mane and grinned back at me. "Let's go, Duke!"

He started walking off, the rest of us following.

"Can I ask you something, Rover?" I said while watching Duke and Amber ahead of us. I took his wagging tail as a yes.

"Why were you excited that he became a horse?"

"He hasn't been a horse yet."

"What do you mean, yet?"

"He's been a dog, a cat, a rat, a cheetah, a cow, a panda and a frog."

"And a guinea pig," Fifi added from behind us.

"Yes, and a guinea pig. He wanted to be a bigger animal again."

"So how many times have you been through that tree?"

"Maybe six or seven."

"And you change to a different animal every time?"

"We have so far. Now, do you understand why animals don't eat each other?"

I thought about it. "Yes," I replied. "It could be a family member or friend."

Just then, the emu from earlier came past us.

"Brand new again!" she yelled out as she went past, lifting her wings.

"New friend?"

I just smiled. "Thank you for letting us tag along. I'm glad Grandpa Duke got what he wanted."

"Just Duke now. He's not a grandpa anymore."

We walked the rest of the way to the cat stop in silence. This world would be worth visiting again, even if it was just to see those centaurs. Wouldn't it be amazing if we had this sort of tree in our world, where you could go in old and come out young again? Or the other tree that healed the sick. That would be even better.

Duke and Amber reached the cat and climbed onto a seat together, chatting away. I sat behind them, leaving Amber to enjoy this moment talking to a horse. That's four places I'd visited now, and in every one of them, there had been something wonderful to see. It gave me a tiny glimmer of hope that the door with the ace of spades might not be as bad as I expected. Watching Amber and Duke talking, I was glad this had been the first place she had seen as she might not get the opportunity to do this again.

Eventually, we reached our original stop, and I saw the glowing light on top of the hill where we had come in. I gave Rover then Fifi a hug and scratched Duke's neck.

"Thank you again for everything. You've all been

very friendly," I said.

"Bye, Duke!" Amber threw her arms around his neck. "Thanks for the ride."

"You're welcome," he replied. "Now off you go, it's time to go back home."

We waved goodbye as we made our way back up the hill towards the light, Amber all the while talking excitedly to me. "That was amazing. The animals could talk. And we rode a caterpillar. Do we have to go now?"

"Yes, we need to go home and get some sleep. There's always tomorrow." I pointed at the glowing light.

"Is that how we get back?"

"Yep. Now hold my hand again so we can go through."

Hand in hand, we went through the light, stepping as usual back into the corridor.

"Wow!" Amber squealed.

Smiling, I replied, "I know. But now I'm tired so let's go back."

"Okay," Amber agreed. "I'm a little tired too."

"You think?" I grinned as she stifled a yawn.

"Maybe more than a little."

Back in my bedroom, I hugged Amber. "Now go sneak back to your room and crawl into bed."

"I'm going to dream of Duke," she said.

"You probably will," I agreed.

"Hey, Morgan," she added, stopping before she walked out of the room. "Duke whispered something weird to me just before we got off the cat. He said 'all is not lost, two must become one'. What do you think that means?"

I stopped and looked at her.

"He said what?"

"All is not lost, then he said two must become one," Amber repeated.

"Are you sure that's what he said?"

"Exactly."

I waited a moment before responding. "I don't know. I'll think about it, and we'll talk tomorrow." I wanted to consider what it all meant before discussing it with Amber. "Now go to bed."

"Alright. Thanks for taking me tonight. Love you."

"Love you too, squirt. Good night."

"Night," she said, closing the door softly behind her.

Why would Duke give Amber those phrases? Why did everyone keep telling us that all is not lost? Nothing in those words gave me any hint of what was going on. Or what they meant. No one had given me a clue either, so I was no closer to working it out. *Am I supposed to do something? Go somewhere? See someone?* I was almost ready to give up trying to figure this out. Eventually, I drifted off to sleep with thoughts of centaurs and caterpillars running through my head.

Chapter 29

The following afternoon we were up in the treehouse, whispering about the previous night. Amber had been very excited about making a new friend, but all I could think about was those eight words that kept coming back to me. Each world I had visited had brought me the same phrase – all except the carnival that had provided the key with the ace of spades on it.

While still clueless as to the meaning of those phrases, I had a bit more of an idea with the key. If it was the key to everything, then we needed to see what was behind that door. Besides, Amber had already decided that was our next adventure.

For me, however, I was torn. I kept coming back to that dreadful feeling I had every time I saw that symbol, from the first card trick Amber had shown me in this very spot to inspecting the key on my bed. I wanted to solve the riddle but I also wanted to stay as far away from that door as possible.

"What are you thinking about?" Amber broke through my thoughts.

Sighing, I replied, "The door tonight. The spade.

Urghh, I don't even like saying it."

"Why?"

"I don't know. I just have an awful feeling that it's something we should stay away from."

"It's the only other key we've got."

"Yep." She was right.

"We have to go," she added.

"We could have a break for a night."

"I don't need a break," Amber said quickly, "and I want to see what's there. What if it's a world full of magic?"

"It's already a world of magic when we step through the purple door," I replied.

"That's not what I mean."

"But what if it really is magic everywhere?"

"Like rabbits popping up out of thin air?" I teased.

"Or people levitating in the air."

"Scarves and silk flowers everywhere."

"Invisible people!"

"Is that magic? Or just fantasy?" I said.

"I don't know, but it could be anything right? If dogs can talk then why can't there be invisible people?"

She had a point. There was no way anything could be ruled out. *Everything is possible.* "I guess we'll find out, won't we?"

Packing for that night was difficult as I had no idea what to expect and, therefore, had no idea what to pack. Frustrated, I gave up worrying about it and decided the key would have to be enough.

Amber and I had the same arrangement as before, except this time I didn't need to get her – she was at my door by 9:30 pm.

"You're early. What if Mum sees you're not in bed?" I said anxiously.

"She won't," Amber replied.

"I hope not."

"She won't," Amber repeated.

"You don't know that for sure."

"I do! Mum went out to the movies with Aunt Leah. I heard her say she wouldn't be home until eleven. And Dad never checks on us."

"In that case, we should be okay then."

"Told ya." She poked her tongue out at me. "Have you got the key?"

"Yes. But I might get you to hold it – I don't want to touch it."

"Cool, can I open the door too?"

"Maybe."

"What are we going to do until the door appears?"

We sat quietly, reading. my eyes skimming over the words, not taking anything in as my brain raced ahead, imagining terrible things ahead for us. I couldn't shake the uneasy feeling I had about tonight. Everything about it felt wrong, but I didn't understand why. I'd played cards many times before and had never felt like this. The only way I was going to figure out what was going on was to use the key and go through that door. We would have to be careful, though: our safety had to come first.

Amber sat fidgeting with keenness to go, having no concerns, despite knowing how I felt. The connection to her magic through the deck of cards was enough for her to anticipate another magical journey. To her, the last world full of talking animals meant more wondrous things were out there.

The clock continued to tick over slowly, and eventually, it was almost 10 pm.

"Are you ready?" I asked her as I gathered my stuff.

"Born ready," she announced in a flash.

Smiling, I nodded toward the desk. "The key is on the shelf. You'd better grab it and put it in your zip pocket, so it doesn't get lost."

In less than ten seconds, the key was safely stowed and we stood side by side, Amber excited, me much less enthusiastic. *If this was the key to everything, then there is no choice. We have to go in.*

Amber grabbed my hand the second the door appeared. "Let's go!"

I entered first but was soon dragged along by Amber as she raced to get to the right door. Within minutes she had us standing in front of it, the key in her hand ready to go.

"I'm still not sure about this …" I murmured.

"We'll be fine," she insisted, her voice slightly high pitched. "Nothing will go wrong, I promise."

Looking sideways at her, I said, "You can't promise that."

"Well, no, but every other place has been awesome, right? Why would this one be any different?"

This kid is way too smart for her age. "Good point. I guess the odds are in our favour."

"Let's go then!"

"Alright," I said. "Go ahead, unlock the door."

Chapter 30

The first thing I noticed was the number of clouds across the sky. Dark, angry clouds, swollen in size like pressure cookers about to explode. Just like the big city I'd visited, no sun shone here. The air was cold and, coupled with the clouds above, increased my reservations. To my left, I could see a vast mountain range. It looked cold and lonely, with the peaks of the mountains hiding behind the clouds. Rocks and sand dominated with minimal grass showing – totally opposite to the green rolling hills we had seen in the animal world.

We had entered at the bottom of a valley, with the mountain range to our left. The valley sides were covered with rocks and sand and looked like they would be challenging to climb. Tree roots poked out randomly, although there were no trees at the top. The base of the valley seemed to be only ten or fifteen metres wide, yet the sides were quite steep and at least five or six metres high. I turned around to see what was behind me, but it was more of the same.

"Okay, we seem to be in some sort of valley or

canyon or something. It looks the same in both directions, so I guess it doesn't matter which way we go," I said to Amber, adding hopefully, "unless you want to go back?"

"No way. I've never seen anything like this."

Neither had I, but that didn't mean I wanted to go exploring. I still didn't like the look or the feel of this place, but I willed myself to go for a short walk to see if the scenery changed. I didn't like being closed in on the sides and knew I would feel better if we could get out of the valley and back up to the top.

"Which way then?" I asked, not caring for either way much.

"Ummmm …" Amber looked both ways and then pointed behind us. "… this way?"

"Why not?"

We began trudging along the valley bed in the direction Amber had pointed, and I immediately noticed the lack of sounds around us. No animals, no wind, no people. Nothing at all.

"Have you noticed how quiet it is?" I whispered to Amber.

"Why are we whispering?" she whispered back to me.

"It's too quiet," I said.

"Probably because we are down in this thing."

"But did you notice there aren't even any birds in the sky?"

"Morgan, stop being such a baby! There's

probably heaps going on up there. We just have to get up there somehow."

"Look at how dark the clouds are up ahead. Maybe we should be going the other way."

Amber heaved a sigh of frustration. "Honestly, Morgan, you'd think I was the older one. We're fine; it's just cloudy."

"I don't like this."

"It's just cloudy," she repeated.

At that moment, I thought I heard a rumble in the distance. "Did you hear that?"

"Morgan!"

"Shh!!" I held up my finger. "Let me listen."

The rumble continued to grow louder as we stood and listened. The clouds up ahead grew almost black, and I could now see lightning amongst them. They were a lot closer than they'd been a few moments ago.

"Amber, we have to go. NOW!"

I had an idea what was coming, not that I'd ever seen a flash flood before but I'd read about plenty in books. Logic told me that a storm was coming this way, and right now, we were in a valley that would channel all the water directly towards us. The rumble fast turned to a roar, and in the distance, we could see the tumbled rush of water heading our way.

"Amber, run!" I screamed.

Panicked, Amber started running back the way we'd come. Being an active child who was partial to all sports, Amber picked up the pace quickly and pulled ahead of me. I pumped my legs as fast as I could while keeping my ears trained to the roar behind us. I shot a look back and saw the rush of water rapidly drawing nearer.

"Faster, Amber, faster!" My voice hurt from yelling so loud.

With Amber still in front, I noticed ahead on the left the gateway where we'd entered. If we timed it right, we could sneak back through the gateway and miss the flood altogether. But I had to grab hold of Amber or she wouldn't make it through. And there was no way I was leaving her behind.

"Amber!" I bellowed. "The door! Go to the door!"

But she was on the other side of the valley floor now. She turned back to me, panic in her eyes as she ran straight past it. The roar of the water behind us now sounded like a freight train rolling over the top of us. Too late to get to the door, our only chance now was to climb up the side.

Pushing myself beyond my limits, I shortened the distance between Amber and me. I needed to get her up the side of the valley, but she wouldn't hear me if I was too far away. The only thought in my mind now was getting her to safety.

"Amber!" I screamed out again. "Amber!"

She looked back for a split second, and I pointed ahead to a section of the valley that had a heap of tree roots and large rocks protruding. "We have to climb out!"

Amber nodded – she'd heard me and started veering off in that direction. I could feel the cold spray of the water creeping up behind me and fear started to curl in my stomach. If we didn't get up the side in time …

I wouldn't let myself finish the thought.

Ahead of me, Amber had reached the tree roots and was climbing up the side. Like she'd done this a hundred times before, she scaled the side of the valley in record time. She was halfway up when I reached the base. Concentrating on where to place my hands, I found a foothold and started hauling myself up, hoping and praying that Amber was still climbing above me. At least if she fell, I would be beneath her to catch her or stop her fall.

For a split second, I glanced to my left. The wall of water was meters away, moving incredibly fast; it seemed impossible to get away from it in time. I leapt for a tree root above my head and grabbed it seconds before the water swept away the sand underneath my feet. I hung on; my legs now ripped out from under me by the rush of water as it tried to take me with it down the valley floor. Glancing up, I saw Amber had made it to the top and was leaning over watching me. She pointed to another tree root just up to my right. I nodded and reached for it.

The water had now risen and dragged against my thighs, my body almost horizontal in its grip. I couldn't let it take me away or Amber would be stuck in here forever. Straining every muscle, I heaved myself up and out of the water. A rock jutted out just above my waist, and I used my knee to hoist myself onto it.

"Hurry!" I could hear Amber screaming above me. Her urgency doubled my efforts and I pushed up off the rock to the next tree root above me. With the water lapping at my feet, washing branches and mud past me, I reached the top of the valley wall. Amber grabbed my arm and tried hauling me over the edge.

I lay on my back on the sand, gasping for air. Amber jumped on me; hugged me with all her might, crying and trying to talk at the same time. I wrapped my arms around her and held onto her until her tears started to slow.

"Shhh … it's okay. I'm okay … we're okay."

"I thought you were going to get swept away," she sobbed.

"I'm not going anywhere, squirt." I kissed her forehead. "I promise. And that's one promise I will always keep."

"I was really scared," Amber said softly.

"I know, but how awesome were you! You went up that side so fast!"

She smiled a little.

"But now we need to move away from the edge. It might crumble, or the water might come up more."

"I don't think it will," Amber said. "Look, it's already slowing down."

Indeed, the water had stopped rushing through the valley and now looked more like a lazy river. I hadn't even noticed that the roar had disappeared; I couldn't shake the idea that it had tried to get us, and when it realised it couldn't, it had given up the chase. The thought scared me.

"I knew this place wouldn't be good," I muttered inwardly. We sat for a few more minutes catching our breath.

"Okay …" I stood up. "… we need to find the gate and get out of here. I don't want to stay in here any longer."

"Me neither," Amber agreed. "But won't it be covered by water?"

I looked back into the valley.

"Yes, it will," I agreed a little sadly. "We'll have to wait for it to go down."

"What do we do until that happens?"

"We can get away from this river for now. Not too far, though. I want to make sure we can get back as soon as it goes down."

So we started to walk back toward where the gate should have been, what had just happened to us heavy on my mind. I never wanted to go through anything like that again, *ever*. I now just wanted to go home. That had scared me more than I wanted to admit, but I wouldn't tell Amber that.

Up on top of the valley, we could see more of our surroundings. A few scattered trees grew here and there, a fence or two dissected the land. Other than that, we may as well have been back in the valley.

As we continued on our way, the wind picked up a little, but not enough to be annoying. Clouds still covered the sky, and I wondered if this world even had a sun. Cold air chilled my legs, made worse because they were wet.

We walked further, and the wind strengthened. The hood of my jacket started to whip around my head, almost out of control.

"Gee, it's getting windy," I stated the obvious.

"Yeah, I noticed that too," Amber replied as she grabbed her hair to stop it from whipping her face. "It's really strong."

"I wonder if there's somewhere nearby we can shelter, just until the wind dies down and the water recedes."

"Over there." Amber pointed to an area a bit further away from the river.

"Really? How can you see that far? I can't see anything." I squinted harder but saw nothing.

"Trust me," she said.

I let Amber lead us towards the shelter she'd seen. The wind had now started to howl, and I had to lean into it just to take a step.

"I can barely walk!" Amber yelled over the wind.

"I know!" I yelled back. "Just keep going. And stay close!"

We linked arms and used our combined strength to push against it, but it pushed against us even stronger as if trying to stop us from going any further.

"I can't … go … any …further," Amber said, her words blowing back into her mouth. Unable to move upright, we crouched low to stop from getting blown away by the wind's anger. The gale swirled, pushed, and hammered against us from every direction. I shoved Amber to the ground. We would crawl to shelter if we had to.

"On your knees," I shouted as I pushed her down.

But the wind seemed to crouch with us, insisting on making every move difficult. We stayed close to each other on hands and knees and fought for every inch of ground we took. Amber looked sideways at me, and I could see the fear in her eyes start to rise again.

"It's just wind," I tried to comfort her. "Do you still know where we're going?" It was better that she focused on moving forward rather than thinking about being blown to the other side of this world.

Amber nodded.

"Stay low!" I yelled at her as she started to rise. Immediately she dropped back down. I couldn't move at all now, and it was all I could do to stay where I was and not get blown away. I'd seen movies with tornados before and knew how bad they could be. I hoped we weren't about to experience one.

I dropped down and lay flat, and Amber copied me. We linked arms and clung to the ground. It was all we could do. Any move we made would most likely result in one or both of us being flung away like discarded rubbish. We stared at each other, a silent conversation going on between us.

I sincerely regretted bringing Amber here. Nothing I could say to her would be enough. No matter how many times I said sorry, it would still never be enough, especially if we didn't survive this world. I was the big sister: I was supposed to get us out of this mess, and I didn't know how.

Chapter 31

Amber

Amber physically trembled as she watched Morgan clinging to the ground beside her. She watched a tear roll down her sister's cheek and *knew* Morgan was blaming herself. But she knew it was her fault, not Morgan's. Because of her stupid magic, she had Morgan bring them here, even though Morgan knew better. She had said this place didn't feel right, but she'd made her go anyway.

She could see that Morgan was scared too, and Amber tried to show she was brave. But the weather in this world was freaky, and it wasn't something fun like snow. If it were snow, they would be making snow angels right now, not clinging to the ground.

As they lay together, Amber grabbed Morgan's hand. Her sister smiled back at her, a tiny smile that was meant to reassure her, but it only made her heart beat faster. Was Morgan giving up? That scared Amber more than anything had so far. If Morgan didn't keep trying, what hope did they have?

The gale-force winds had them pinned down; her ears hurt because she couldn't cover them up, and her sister was giving up on them?

At that moment, the wind around them stopped. Amber didn't move, afraid that if she did it would start up again. Amber loosened her grip, and Morgan wiggled her fingers.

"Did it just … stop?" Amber asked.

Morgan lifted her head. "I think so."

She sat up and, brushing herself off, looked around. Amber sat up too.

"How is that possible?" Morgan wondered out loud.

Amber stayed quiet, not knowing how to answer. She looked around for the shelter she had seen earlier.

"That building … it's over there," Amber pointed. It was still a long way away, but at least she could see it.

"So it is," Morgan said. "You were right."

"We should get there fast, in case something else happens."

Morgan nodded.

"Come on," she said, grabbing Amber's hand again.

As they drew nearer, she realised it was a small cottage standing by itself in the middle of nowhere. Amber wanted to get inside where it would be safe, but her arm jolted as Morgan stopped suddenly.

"Morgan? What's wrong? Why did you stop?"

But Morgan didn't answer. She just stood statue-like, staring.

"Morgan?" Amber prodded again, but still nothing.

"Morgan!" she shouted. "You're starting to scare me!" Amber tugged at her arm.

Morgan tore her gaze away from the cottage and turned to Amber. Her face had gone pale, and her eyes were wide. She looked afraid. "The cottage. It's the same as the one in my snow globe."

Chapter 32

Impossible! I looked closely, remembering the lifelike details in the globe. From the noticeable wood-grained windows to the purple door and the curtains swaying in the breeze – *it's all there in front of me right now in a real life-size version.*

Amber tugged on my arm. "You're starting to scare me!"

I looked at her and said, "The cottage. It's the same as the one in my snow globe."

Amber looked at the cottage then back at me again. "Cool! What do you think that means?"

"I don't know," I murmured, "but we still need to get inside before anything else happens."

Amber ran up the cottage stairs and tried the door handle as I reached the steps.

"It's open!" she said as she pushed the door open, chatting to herself as she entered the cottage. "Oh, cute! There's a cute little kitchen here. Oh, look at this! This chair is so cute; I wonder if there's a bedroom here and if it's tiny too. Who are you?"

Hearing the last sentence, I bolted up the stairs as fast as I could. *Someone's in there with Amber.* I quickly pushed my way into the cottage. Amber stood in the middle of the room, her gaze on an elderly gentleman sitting in a rocking chair in the corner. He seemed rather ordinary – could have been anyone's grandfather. His grey hair framed a round face, while glasses sat on the edge of his nose. Rushing over to her, I pulled her out of harm's way and turned to the man.

"Who are you?" Amber asked again, peeking out from behind me.

The man ignored her question, and just sat there, rocking slowly, hands clasped together under his chin, index fingers pointing upward.

"It took you two a while to get here," he started. He had a smooth voice that sounded surprisingly young for his age. "I've been waiting for a long time."

"What do you mean?" I said. "What have you been waiting for? What are you doing here?"

"Now, Morgan, it's not polite to ask these things, especially seeing as you are the one who walked into my cottage."

My face heated, and I imagined it going a little red: he was right; we were the ones trespassing.

"Hey! He knows your name, Morgan!" Amber said from behind me.

He smiled patiently. "Of course, Amber. I know who you are. As I said, I've been waiting for you. She will be so pleased to know I've found you."

"She?" I asked. "Who is she?"

He smiled again. "Patience. First, we need to get you to the city."

"What city? What are you talking about? There are no cities around here."

"Oh, you've explored everywhere, have you?" he replied.

I felt myself going red again. "Um, no."

"Well, then. Off to the city we go."

"I'm not going anywhere with you," Amber declared. "I know all about stranger danger. And I don't know you."

"You may not know me, but I know you. I know both of you. You, Amber, love magic tricks and have been perfecting a scarf trick. You love your treehouse and your sister very much. You recently performed a coin trick and a card trick that led you and your sister to this world. Morgan, you are older by five years, and you're starting high school this year. You're worried about making new friends and if you'll be smart enough. Your father is a scientist, and your Aunt Leah has a flower business. I know both of you," he finished.

Amber stepped out from behind me. "How do you know all that?" she asked.

"Please, you need to follow me now. I need to take you to the city."

"But we won't know how to get back," I pointed out.

"I will bring you back myself," he replied. "Please, follow me."

"Can we at least know your name?" I asked as he rose from his chair.

"My name is Merrin."

I looked at Amber. "What do you think?" I whispered to her. "Do we trust him?"

"I say yes," she replied.

Every other world had led me to someone who helped me understand things. There was no reason to think this one would be any different. Therefore, I nodded.

"Okay," I said. "Let's go."

Merrin turned to a door by the kitchen that looked like a pantry. Opening it, he beckoned us to follow and headed down some concrete steps to another room.

"A secret room!" Amber whispered excitedly. "Maybe we'll teleport to the city like they do in Harry Potter!"

Merrin chuckled. "Not today. Follow me."

He then opened another door and stepped through that.

Trailing behind him, we entered a tunnel made of dirt. It smelled damp, and the temperature was a lot colder down here. Merrin turned on a torch, lighting up the path ahead as we made our way through.

"What is this?" I asked.

"This is one of the many tunnels built over the years to get us safely to the city."

"Many tunnels?"

"Yes. We built hundreds of tunnels to keep us

safe. It's not safe up there." He looked toward the ceiling.

"We know." I grabbed Ambers' hand again; it was comforting having her nearby.

The only sound was our footsteps as we made our way further into the tunnel. Occasionally came the sound of dirt running down the wall, dislodged by things we couldn't see. Little rocks and handfuls of earth landed on the floor behind us.

"Is this tunnel going to hold up?" I asked, hearing more sounds behind me.

Again, Merrin chuckled. "These tunnels have been here for many years. I have used them often to wait at the cottage for you to arrive."

But the clumps of dirt continuing to litter the ground behind me made me feel unsafe.

"How much further do we have to go?" I asked, anxious to get out of the tunnel.

"Not far now," he replied. "Another few minutes."

I squeezed Amber's hand to reassure her. She hadn't said anything in the tunnel, just followed us quietly. I hoped she wasn't feeling too overwhelmed. I felt better when she squeezed my hand back. She was okay for now.

A large clump of dirt hit the ground behind me.

"What was that?" I exclaimed, leaping forward in fright.

"I don't know." Merrin turned the light behind us to look. "I can't see anything. Let's continue." But this time he sounded a little more worried.

We picked up the pace a bit. Clumps of dirt continued to fall behind us, and after everything that had happened to us today, I grew even more worried.

"Ow!" Amber cried out.

"What happened? You okay?"

"Something hit my head."

I felt the top of her head and pulled some dirt away. "A pile of dirt landed on you. We need to get out of here, Merrin," I said firmly. "Now."

He didn't answer but picked up the pace again. Behind me, the noises became more frequent. It began to sound like rain as the soil continued to drop from the ceiling and walls. A pile of mud the size of a dinner plate landed on the ground in front of me, nearly tripping me up. It seemed to be a trigger as more large clusters started falling from the ceiling.

"Merrin!" I couldn't keep the panic from my voice. I wasn't going to survive a flood and a windstorm only to be buried alive in a collapsing tunnel. A mass of soil hit my back and almost knocked me to the ground. Torrents of dirt now showered over us from above.

"Merrin!" I yelled again.

"We must run," he yelled back.

Once again, we ran for our lives as soil and small rocks rained down upon us. The tunnel seemed to be breaking up around us, trying to bury us with it. I didn't dare look back; the sounds alone told me the tunnel was closing in behind us – there was no going back. Dirt continued to fall, making running difficult. We had to leap over piles of soil and rubble, which slowed us down as we tried to navigate the different levels under our feet.

"There it is!" Merrin cried out, running at a speed that belied his age.

Ahead of us was another set of steps, this time leading up. We followed Merrin up the steps and nearly fell over each other in our haste to get through the door. He slammed it shut behind us and leaned against it, breathing heavily. We listened at the door, ready to block it if the onslaught tried to enter, but eventually, the noises subsided, and Merrin opened the door again.

The earth was piled up against it, hiding the stairs underneath. The tunnel was gone. He closed the door again and looked at us. "We won't be going back that way."

"Why is this place trying to kill us?" I complained. "I've never run so much in my life."

Amber stood very still. "I want to go home," she said quietly.

"I know, squirt. I do too."

"You're safe now," Merrin said.

"How can you be sure?" I asked.

"I want to go home. Now. I hate it here." Amber repeated.

"You are inside the dome. You are safe." Merrin assured us. "Look around you. This is the tree of safety. It can't get you here. Now you need to follow me."

Recovering slightly from my fright, I looked around. *The tree of safety?* It looked like the inside of a tree ought to look, or how I imagined it should be. What was it with all the trees I had seen lately? The dream tree, the rejuvenation tree, the healing tree and now the tree of safety? I continued to stare at the walls of bark that surrounded me.

"It's remarkable. I've never been inside a tree before," I murmured to Amber.

"This way," Merrin said.

Over in the corner hovering just above the ground lay a cloud – a fluffy, white cloud. We went forward for a closer look. Merrin stepped onto it and gestured for us to follow.

Unsure, we hesitated before climbing on board. It felt like cotton wool to touch, yet sturdy as the ground beneath our feet. We still held each other's hand tightly. Merrin just smiled. He seemed more relaxed now we were here. The cloud began to rise, and as it did, my fear diminished. Something about this cloud and this tree made me feel better about everything. Even Amber smiled as she moved her hand delicately across the cloud.

We seemed to reach the top as the cloud came to a halt. Merrin stepped off first onto another bed of clouds then he turned and offered a hand to help us.

"Thank you," I said as he assisted Amber and then turned to us.

"Well, it's been fun," he said. "But this is where I leave you."

"You're leaving us alone up here?" Amber asked.

"Oh no, Amber, you're not alone," and with that, he turned and disappeared into the clouds.

"Hello," a melodic voice straight away sounded from behind us.

We turned to see a stunning girl, not much older than me. She wore the most beautiful pale-yellow gown I had ever seen.

"My name is Queen Tia," she said. "Welcome to my city."

Chapter 33

I couldn't help but stare at her. Her long blonde hair was wound around her head in a beautiful braid, with small flowers intertwined, almost like a crown it was so perfectly placed.

"Hi?" I offered uncertainly.

Queen Tia hurried forward and scooped us up in a big hug.

"I've been waiting for so long! Now you are right in front of me," she beamed. "I wasn't sure when you would arrive, but we've been looking out for you for such a long time."

"We?" I asked.

"Yes, I've had scouts out there searching every inch of this place. I knew one day you would come." She smiled warmly. "Please, come with me. We will sit down; there is so much to talk about."

Queen Tia released her hold on us and started walking away. We had no choice but to follow or be left behind. *But how did she know we were coming? And she seemed so genuinely happy to see us.* I frowned as Amber and I walked behind the Queen as she made her way down a pathway lined with tree branches.

The floor, completely covered in clouds, felt as reliable as any ground I'd ever walked on. Branches surrounded us, changing continuously and forming pathways, pushing us in a specific direction. Now and then other people appeared through them, keeping busy with whatever their day's task was. We reached a structure – a treehouse in a cloud – and followed the Queen inside.

Inside was much more luxurious than the outside, and it seemed more extensive than the outside portrayed. Furniture was scattered throughout the space. She pointed to the couch in the corner, and we gratefully sank into the softness of the cushions with sighs of happiness. After all the running we'd done, it was nice to take a break.

Queen Tia sat on another couch opposite us – red velvet, with gold trim lining the edges and the legs. Despite being so large and fancy, it looked very comfortable. She surprised me by lifting her legs and curling them under her body, sitting as any average person would. I always thought a Queen would sit up tall and look down on everyone.

An older lady came in with a tray of biscuits and drinks and placed it on the table between us then left quietly.

"Go ahead," Queen Tia offered, tilting her head toward the tray.

Amber leaned straight in and grabbed a handful of biscuits. "I'm hungry," she declared.

Queen Tia just smiled. "Take as many as you

want."

"Thanks," Amber mumbled, her mouth full.

"Where do I start?" the Queen said, then she clapped her hands together. "I'm so excited you're both here!"

"How did you know we were coming?" I asked.

She leaned forward and said, "My vision cloud showed me that two young girls would come to us one day. It said that you would be the key to putting this world back the way it was."

"Vision cloud? What else did it show you?" I found it hard to believe this.

"Many things," she smiled. "I couldn't see when you would arrive, but I knew you would come. The cloud is never wrong. That's why I sent scouts out each day. Many people thought the prophecy was just a story grown over hundreds of years. But I knew."

"The prophecy?"

"Yes. It has been foretold that a pair will destroy the balance of this world. It says that we shall live in hiding above the clouds until the day another pair would come. The prophecy says that you will be able to restore the world to what it used to be."

"How do you know it means us?"

"The vision cloud showed me both of you walking across the plains of this world. That's when I knew it had to be part of what had been forecast."

"But how are we supposed to fix things?" My head was spinning. "I don't even know what's wrong."

"The first two that arrived unleashed the elements of this world. They had always been kept under control by the Peace Stone. The stone was found by this first pair and broken in half. One half remains in this world, but the other must be found and returned."

"And you mean by the elements …?"

"Earth, air, fire and water. The four elements. Now we are hunted by them when we go beneath the clouds. We are safe once we are up here, or in the tree of safety. Outside of those boundaries, we are always in danger."

"We nearly drowned in the valley," Amber piped up,, annoyed by the memory. "And then we nearly got blown away."

"The tunnel collapsing …" It dawned on me. "… that was the earth element."

The Queen looked unhappy. "Yes. So you have already seen three of them. You can see why it's important to fix what is happening."

"I'm sorry for what's happening here, but I really can't see how we can help you. Can you tell us where the other piece is?"

"I don't know where it is," the Queen said sadly. "I just know it's not in this world. It's somewhere else, I can feel it."

"I don't understand how we can help. If you don't know where the stone piece is, how are we supposed to find it and bring it back?"

The Queen leaned forward, took both of my hands in hers and looked at me intently. "You are the key to everything. The prophecy says that it is you that will find the stone. We all have our part to play. Even me." She turned away for a second as if to hide from us.

I briefly wondered what she was hiding.

"What does the stone look like?" I asked.

"It has an indentation on the smooth side that looks like the ace of spades. You'll know it when you see it."

"I'm not sure that I would."

"You must try," she insisted with urgency. "Our lives rest in your hands."

"But I don't know how," I repeated.

"You do. Deep down, you know."

But I don't. I have no clue where to find a stone that I've never even seen. And I don't want to get caught up in your world of problems either. I just want to go home, and forget this world ever existed.

Yet I said, "I can't promise anything, but I'll try." *What harm can there be in making that statement?*

The Queen rose and hugged me. "Thank you! It is your destiny. This has appeared to me. You are the key, and once you return the stone, you will restore our world."

Wow. That's a lot of pressure for a thirteen-year-old. And now I'm the key to everything? I was a little overwhelmed. I looked across at Amber. She still sat silently with her legs crossed on the couch – she'd been through so much already; it was too much for her; it was too much for me. Whatever happened moving forward, I would leave her out of this world from now on.

"I suppose we should go," I began, realising how long we'd been gone. "Thank you for everything."

"It is my pleasure. We've been waiting for so long. I can't believe the prophecy is about to come true," the Queen gushed excitedly.

Uneasy, I stayed silent. I had a fair idea that once we left this world, we would never come back again. I didn't want to lie to Queen Tia, but the odds of finding a stone I would recognise – despite never having seen it – would be minuscule.

"Come. Merrin will be waiting at the tree," she said, beckoning us to follow.

Sure enough, Merrin was standing at the tree exactly where we'd arrived, his hat in his hand, waiting for us to come back. He bowed slightly to the Queen as we approached.

"Merrin," she said warmly, "it is time to take the girls back. Can you ensure they get there safely?"

"Of course," he said. "I will give my life before any harm comes upon them."

"Excellent. Then go, and I will pray for your swift return." She kissed my cheek and ruffled Amber's hair before pushing us gently towards the tree.

"Bye," Amber said, as she stepped onto the cloud that would take us back to the ground.

"Goodbye," I said to Queen Tia. "I hope you get

what you want."

"You won't let me down," she smiled. "I have faith."

I said nothing, uncomfortable with the confidence she'd bestowed on me as I followed Amber onto the cloud and took one last look around. I would probably never see a city in the sky again. The Queen stood watching us as we started our descent. She locked eyes with me and didn't break her gaze until the cloud lowered past her line of sight.

Turning back to Amber, I said, "A city in the clouds. Who would have guessed that one?"

She smiled back at me. "The biscuits were good."

"Of course, that's all you think about," I teased. "You're a bottomless pit."

"Am not!" she exclaimed.

"I'm just joking," I added, trying to take her mind off how we were going to get back home. In truth, I needed the distraction too, but being the older sister, I had to get her back safely. I couldn't ignore that fact.

"Merrin, how *will* we get back? The tunnel collapsed on our way here."

"We have many tunnels," he told me. "It's the only way to get where we need to go."

"Why did the tunnel collapse then?" I asked.

He sighed. "I would guess the elements are aware of you and how you can help our world. They want to stop you."

"You know about all that?" Amber asked.

"The prophecy has been around for hundreds of years. The Queen has spoken for years of two people not from our world who would come and save us. You are the first people I have seen in over thirty years."

"You were here before things changed …?"

"Yes. I was a farmer living off the land with my wife. That cottage you came upon? My house."

"What was this place like before it changed?"

"Just like any other," he said. "People were going about their lives … Now we have to live above the clouds."

"At least you're safe up there," I remarked.

"We are, but it's very limiting. I prefer down here on the ground."

"We live on the ground," Amber added.

"You do," Merrin smiled. "And if you come back with the Peace Stone then I will be able to live on the ground again too."

"The Peace Stone? Is that what it's called?"

"It is. And such a beautiful stone it is too."

"You've seen it?" I held my breath.

"I have."

"You know what it looks like then?"

"I did. Before it became broken. I'm not sure what it would look like now."

"What did it used to look like?"

"It shone with the most beautiful iridescent colours, hundreds of different hues depending on how the sunlight hit it. Every colour you could think of, better than any rainbow you've ever seen."

"Why didn't the Queen tell me what it looked like?" I wondered.

"I don't know. The Queen has seen it, I'm sure of it. It always seemed to dance with colour, no matter which angle you looked at it."

He stepped off the cloud into the tree of safety and motioned for us to follow him to another door.

"How did you get to see it? I got the impression that no one knew what it looked like." *Strange*, I thought.

"I was the Keeper's friend. He spoke of the prophecy often."

Silently, I followed Merrin through another tunnel. Why wouldn't the Queen tell me what the stone looked like if she wanted me to find it? It didn't make sense. At least I knew what to look for now. I was sure if I ever saw a stone like that, I would remember it.

The elements seemed to keep their distance as we completed the journey back to our gateway. We surfaced through a wooden door and stood outside the valley where we'd first entered this world.

"The gateway is there," he pointed. "Hurry before the elements awaken and come for you again."

"Thank you for keeping us safe," I said.

He just nodded and said, "Hurry now."

We turned back to see the gateway visible at the

bottom of the valley. The water had receded completely – it was like the flood had never happened. I turned to look at Merrin one last time, unsure if I would ever see him again.

"Hurry!" he said urgently as the wind around us began to rise again. We slid to the bottom of the valley, using whatever we could to slow our descent. Still, we both managed to land on our butts. Scrambling to my feet, I brushed the dirt off and helped Amber to hers.

"Let's go." I pushed her forward and grabbed her hand, and we stepped through the gateway back into the corridor and hurried straight back to my room.

I was back home. Safe. I hugged Amber. "I'm so sorry. I would never have taken you in there if I'd known."

"It's okay," she said. "But I don't want to go back there again, even if it does have a Queen that lives in the clouds."

I smiled and said, "That part was pretty cool, hey."

"Yeah. Merrin was nice too."

"He was. But now it's time to go to bed before we get in trouble."

"Okay. I'll see you in the morning."

"Night, squirt." I closed the door softly behind her. The purple door was gone from the wall as if it had never been there. It would have been easy to make myself believe it had all been a dream if I tried. I knew better though. As much as I wanted to forget this last world, I wouldn't be able to let it go now someone depended on me to save their world. *I'm not a superhero. What am I supposed to do? Start looking at all the rocks in my garden? The next-door neighbours? With all the trillions of stones in the world, how am I supposed to find this exact one? The Queen doesn't realise just how big a task she has set for me.* All these thoughts ran through my head as I settled into bed, destined for a night of tossing and turning.

Chapter 34

The next morning passed quickly as Amber and I sat in the treehouse and talked about what had happened the previous night. She had already forgotten how scary it had been and keenly talked about the Queen and the city in the clouds more than anything else.

"Did you see her room? All those fancy chairs?" Amber said.

"I did."

"She must be rich!"

"I didn't see any money anywhere, did you?"

"Well … no," Amber replied. "But she wore fancy clothes."

"It was a beautiful dress," I admitted.

"And did you notice that once we got to the top, the tree didn't have any leaves?"

"It didn't?" I asked.

"Nope. The branches all went into clouds. I didn't see any leaves at all."

"Wow, I didn't even notice. I was looking at the ground or the Queen most of the time."

"You'll have to have a look when we go there

again."

"Who said we're going back?" I said.

"You have to take the rock back, remember?"

"You heard that? I didn't think you were paying attention. I don't have the stone to give them. Where am I supposed to find a stone with lots of colours? Where do I even start? Do you have any idea how many rocks there are in this world? Probably millions, or even gazillions. There's no way I can find one stone."

"But you have to! She's counting on you!" Amber looked horrified at the thought of not saving her.

"Amber, exactly where do you think I'm supposed to go to find it? Please tell me, and I'll go get it now."

"I don't know, but I know you'll find it. You won't leave the Queen there forever wondering about whether you'll ever come back and save her."

How did Amber know that was what I'd planned on doing? The chances of finding her rock were so small I didn't believe it was worth even trying. I figured if I never went back, then she would just think I was still looking. If I never went back, I wouldn't have to stand in front of her and admit that I couldn't do what she'd asked me to do. I was just an ordinary 13-year-old girl enjoying her school holidays who happened to find a mystery chest.

Sighing deeply, I said, "I can't do it. It could take me hundreds of years to search without ever finding it. The Queen may still be waiting forever for me to come and save her."

"You have to try. You can't promise someone and then go back on your word." Amber looked shocked.

"Do you want to go back and get attacked by those elements again? Don't you remember running through that valley, the water behind us? Or the wind that had us pinned to the ground so we couldn't go anywhere?"

"Yes, but we still got away, and we're okay now."

"The tunnel. Remember the tunnel? Falling around us?"

"Yes," Amber repeated. "But again, we got away. We're safe."

"But you want to go back and face more of that. What if this time it's a fire? Or an avalanche? A tornado? An earthquake?"

"It won't be."

"You can't know that." She had no idea just how dangerous it was. "There's no way you can know that."

"No, but ..."

"Exactly. Even if I do find this rock, which I don't think I will, you won't be going back in there anyway."

"What do you mean?" She narrowed her eyes at me.

"You heard me. I'm not risking your life again. If I must go back, I will, but you'll stay behind."

"No, I won't! I'm coming with you!"

"You're not." I said firmly, "and you won't change my mind on that."

"That's not fair!" She pouted at me.

"It is. What do you think I would say to Mum and Dad? What if there was an earthquake and you fell through a crack in the ground and died? How do I explain that? Yeah, sorry Mum, I took Amber into a magic world through a magic door, and she fell through the ground, and now she's gone. My bad."

Amber started giggling. "Yeah, you might get in trouble for that."

I smiled back at her. "Doesn't matter anyway, squirt. I'll never find the rock. Not in my lifetime."

"You never know," Amber replied. "We could start looking now. Maybe with both of us looking, we can find it faster."

"What, in the backyard?"

"Why not?" Amber jumped up. "Let's go look."

"Sure," I muttered. *Like it's going to be in the backyard.* I didn't want to waste my time, but Amber was already climbing down the ladder, so I obediently followed.

Back on the ground, Amber took charge.

"You look over there." She pointed across the lawn to the garden bed on the far side of the garden. "I'll look over near the driveway."

I just nodded and walked over to the garden bed. *Does Amber really expect the rock to be sitting there in the garden?* I kicked one with my foot. *No fancy colours here.* One by one, I slowly kicked them over, not expecting to see anything. There was no way a rock from another world would just happen to be in my yard. That would be way too much of a coincidence.

"Any luck?" Amber called out from across the yard.

"No," I yelled back.

I turned back and continued to kick rocks over. I'd never noticed just how many rocks we had in our yard before. As I continued to check, I realised that she hadn't even told me what size the stone was. What if it was the size of a football? How would I carry that back to her world? What if it was so small that you could barely hold it between two fingers? You could lose that in seconds and never find it again.

I was interrupted by a tug on my sleeve.

"Could this be it?" Amber held up a rock.

"No, that's not the one."

"Okay," she said. "Let's try those next."

She was looking over at the garden beds near the house.

"Okay." I started heading that way. "You going to help me?"

"Yep." Amber skipped back to me. She was enjoying this scavenger hunt. She kneeled at the edge of the garden bed and looked up at me.

"What?" I said.

"Come on. You can't search from up there. You have to get down on the ground."

Sighing, I knelt beside her. The garden bed ran

the whole length of the house. It would take us forever to search.

"You start on this side of the door, and I'll start on the other side," Amber ordered.

"Yes, ma'am," I said, saluting her.

She poked her tongue out at me and moved to the other side of the kitchen door. We sifted in silence for a few minutes, both caught up in our thoughts.

"Do you think Merrin will be okay?" Amber asked.

"Why wouldn't he be?"

"I don't know. What if he gets hurt?"

"He lives in the city. He's safe."

"That's assuming he got back okay."

"True. But he seemed to know his way around. I'm sure he'll be fine."

"Yeah, I guess so." A couple more minutes went by, then: "The cottage was cute."

"It was."

"It was Merrin's house."

"What's with the fascination with Merrin all of a sudden?"

"He was nice. He reminded me a little bit of Grandpa."

I hadn't thought about Grandpa in a long time. He'd died years ago and I was surprised Amber could even remember him.

"You remember Grandpa?" I asked her.

"A little bit. I remember he was nice to us. So was

Merrin."

"Yes, but other than the grey hair there's not much more in common."

"I dunno. He just reminded me of Grandpa."

"Well, I guess lots of old men look the same." I laughed and added, "How are you going? Find anything?"

"Not yet. But I'm sure we'll get lucky if we keep looking."

I turned back to the garden bed and kept sifting.

Chapter 35

Courtney

Standing at the counter in front of the window, Courtney could hear the girls outside. There was nothing better than listening to the sounds of the birds singing, or the cicadas chirping at this time of year. This was her favourite place in the summer: making lunches or doing the dishes in front of this window. For some reason, it calmed her, gave her a feeling of peace, and brought sense to the world.

Now standing there, preparing sandwiches for lunch, she'd watched the girls climb out of the treehouse, which was helpful as she wasn't looking forward to climbing the ladder to deliver lunch. Courtney liked to think that she could keep up with the girls if she wanted to, but she never enjoyed that climb.

Spreading the butter across the bread, she listened to their chatter outside. From where she stood, she couldn't see them, but she could hear them talking about someone called Merrin. An unusual name. Courtney didn't know who that was, but it sounded like Amber was keen on wherever this character had come from. She loved the way Amber could create anything from her imagination. This was the girl who pulled chairs together when she was five, grabbed a paper plate and told them all to get in the "car" she had made so she could take them all for a drive.

Right now, they were on a mission to find a rock. What type of rock Courtney didn't know, and it didn't sound like they knew either. Yet they continued to explore the garden. She listened absently as they discussed their search and this Merrin character.

When they brought up their grandfather, she was surprised. Amber had been four years old when he had passed away. He'd never really been a big part of the family, living so far away from them and he'd rarely visited. For Amber to remember him at all surprised her.

"Have you found it yet?" Courtney heard Amber ask.

"Not yet." Morgan had the patience of a saint when it came to her little sister.

"What was it supposed to look like again?"

"Lots of colours," came Morgan's reply.

More silence as they continued to search.

"What about this one?"

Morgan sounded unsure when she answered. "I don't think so?"

"I don't know what I'm looking for."

"I don't know either, squirt."

"Did she say anything else about it?"

"Not really. Something about an indentation, but that was it."

"So, we're looking for something with a hole in it?"

Courtney wondered who 'she' was. Had someone told them to go looking for a rock? Or was this all part of some game Amber had dreamed up?

"Not a hole … an indentation."

"Right." It didn't sound like Amber was any less confused. Maybe it wasn't one of Amber's games after all.

"I wish she'd told you more about it."

"Me too," Morgan replied.

"Otherwise, how are we going to find it?"

"That's what I've been saying!" Morgan sounded frustrated.

"Do you think Merrin and the others have been building tunnels for years?"

"I think they had to, or they wouldn't be able to go anywhere, or get to the tree."

"But where did they put the sand they dug out?"

"I don't know. I didn't see any piles of sand anywhere."

"But it had to go somewhere. Hundreds of tunnels would be lots of sand."

"I don't know, Amber. I didn't build them. I don't have the answer for you."

Courtney smiled, knowing firsthand how relentless Amber could be with her questions. She'd been at the receiving end many times. She wondered once more about which movie they were discussing. Tunnels, trees, rocks, and someone called Merrin. It didn't sound like something she'd ever seen. Considering the mysterious 'she' they spoke of still didn't give Courtney any further clarity. She was lost on this one, although it sounded like an intriguing storyline.

"Morgan, will you really never go back?"

Courtney's ears pricked with concentration. This was a new line of conversation.

Morgan sighed and replied, "I don't know. It was pretty scary. I'm not really in a hurry to get back there again."

"But if you find the rock?"

"If I do find the rock, then I'll go back. But not until then."

Courtney frowned. When had Morgan had a chance to go anywhere? It was school holidays, and other than shopping with her neither of them had gone anywhere. *It must be an elaborate game they've thought up. Maybe they're role-playing.* Yes, that made more sense to Courtney.

"Do you think Merrin will be waiting when you go back?"

"*IF* I go back," Morgan said. "Probably, if I go in at the same place."

"Oh. Could you get there a different way?"

"I don't know. There's so much I don't know! I've never gone back to any of them before."

For reasons Courtney couldn't understand at that moment, her heart started to beat a little faster. She paused, knife in hand, tomato in the other. She wanted to hear this.

"Maybe you could go straight to the tree and skip all the bad stuff," Amber suggested.

"That would be easy, wouldn't it."

"Yeah, and then Merrin wouldn't have to wait around for you. And the Queen would be ready when you came and wouldn't have to send anyone out."

"Still, I don't know if the entry point would ever change. Maybe we'll find out someday."

"Then what? Do we try another one?"

"You want to go again?"

"Yeah! It's so much fun. The first one was so cool. Duke was the best. I'd go back there again."

"That was good, wasn't it? But there are so many more to see."

"But you haven't got any more keys."

Keys? Courtney involuntarily stopped breathing.

"I've got lots of keys. I just haven't matched them up yet."

"You're so lucky that you got the magic door, Morgan. I wish it had come on my wall."

The knife slipped from Courtney's hand and just missed her foot as it fell to the floor unnoticed. She held onto the edge of the counter as she struggled to breathe. *The magic door. It's open, and the girls have been exploring.*

Chapter 36

Robert

Robert's full attention was fixed on the computer in front of him when the phone rang. Not the regular office phone, which everyone used, but his mobile. He frowned, wondering who would be calling him during work hours. Those close to him knew to call the work phone as he didn't always keep his mobile nearby while he was working. He picked up the phone and looked at the screen. *Courtney?* Why would she be calling him now?

Puzzled, he tapped Bryan next to him and gestured toward the door. Bryan nodded as Robert hit the answer button and headed out.

"Courtney? What's going on?" His question was met with silence.

"Courtney?" Robert tried again.

"Rob, you have to come home." Her voice had wavered. "Please."

"Why? What's happened? Are the girls okay?"

"Yes … no … yes … they're okay for now."

"What do you mean, for now?" he asked, frantic for some real information.

"They're in the garden," she replied.

He let out a sigh of relief. The girls were okay. "Court, I can't leave at the moment, I'm analysing some data that needs to be ready tomorrow."

"Please," Courtney begged. "I need you now. You need to be at home. It's an emergency."

"Unless you have a good reason then, Court, I'm sorry, but I just can't leave right now. Whatever it is, can you handle it?"

"Can I handle it?" Courtney almost screeched down the phone line. "I can barely breathe! Robert, the girls have opened the door."

"What door?" He frowned, confused.

"The purple door!"

His knees buckled, and he sank onto the bench seat behind him. *They know about the door.* Robert didn't understand how this had happened. They'd gotten rid of the chest and the key; hidden it where it would never resurface. *How did they find it?*

"Oh," was all he managed to get out.

"Now will you come home, please! We need to talk to them, and I don't want to do it without you."

"I'm on my way," he replied.

Chapter 37

We continued searching for a few more minutes until we both grew bored. We were kidding ourselves if we thought we were going to find it in our backyard.

"Oh well," I said to Amber as we sat down under one of the big trees. "We'll just have to find it somewhere else. Maybe next time we ride to the park we can have a look there."

"Great idea! There are tons of rocks around the pond."

"A good place to start then. Are you hungry?" I asked.

"Starving."

"I'll run in and check with Mum if lunch is ready. We can eat here under the tree if you want."

Amber stretched out on her back, looking up at the leaves. "Sounds good."

I raced into the kitchen and found Mum sitting at the table. Half-made sandwiches lay on the counter, and a knife lay on the floor. I looked around, puzzled. "What's going on? Everything okay?"

I picked up the knife and put it in the sink. The

cheese slices were in the packet off to the side, not yet on the bread. I added the cheese to the ham and tomato and slapped another piece of bread on top.

"Perfect," I announced. Picking up the plates, I headed outside again. On the way past, I pecked Mum on the cheek and said, "Thanks for the sandwiches." I smiled and exited the house.

Back under the tree, I handed a plate to Amber. "There you go."

We sat in silence, enjoying our lunch but wondering why Mum hadn't said anything to me. Not a single word. Whatever it was, it was probably adult stuff. I knew she would tell me if I had done something wrong. I lay back on the grass and put my hands behind my head.

I had nearly dozed off under the tree when I heard tyres crunching on the driveway. We weren't expecting anyone as far as I knew. Opening one eye, I peered over and saw Dad's car pulling into his usual spot. *What's Dad doing home? He's supposed to be working.* Deciding it wasn't my problem, I closed my eyes again and continued to lay enjoying the shade and the peace.

I only half-listened as Dad walked towards the house, opened the door, and went inside. It was a little strange that he didn't call out hello on his way past, because he always made sure we knew he was coming or going. Not today.

I sighed, still contented. This was the perfect place to be right now. Under the tree in the shade, the sound of summer in the background. With school starting soon I wouldn't have time to enjoy this. I could hear Amber breathing deeply next to me, and was sure that she had fallen asleep. It was the perfect summer's day.

A couple of minutes later, the back door opened again, and Dad came out.

"Girls," he called out.

I opened my eyes and looked over at him.

"Can you come inside, please?"

Without waiting for an answer, he closed the door.

A feeling of unease washed over me. *What have we done? We're in trouble for going through the garden? Maybe Aunt Leah is sick again?* I hoped it wasn't that.

I poked Amber in her side. "Hey, squirt, wake up."

Nothing. She had always been able to sleep through anything.

"Amber!" I pushed her arm. "Wake up. Dad wants us inside."

She opened her eyes and yawned. "Why did you wake me? I was having a dream about Duke."

I sat up. "Dad wants us inside."

"Dad's here?" She looked confused.

"Yes," I repeated, grabbing her arm, and pulling her up. "And he wants us inside."

We walked into the house hesitantly. Both Mum and Dad sat at the kitchen table, faces unhappy.

"Come sit down," Dad instructed.

Straight away, I felt I was in serious trouble. I took a seat at the table and looked at them.

"What's going on?" I asked. "Is Aunt Leah okay?"

Amber sat next to me and took my cue. "Is Aunt Leah sick?"

"No, no, you're Aunt is fine," Dad reassured us.

"Is Mum sick?" Amber sounded alarmed. I had to admit she didn't look well.

"I'm okay," Mum replied. "But we need to talk to you both."

"Have we done something wrong?" Amber asked in a small voice.

"No, hon." Mum reached out, smoothed Amber's hair and looked over at Dad.

Dad cleared his throat. "There's no easy way to say this …"

I waited, holding my breath for whatever was about to come.

"We know," was what he said.

I looked at Dad, then at Mum, who both looked straight back at me. Confused, I checked Amber, who seemed as puzzled as I was.

"Know what?" I asked.

"The door," came Dad's response.

"The door? What door?" I said innocently, although my heart started beating out of my chest.

"The magic door."

"That's silly," I said weakly. "There's no such thing as magic. Certainly not a magic door. I think you've been smelling too many chemicals at work, Dad."

"It's real," Mum added. "As real as you and I. I've been through the door myself."

I looked at her, my eyes at first widening, then narrowing. *What's she trying to do? How can she possibly know about the purple door and what's behind it?* I didn't know what to say, so stayed silent.

"It's purple, and it appears on your wall at the same time every day," Mum continued.

Has she seen the door?

I worked back in my mind trying to figure out when she would have seen it. Maybe during those five minutes when the door was there she had come back into my room to find me gone. That didn't make sense, though, because if that had happened, I'm sure she would have been waiting for me when I came back.

"I don't know what you mean," I replied softly, not sure where this conversation was going.

"Yes, you do!" Amber chipped in. "The one on your wall every night. Remember? With the keys and all those doors."

Inwardly I groaned. Outwardly I glared at Amber. She had just given away my secret; something she had promised she would never do.

"Yes, that one," Mum smiled at Amber.

"Am I in trouble?" I asked.

"For what?" Mum asked me.

"I don't know." I didn't understand what was

going on here.

"Let me explain," Mum said.

Dad rose and returned with a pack of biscuits which he put on the table. What was it with people and biscuits? First Queen Tia and now Dad, like it was going to fix everything.

"I was only thirteen when the door first appeared to me," she said, staring straight at me. "I started exploring all those worlds inside that corridor. I even took your father and your aunt in there a couple of times."

"You saw the door too?" I asked.

"I did. And I had a wonderful time exploring it."

"You were thirteen as well. I wonder why that was?" I considered.

"I don't know why it happens at thirteen, but it did for me, and my mother too."

"Grandma knows?" I was shocked.

"Yes, she knows about the door. How did you find the chest? I thought I had hidden it well."

It had become a conversation between Mum and I, as Dad and Amber watched on in silence.

"The dreams."

"You were having the dreams after all. You told me you weren't." Mum seemed disappointed.

"You were so worried that I had them all the time," I said a little defensively.

"I was," she replied. "Because once you start dreaming every night, you know the door is coming."

"Well, how was I supposed to know that?"

"You weren't," Mum said. "How did you find the chest?"

"The dream changed one night and showed me the chest in the attic. I went up and had a look. It was exactly where it was in my dream."

"And the golden key?"

"This might sound crazy, but it flew out from under the floorboards and straight into the lock on the chest."

"It's not crazy," Mum reassured me. "I've seen enough in my lifetime to accept almost anything is possible."

"How long have you seen the door?" Dad asked me.

"I don't know. A week or two, maybe?" I replied.

"How many doors have you been through?" Mum asked.

I counted on my fingers as I spoke. "The dream one, the carnival, the one with me, the wind one. Four."

"And the animal one, "Amber added.

"Oh yeah, so that's five."

"Five," Mum seemed relieved.

"But there's so many more to explore. I have the keys; I just haven't matched them all up yet."

"I don't want you exploring anymore," Mum said sharply.

"Why not?"

"It's not safe. You don't know what's in there."

"Neither did you," I pointed out.

"True," Mum agreed. "But I'd rather not risk your life."

"We've been fine up to now. Nothing has happened." I couldn't believe Mum was going to stop me from exploring. "How did you find out that I had the door?"

"You girls were talking outside the window. Amber said something about keys and doors and how she wished she had the magic door. That's when I knew."

Amber and her big mouth. I was angry for a split second before I realised we were both in that conversation. We also had no idea that Mum was listening in from the kitchen either. It wasn't anyone's fault.

"Do you know why it appears at the same time every day?"

"We worked out it had something to do with the time the chest opened," Dad replied. "What time does it appear for you?"

I thought briefly about lying but being an honest person, it just didn't feel right. Besides, I'm sure they would have sat in my room and waited until it appeared, just to be sure. "Ten at night."

"That must have been the time you opened the chest. You said the dream showed you and you went to check it out," Dad said, thinking out loud.

"Yes, and when it unlocked, there was a huge bang, and I raced back to my room with it. I'm pretty sure that it was around ten o'clock now that I think about it."

"I remember that night!" Dad exclaimed. "It woke me up. I thought there was a burglar, so I checked the house. But you were in bed asleep?"

"Well … I was in bed," I said a little sheepishly.

"Uh-huh. You fooled me," Dad said.

It was hard to wrap my mind around the idea that this wasn't as much of a secret as I thought. The whole family knew, including Grandma and Aunt Leah. It had taken me ages to accept what was happening to me, and I was having just as much trouble digesting the fact that everyone knew. I never thought I'd be talking to Mum and Dad about magic doors.

We sat in silence for a minute, each in our own thoughts. Running through the conversation, I realised something. "Hey Mum, why did you hide the key and chest? Why would you want me to stop exploring?"

"We'll get to that. First, I'd love to hear about your adventures. Why don't we move into the lounge room where it's more comfortable, and you can tell me all about it?"

Chapter 38

Courtney

That could have been a lot worse, Courtney thought as they made their way to the other room. Morgan and Amber were both forthcoming with what they'd been doing. Amber hadn't spoken much, but she suspected that was because it was Morgan's door. Courtney assumed that meant she hadn't been in there as much as Morgan had. Amber also had a very keen sense of when to stay quiet – except for the moment she had given up the door and the keys. Courtney had a feeling Morgan wasn't too pleased about that.

Still, she felt relieved it was now all out in the open. Now she could protect her girls and make sure they stayed away, even if that meant sleeping in Morgan's room with her to make sure she didn't go anywhere.

After making themselves comfortable, the conversation resumed.

"Tell me everything. Where did you go first?" she

asked Morgan.

Morgan still seemed hesitant but once she started speaking the excitement soon took over.

"The first one was a dream tree."

"That was probably my favourite door of all," Courtney said fondly, encouraging Morgan to talk.

"Really?" Morgan's eyes shone brightly. "That's where I met Flora, one of the fairies."

"Did you meet the lady in white?"

"I did. She showed me the tree and Flora."

"It's a beautiful place. Unusual, but beautiful," Courtney added. "What I liked most was the concept of the tree. Wasn't it amazing to think that every person in the world that was having a dream had a leaf on that tree?"

"I know! And when they changed colours and fell off. It was pretty cool," Morgan replied.

"I want to see *that* tree!" Amber complained loudly.

Courtney laughed. Why the door went to the oldest child, she didn't know. Amber would have seemed like the more obvious choice to her. With her childlike wonder and her love of magic, she would have been the one to leap in headfirst. She would have wholly accepted the concept without question.

"Maybe one day," Courtney told her, knowing she would do everything she could to make sure that didn't happen. She didn't like lying to her kids, but sometimes a small white lie for their safety and happiness was necessary.

"Where did you go next?" Courtney asked.

"After that was a bizarre place where every person in there was me."

"What do you mean?" Robert asked.

"Each person I came across was just me but at different ages. I met a family – a mother and two daughters. One was around five, and the other was older than me. They all looked like me and had the same story. It was kind of freaky."

"Interesting …" She could see Robert's scientific mind ticking. "The same person at different ages. Could you tell it was you?"

"The one closest to my age was easy. So was the young girl, and even the Mum. At least I know what I'll look like when I'm old."

"Fascinating," Robert replied. "I'd love to see that world. Which symbol was that one?"

"Um, I think it was a rectangle with an oval inside it?" Morgan said uncertainly.

"A mirror," Robert said, "… with a face reflected in it. That's very clever."

"That makes sense," Morgan said.

"What was next?" Courtney asked.

"Next was a carnival," Morgan replied.

"I don't think I've been to that one. What was it like?"

"Fun, and then a bit weird. I was a celebrity in that one."

"A celebrity? What sort of celebrity?" Another

impressive door she'd never had the chance to visit.

"I don't know," Morgan said, and then she smiled at Courtney. "It was funny being ushered in and having my hair and makeup done."

"I want to go see that one too!" Amber interjected.

Morgan ignored her and continued, "but then they pushed me out on stage in front of hundreds of people. I didn't know what to do."

"What did you end up doing?"

"Nothing. I just said that I wasn't sure what I was supposed to do."

"I bet that didn't go down well," Courtney said.

"Actually, they all cheered and clapped, and then I got out of there as quick as I could." Morgan smiled. "But they were all waiting outside for autographs when I left."

"Then Morgan took me with her for the next one," Amber piped up.

"Really?" Robert smiled at her and said, "and where did you go?"

"We went to an animal place where there were talking dogs and horses and half men and everything," she said, her enthusiasm still alive from the journey.

"We rode a centipede bus and saw three doors that led to rejuvenation and healing trees. It was beautiful and the centaurs, or half men as Amber said, were almost unreal," Morgan added.

"Sounds like fun," Courtney agreed. "And what

about the last one?"

Morgan frowned. "That place wasn't very nice. To be honest, it was scary."

"Yeah, we nearly drowned and then nearly got blown away, and then we nearly got buried," Amber rapidly recounted.

"It wasn't as bad as that," Morgan said quickly, knowing her parents' immediate reaction. But her face told a different story. Courtney had the feeling it *was* that bad. It was the very thing she had worried about all along, and for a good reason. That place sounded like the door Tiana and she had gone through. She could feel her body almost going into shock as she realised that the very thing she had feared most could possibly have already come true.

Chapter 39

I was watching Mum when Amber finished her last sentence. It's funny, I've read in books when they say things like "you could see a storm brewing in her eyes," but I swear I really could. The moment Amber mentioned all the problems we'd had in that last world, Mum's eyes clouded over, and her face froze. She looked like she'd seen a ghost, and not a friendly one either.

I stared at her. "You've been in that one, haven't you?"

Mum nodded, unable to speak.

"That's why we've been so afraid that you might have seen the door," Dad added. "That world is one to be avoided at all costs."

"Too late," I replied. "We've already been in there."

Alarmed, I noticed a tear roll down Mum's cheek.

"We're okay," I said, trying to calm her. I wasn't sure what was going on in her mind, and I didn't want to upset her, but I didn't want to lie to her either. It worked because she seemed to gather herself up and sit taller.

"Tell me exactly what happened … please." She leaned forward in her chair. I could tell that whatever I said next was incredibly important.

Taking a deep breath, I said, "Well, we arrived in some sort of valley and started walking along the valley floor when we heard a strange sound. It turned out to be a rush of water coming down the valley. We ran up the side and managed to get out in time."

"I don't think it was a valley," Mum countered. "I think it was a path of destruction caused by a tornado."

"What makes you say that?"

"I'm pretty sure. What happened next?"

I shrugged. "Next, we decided to go to a little building that Amber had seen. We headed towards it, and then out of nowhere, a powerful wind came up. Eventually, we had to lay flat on the ground, or we would've been blown away."

"How did you get away from it?" Mum asked.

"It just stopped."

"It just stopped?" Mum repeated.

"Yes. So we continued to the building, which is where we met Merrin."

"Merrin was waiting in the cottage for us," Amber added brightly.

"What do you mean?" Dad asked.

"He said he'd been waiting for us. He had to take us to the Queen."

"The Queen?" Mum's brow creased deeply. "The Queen of what?"

"The city in the sky," I finished.

"How do you get to a city in the sky?" Mum looked flabbergasted.

"Merrin took us through a tunnel," I started.

"… which collapsed around us," Amber added.

"Yes, which collapsed. We ended up at the base of the tree of safety and rode a cloud straight up to the sky."

"Then we met the Queen," Amber said.

"Yes," I said, giving Amber a sharp look for butting in. "The Queen took us to her rooms to talk. Then Merrin took us back to the gateway, and we came back. That's pretty much it."

"What did the Queen want to talk about?" Dad queried.

"Some old prophecy. But it's not important. What she wants is impossible."

"What's the prophecy, Morgan?" Mum asked a little more sharply than she intended.

"Something about tearing the world apart and putting it back together again," I sighed. "But honestly, Mum, there's no way I could do what she's asked. As I said, it's impossible. To be honest, I don't know why it's up to me to save the world."

"Well, you're not going back in there again." Mum sounded pretty definite about that. "I don't care whose world it is."

"Fine with me." I smiled. "I don't want to battle the elements again anyway."

"The elements?"

"Yes. There was a couple of people who unleashed the elements of the world. That's what caused everyone to have to live above the clouds where they were safe. Earth, air, fire, water. The four elements are what keeps everyone away."

"How are you supposed to save the world then?" Dad asked. "How do you fight and win against the elements?"

"I don't think I'm supposed to fight them, Dad. But there is some special stone somewhere that is supposed to restore everything to the way it was. And apparently, I'm the one destined to find it."

"Is that what you girls were talking about out in the garden?" Mum asked.

"Yes. But I didn't expect to find anything, and we didn't."

"Tell me more about this conversation with the Queen. What does the stone look like?" Now Mum was throwing questions at me.

"There's not much to tell. We talked about the prophecy. The Queen said her crystal ball …"

"Vision cloud," Amber interrupted.

"Sorry, her vision cloud showed her that two people not from her world would come and restore the balance. Something like that. She said I had to find the missing rock …"

"Peace Stone," Amber interrupted again.

"Do you want to tell it?" I snapped at her, then continued. "Those two people broke the Peace Stone, and I'm supposed to find it again. Except she couldn't tell me what it looked like, or where it could be."

"Merrin knew what it looked like," Amber cut in again.

"Did he? What did he say?" Dad asked.

"He said it was beautiful with lots of colours." Amber grinned. "That's right, isn't it, Morgan?"

"Yes," I replied, smiling. "With an indentation. Merrin was much more helpful than the Queen, who only told me I would know it if I saw it."

"Sounds like your old rock, hon," Dad said, looking over at Mum. Straight away, Mum looked up at the rock on the mantlepiece. It had been there for as long as I could remember. *Wouldn't it be funny if that's the stone we're looking for and it's been under our noses the whole time?*

The silence between us grew as we all contemplated the possibility.

Finally, I rose off the chair and walked to the mantlepiece. The stone was a bit smaller than my hand. It sat flat on the shelf, while the exposed section had all the typical crevasses and abnormalities you would expect to see on a rock. I put my hand on it, a little afraid to pick it up, and looked back at Mum, Dad and Amber, all staring at me expectantly.

Holding my breath, I lifted the rock and turned it over.

Chapter 40

Courtney

Courtney found herself forgetting to breathe as she watched Morgan lift the rock. She had been in that world, and a tornado had thrown her out. She also knew her best friend had been left behind to die. The loss of her friend had overshadowed so many memories of that time. Had she taken a stone from there? What happened that day was buried so deep inside to save her from more pain and heartache. *Is it possible that I caused all this?*

Morgan lifted the rock and paused again before turning it over. Courtney knew the stone was full of many colours; it was what had drawn her to it in the first place, the reason it remained on show in the house. But was it the rock Morgan was looking for? That would change everything.

Morgan turned it over and stared at the other side. Gradually, she sank to the floor. "It's the one," she said weakly.

"What do you mean it's the one?" Robert

spluttered.

Morgan didn't reply straight away. She just sat there, looking at the rock in her hand. Then she said quietly, "This is the stone that will save their world."

Every part of Courtney's body stopped moving as memories flooded back in. In her mind, she saw the circle of stones again; in the centre the most beautiful colourful stone floating in mid-air. On the outside, two young girls, awed by what they were seeing, too selfish to understand that taking this could cause so much damage. Fast forward ten minutes to the same two girls running away after having taken and dropped the stone, causing it to break in two, ending with being caught up in a tornado, with Courtney coming home and her friend left behind.

Courtney didn't feel the tears that now ran down her cheeks and fell from her face. She didn't feel Robert's hand as he reached out to comfort her. She didn't see Amber, staring at her from her seat, watching her mother break down in front of her. All Courtney saw was the memories that flooded her mind, taking her straight back to that world and the problems they had faced. Her heart broke for the trouble that Tiana and she had caused these people.

"Are you sure?" Robert asked Morgan. "Are you really sure?"

"Yes," Morgan nodded. "It has the indentation in it, the ace of spades. This is it."

"So that means we can go give her the rock and

save their world then." It came from Amber, keen to help.

"No!" shot out of Courtney's mouth before she could stop it. Her family looked at her in disbelief. "No. It's not safe. You girls said yourselves that you nearly drowned and were almost buried alive. Do you think I would let you go back in there?"

"But we have to help them!" Amber cried out.

"It's not safe!" Courtney repeated. "It's not safe."

She remembered the fear she'd felt as the tornado picked her up and carried her away, afraid that she would never set her feet on the ground again. She had feared that she'd be thrown to her death, as it turned out Tiana had been.

"Come with me for a minute," Robert gently spoke as he pulled Courtney up from the lounge. Reluctantly she followed him into the kitchen where he sat her in one of the chairs and turned on the kettle. Waiting for it to boil, he prepared two cups with coffee and sugar as she sat there quietly watching.

"We have to go back in there," Robert said softly.

"No, we don't!" Courtney shook her head fiercely.

"Hon, you have a chance to right a wrong here. You have the key to their world, a world you unbalanced. I know you don't like it, but you must do the right thing. You have to fix it."

"The girls are *NOT* going back in there. You know only two people can go in. It's Morgan's door, and she must be one of them. I don't want anything to happen to her ..." She was nearly in tears again. "I can't lose her."

"You won't. But you need to tell them the truth about what happened in there. If Morgan goes back, she needs to have all the facts so she can stay safe. You have to tell her."

"I said she's not going in there!" Courtney growled this time, her jaw clenched.

"What if I went with her? I could protect her and get the stone back to its rightful place. I'll make sure nothing happens to her."

"What if I lost you too? I couldn't bear it."

"You won't. The girls know what to expect and where to go. Morgan can show me, and I can keep her safe. We can restore the world to what it was, and you can sleep at night, knowing you did the right thing."

"I don't know ..."

"Yes, you do," Robert answered. "You couldn't live with yourself knowing that you could help someone and did nothing about it."

"Do we need to tell them about Tiana? How do I tell my girls that I let my best friend die? They will never look at me the same again."

"If anything, they will understand better than they ever would have before the door. They've been through this place and know how dangerous it is. You are their mother; they'll be okay."

Courtney sighed. Robert was right. They needed

to do something to save that world, and the stone in their lounge was the key to that. They could help them, and they *should* help them. Robert finished pouring the coffee and handed a cup to her.

"Are you ready for this?" he asked her.

"Not really," Courtney replied. "But it needs to be done. Let's go."

Back in the lounge room with coffee in hand, Courtney stared at her girls where they sat on the floor and wondered where to start. They looked back at her, so innocent. Both girls knew something was wrong, but she also knew they were too considerate to pry. Robert nodded at her, silently giving her the confidence to tell her story.

Courtney took a deep breath and said, "When I was your age, I used to explore these worlds too. I took your father in, and your Aunt Leah too. I even took my best friend a couple of times."

"Best friend?" Morgan looked puzzled. "Who's that?"

"She was very close to me; we did everything together. She didn't have the easiest life. Being a foster child, she was always moving from home to home. These worlds were a highlight for her, and to see her truly happy made me happy."

"You've never mentioned her before," Morgan interrupted.

"No." Courtney smiled sadly. "That's because she's not with us anymore."

"What happened?" Amber asked.

"We were young. We didn't know what we were doing. We went through a door and started exploring this beautiful world. We came across a clearing surrounded by rock, and floating in the middle was the most beautiful stone we had ever seen. We wanted a memento of our trip, so we decided to take it back with us."

She stopped for a moment to let this sink in, watched the girls' faces as they digested the information. Morgan was the first to realise what she was saying.

"You mean …" She stopped short, one eyebrow rising.

"Yes. We took the stone. We were the ones that unbalanced that world in the first place."

"Why?" Morgan seemed disappointed with her.

"It's easy to see why it's a bad idea in hindsight. But at the time, it was a beautiful stone that would remind us of a time in our lives where everything was amazing. We didn't know what would happen. As soon as we moved it, the ground started shaking. We dropped the stone, and it broke in two. We both grabbed a piece and ran."

"Then what happened?" Amber this time.

"Well," Courtney answered, "the wind started howling, and we started running. It got worse and worse, and as we ran, it turned into a tornado. We were both picked up and taken along with it." She paused. "Eventually I was thrown out of the tornado, and straight through the gateway back into the corridor."

"What about your friend?" Courtney could tell from Morgan's voice she knew what she was going to say next.

"She didn't make it," she said sadly.

"What do you mean she didn't make it?" Morgan narrowed her eyes at her.

"I can only assume she was thrown somewhere in that world and died." A tear rolled down her cheek.

"Didn't you go back to find her?" Morgan asked.

"I couldn't. I lost the key somewhere along the way. The door locked behind me, and I was never able to get back in. Your father and I tried everything to get that door open, but we couldn't. She was gone."

"I have the key. How do I have the key if you lost it? We can go back in and look for her."

"Morgan, it was thirty years ago. That tornado was like nothing I had ever experienced. That valley you landed in? … that was the path the tornado tore through the land as it travelled. No one could have survived that."

"You did," Amber said matter-of-factly.

"True, but I was lucky. There's not a day goes by that I don't think of her. The stone was the only thing I had left of her. I put it on the mantelpiece and forgot all about it, but I never forgot her."

The girls sat silently.

"I'm sorry, but that's why I wanted you both to stay away. It's dangerous, and I had no idea that you had already gone in there."

"But we have to save them!" Amber insisted.

"I know we do." Courtney knelt on the floor with the girls and took their hands in hers. "I have to undo what I've done. But it's also dangerous in there, so we have to be careful."

"We will be," Amber squeezed her hand.

"You won't be going," Courtney told her firmly. "Only two people can go through the door at once. One must be Morgan. The other will be your father."

"*What?* No, I want to go back and see Merrin!"

"I'm sorry, Amber, but your dad needs to keep Morgan safe."

Courtney turned to her other daughter. "Are you up for going back in there? Dad will be with you all the way."

Morgan struggled with her decision. It wouldn't be easy; they all knew that, but she also knew her daughter was a lot stronger than she gave her credit for.

"I guess so," she said, "if Dad's with me."

"I'll be right beside you all the way," Robert assured her.

"Okay. I'm sorry, Amber. If I have to go back, I should have an adult with me."

Typical of Morgan to be worried about her sister, Courtney mused.

"Fine." Amber seemed resigned that she wouldn't be going. "I suppose it doesn't matter who saves the world as long as someone does."

Courtney sat back and picked up her coffee. She had raised two awesome kids. As scared as she was to send Morgan and Robert back, she had to admit it felt good to be able to do something to help restore the world, especially considering it was Tiana and she that ruined it in the first place.

"When do we go?" Morgan looked at her father.

"Tonight, I suppose," he replied with a shrug.

"Make sure you take it straight to Queen Tia," Amber pointed out then added, "and don't break it and don't lose it."

Courtney looked up at Robert. *Did he hear it too?*

"Queen who?" Courtney whispered.

Amber frowned but answered straight away. "Queen Tia. The one who rules the city. We told you about her, remember?"

"I remember. Tell me, what did Queen Tia look like?" Courtney could barely get the words past the lump in her throat.

Amber smiled. "She was real pretty. Long blonde hair, really blue eyes like my bike."

"How old?"

"Around my age. Maybe a bit older," Morgan answered.

Courtney's world stopped turning. *Is it possible that Tiana survived?* For as long as she could remember, she had always called her Tia. Her friend never liked 'Tiana'. She always said it sounded too snobby. If it was her, how was it possible that she hadn't aged at all? Could it be her? *There's no way it can be her, can it?* Courtney looked over at Robert who seemed as shocked as she felt.

"Do you have any pictures?" he asked Courtney.

"Attic," she said weakly, kids forgotten.

He came back a few minutes later and handed her a picture. Courtney stared at the photo for a minute and then turned it toward the girls.

"This is my friend, Tiana."

She watched their eyes widen.

"That's Queen Tia!" Amber squealed.

"Yes, that's her," Morgan confirmed, nodding.

Courtney looked at Robert.

Robert looked at Courtney.

"I'm going in," she said firmly.

Robert just nodded.

Tiana was alive.

Chapter 41

At nine-thirty that night, my whole family, including Aunt Leah, were in front of me in my bedroom. Mum and Dad sat on the edge of my bed, Aunt Leah leaned against the wall and Amber sat cross-legged on the floor. It had been one of the strangest days of my life.

After our conversation in the lounge, I'd returned to my room to digest everything. Never in my wildest dreams could I have ever guessed that Mum knew Queen Tia, or that she even knew about the door. It seemed like a tradition passed down through each generation. Mum and Dad had hidden the chest and the key to stop me from going through the door, all because Mum had lost a friend in one of those worlds and thought she was gone forever, a friend I didn't even know she had because she'd never spoken about her. And this friend turned out to be the Queen of the City in the Sky.

At least Mum had been able to answer my questions, like why I was the one who saw the door, and how the chest and the golden key were hidden in the first place. There were still so many more that

I wanted to ask … like how the key ended up at the carnival if Mum had lost it behind the Ace of Spades door. I had no idea how it could go from one world to another. As far as I knew, the only thing to go through the doors between worlds was me, and I know I didn't do it.

Then there was the rock. This whole time I believed I would never find the Peace Stone. Yet here it was, in my house, and it was Mum who'd brought it back, inadvertently destroying the peace in that world.

Now that I knew about Mum and Queen Tia, I knew where the other half of the rock must be. It made sense now as Queen Tia had said she had played her part in all of this. She knew what she'd done and I guessed that she still had the other half.

Just then, a thought occurred: did Queen Tia know I was her best friend's daughter? Is that why I was the only one that could help her? Did she know the rock was in my house the whole time? Maybe she made up the entire prophecy as she'd known all along who I was and how I could help her. If that was true, it meant she could see into the future, or at the very least was watching over us somehow. Despite everything I'd seen, it was hard to believe that this could be true.

Either way, I was going in there tonight with Mum, whether I was ready or not. The plan was to get straight out of the valley and make our way back to the cottage where Merrin was hopefully waiting.

We needed him to get us back to the Tree of Safety and the Queen. From there we would collect the other half and take it back to where it came from. I wasn't sure how we would put the rock back together yet – that was something we would have to work out once we were there. All of this was assuming Mum remembered how to get back to the origin of the stone.

The other problem we would face was the elements themselves. While I was quietly confident we could safely get to the cottage, I had no idea what would happen after that. We just had to hope we could get through it like every other time.

I rechecked my backpack, making sure our half of the Peace Stone was safely tucked away. No way could we lose the key to saving their world, so I zipped it shut again and looked up to find everyone staring at me.

"What?" I said, so deep in thought I'd filtered out their conversation and hadn't noticed they had stopped talking.

"Are you sure you're ready for this?" Mum asked me.

I wasn't, but I would never say that knowing what was at stake. I simply wouldn't be the one to stop Mum from meeting the friend she thought she'd lost forever. "Nope. Just double-checking to make sure nothing's going to fall out."

Mum's eyebrow rose as she viewed me intently. "Because we don't have to go if you don't want to."

"No, it's fine. We're going to go save a world and reunite two long lost friends. Why would I want to miss out on that?"

"I can't believe all of this," Aunt Leah said. "Yesterday was a normal day. Today you are about to go and find a person you haven't seen in over thirty years and save a world at the same time by going through a magic door. Yesterday I was arranging flowers, and today I'm in my nieces' room waiting for my family to return from a dangerous mission."

We all stared at her.

"Well, I thought I'd be having a coffee and watching a movie tonight …" she defended herself.

We all burst out laughing – it was a good break to the tension.

"Sorry …" Mum smiled at Aunt Leah. "I knew you would never forgive me if I didn't tell you what was going on."

"Exactly!" Aunt Leah replied, stepping forward and hugging me. "You be careful in there."

"I will," I promised. I glanced at the clock. Ten more minutes to go.

"Do you want to go over the plan one more time?" Dad asked us.

"I think we've got it," Mum replied.

"Once more," Dad countered. "Just to make me feel better."

Mum sighed and winked at me. "In the door, rescue the princess, save the world and return home a hero."

Amber smiled as we all laughed.

"Okay," Dad conceded, smiling. "I get the hint."

"Do you have the key?" Amber looked at me.

I patted down my pockets until I could feel the shape of the key under my hand. "Yep, got it."

"Tell Merrin I said hello," she said.

"I will, squirt, and I promise when this is all done, I'll take you back in there to see him again."

I could see Mum frowning out of the corner of my eye, but I meant it. I would take her back there again.

Amber jumped up from the floor, ran to me and squeezed me tight.

"Even if we have to sneak out …" I whispered in her ear, making her smile.

Amber moved to the bed and sat next to Mum, who put her arm around Amber's shoulders. We stayed silent, lost in our thoughts. I watched the clock as it slowly marched towards 10 pm. I was as ready as I would ever be.

Finally, the wall started to pulse.

"Look," I said.

There was a stillness in the air as the outline of the frame appeared. As it had done every night since I found the chest, it pulsed its way in and out of this world until it finally rested in place.

"Wow," Mum said, almost breathlessly. "I'd forgotten how it appeared each time."

"It's beautiful," Aunt Leah said softly.

Dad cleared his throat and said, "It's time."

Mum stood up and hugged Dad tightly.

"We'll be fine," she said to him, although it sounded more like she was trying to convince herself. She kissed the top of Amber's head and then looked at me.

"Ready?"

"Ready," I replied.

"Um … how does this work again?" Mum asked me.

I just smiled and opened the door. Looking over to Mum, I held out my hand, and without hesitation, she took it and stepped forward.

"We'll be back in five minutes," I said to the rest of the family.

"I think it'll take a bit longer than that," Aunt Leah said.

"Not on this side." I liked being the person who had the answers. "The door is here for five minutes. On the other side, time is different. No matter how long it takes, only five minutes will pass here."

"Oh. Well, that's good for us, I guess. We don't have to wait long for you to return." Aunt Leah smiled. "Now go, and be safe!"

I ruffled Amber's hair and squeezed Mum's hand. As soon as she pressed back, I knew it was time. I stepped through the magic door, Mum in tow.

On the other side, we stopped and turned around. Behind us, we could see the three of them standing close together, watching the start of our journey from my bedroom.

"We're fine," I told them.

"Absolutely fine," Mum added.

Amber waved, and Mum waved back at her. Turning away, I continued to hold her hand as we made our way down the corridor.

"Do you remember all this?" I asked her.

She looked around for a moment. "The doors look the same, but I don't think they are in the same order."

"That's the dream tree," I pointed as we passed the tree symbol on the door.

"Yes, I've been there, remember?"

"Oh yeah, sorry, I forgot. Too much on my mind," I replied.

"Understandable," Mum said absently. She was studying the symbols on the doors as we kept walking down the corridor. "I forgot just how long this place was."

"It's not much further now."

"Last chance to pull out then?" Mum questioned. "We could turn around and go back right now."

"No," I responded. "We have to fix their world. Someone once told me to take ownership of mistakes I made, and to do whatever I could to fix them."

"Sounds like a wise person," Mum said, knowing full well she had given me this advice.

"We have to make this right," I finished.

"You are such a beautiful person, Morgan.

Whatever happens, I want you to know that I am so very proud of you and the person you've become." Her eyes shone with tears.

"Don't be embarrassing, Mum," I said, trying to get the words past the lump in my throat. At that moment, I noticed the Ace of Spades coming up on the next door. I pointed to it, and we stopped.

"I'm nervous," Mum admitted.

"Why?"

"I haven't seen her for thirty years. What if she doesn't recognise me? What if she does recognise me but doesn't want to have anything to do with me? I couldn't bear it if I lost her again."

I could almost feel Mum shaking. "Why would she not want to have anything to do with you? You were best friends, right?"

"She might blame me for what happened."

"Well, you won't know until you talk to her."

"True."

"So, are we going to do this?" I asked.

"Yes," she said, but we both stood there, neither of us moving.

Someone had to move first so I pulled the key from my pocket and slipped it into the keyhole. Looking up at Mum, I waited for her to give me an indication that she was ready to go in. With one hand still on the key, all I needed was her final approval. I wasn't doing this without her.

Finally, she took a deep breath and nodded. "Let's do this," she said, so I turned the key.

Chapter 42

The door swung open and we stepped into the valley at the same place Amber and I had before. The canyon was still there, the walls looking as impossible to climb as they had previously. But climb was what we needed to do, and fast, before the water came rushing at us like last time.

"I did this?" Mum turned on the spot, looking around the channel she now stood in.

"Well, if your theory is right, then technically a tornado did this."

"I did this." Her voice changed from questioning to sad.

"And you can also fix it," I replied. "Let's move before something bad happens."

"You're right," she agreed.

I looked around.

"Over there," I said, pointing to an area that looked safe enough to climb. I took off, not waiting for a reply, Mum trailing behind me, still scanning her surroundings.

"C'mon!" I hurried her along. I knew how fast this had filled last time and didn't want to go through it again. "Now is not the time to be dawdling and taking in the scenery."

"I'm sorry, hon," she said. "It's just been so long since I've been in here. I've forgotten most of it."

"I'll go first."

After studying the wall for a few moments, I started to see the track that would get us to the top. Placing my hand on the first rock, I pulled myself up while working on a toe hold in a little crevasse of the wall. Slowly, using the tree roots and rocks buried in the soil, I made my way to the top edge of the valley. It was certainly more manageable when taking the time to work out the best way to go.

I looked down at Mum. "Your turn."

It didn't take her long to scale her way to the top.

"That was easier than I thought it would be," she said as she dragged her leg over the edge.

"I know," I frowned. "Where is the water? Why didn't it come this time?"

"I don't know, but I'm grateful it didn't. Which direction now?"

I looked around at the vast open field where dried grass tufts poked up everywhere. "I'm not sure. The grass is taller here than it was the other day." I turned and looked back down the valley. "We went the other way first. Then when we heard the water coming, we turned back and ran this way. We passed the gateway and kept going until we saw a safe place to climb."

"So it might be further down?"

"I think so. We were running fast; I guess we could have gone a bit further than I thought."

Turning both ways again, I made up my mind. "This way."

"Tell me more about Tiana," Mum said as she fell in step beside me.

"There's not much to tell."

"Did she look happy? Was she friendly?"

"She was very friendly. She seemed extremely happy to see us; she gave us a huge hug when we first met."

"What else do you remember?"

"I remember that she didn't sit like a Queen. When she sat on the lounge, she sat like we were going to watch TV."

"She always loved to curl her legs up underneath her."

"Yes!" I exclaimed. "That's exactly what she did."

"I can't believe it's her," Mum said.

"We have to get to her first," I said. "But something's not right ... no water and we haven't had any wind yet either. Last time the elements were thrown at us pretty much straight away."

"Maybe we're just lucky. Maybe we've slipped under the radar somehow."

"Maybe." But I wasn't convinced. Something was coming; it was just a matter of what and when.

"There it is," I said as I spotted the cottage in the distance.

"What's that?" Mum said at the same time.

"The cottage," I repeated.

"No, not that. What's that sound?"

Straight away, my stomach curled in knots. The water rush began with a sound. What was coming now? We stopped and stood in silence as I tried to catch what Mum was hearing.

"I can't hear anything," I said.

"Shhh," Mum held a finger to her lips.

That's when I heard it – a crackling and snapping in the distance. Mum turned in the direction of the sound. Black smoke filled the sky. Panicked, I looked at Mum for help.

"It's okay," she tried to comfort me. "It's miles away."

Just as she spoke, a fierce wind came up and started blowing past us.

"It's heading this way; we'd better get moving." Mum grabbed my hand and walked briskly towards the cottage. Behind us, the wind continued to thrive, pressing against our backs as if trying to help us get there faster. The sizzling and popping sounds grew louder, even with the wind in our ears. I turned my head for a second and went cold. A blazing fire roared behind us, the orange flames reaching high into the sky, reaching higher than they should have for the length of grass beneath our feet. The wind pushed the fire, helping it to cover the ground with astonishing speed.

Other than the water, wind, and tunnel collapse before, I'd never truly felt my life was in danger. This fire, however, was like nothing I'd ever seen or heard. It covered the ground much faster than we could, and at this rate, it would catch us before we could reach the cottage. The roar behind us filled me with terror.

We began running for our lives.

And the wind pushed the fire faster and faster. Grey flakes of ash floated past us, followed by embers that landed on the ground and started little spot fires. The wind then fanned the spot fires, turning them into larger ones.

The heat from the primary fire began to touch my back. I wasn't even looking at Mum now: blind fear had me running without conscious thought, survival the only instinct I now had.

Sweat ran down my face from running and from the heat of the fire. My senses heightened. Every crackle of the fire I could hear, every bead of sweat I could feel, every speck of ash was in my sights. I didn't know how it was possible, but I swore I could taste the smoke. My back felt like it was in an oven, my hair curling in the heat of the flames.

I focused on the safety of the cottage up ahead rather than focus on the fire and, like a switch changing inside, I realised I might get through this. Panic subsided a little, and I finally registered Mum in my peripheral vision. *Thank God she's still with me.*

As we drew closer, I noticed the porch of the cottage had caught fire. The blaze raged right behind us now; it was going to be a tight race to see whether we would make it to the cottage before the flames. Leaping over the stairs in stride, we avoided the railings which were now also on fire. The door flew open as we reached it, and we fell through onto the ground together.

I reached for Mum, tears mixing with my sweat. She gasped for air, rasping to fill her lungs, but I didn't care. I felt like a five-year-old again. All I wanted was my mum. She held me tightly until I stopped crying.

"Are you okay, hon?" she asked as her hands checked me over.

I nodded, not trusting myself to speak.

"Wow, that was something." Her voice shook as she spoke, and I knew she was trying to be brave for me. That's when I noticed Merrin standing by the door, waiting for us to see him.

"Merrin!" I cried out.

He smiled as he looked out the window. "Hello again. I'd love to chat, but we have to move now. The fire is almost on us."

Terrified, we peered out the window. Merrin was right. The porch was now totally engulfed in flames, and we could feel the heat saturating the wall.

"Your house, Merrin," I said sadly.

"It's okay. It's just a house. We must go. Now."

He hurried to the secret room just like last time and took us to a white door. Opening it, he signalled us to follow.

"Through the rabbit hole …" Mum muttered

under her breath as we followed him in.

The door closed behind us, but not before we heard a massive crash from the cottage.

"There goes the roof," Merrin noted.

"We can't come back here, can we?" I realised.

"Hopefully we don't have to," he replied.

"Will this tunnel collapse too?" I asked.

"Not while that fire's burning. We have a small window of time – we should take advantage and get through as quickly as we can."

"Let's go then," Mum urged.

Without another word, we headed through the tunnel. I trailed my hand lightly against one of the walls, wondering when it was going to start falling in around us. If we weren't already committed to saving this place, I would have turned around and gone straight through the gateway and back home.

Even though I was the child in this, I felt the need to look out for my mother. Maybe it was because I had been here recently, and she hadn't. Indeed, it was because she was family. I could tell she felt the same as she walked through the tunnel with one hand on my shoulder, making sure I was still there with her. Whatever it was, this invisible bond that held us together was the only good thing since we had entered this world. Crazy, but I had never felt closer to her.

We reached the end of the tunnel without incident and entered the Tree of Safety once again. Mum looked around in awe as it dawned on her that she was inside a tree trunk.

"This is amazing," she said breathily.

"Sit for a minute," Merrin said, "and catch your breath."

I plopped down on a small tree stump and heaved in a deep breath. We hadn't stopped since we'd entered the gateway between the two worlds. Mum moved slowly around the space, looking at all the doors, the walls and everything in between.

"What are all these doors?" she asked Merrin.

"The tunnels," he replied.

"Tunnels to where?"

"Everywhere."

"That's how they move around," I added. "Or the elements hunt them down if they are above ground like it just did with us."

"Are we safe in here?" Mum asked no one in particular.

"This is the Tree of Safety," Merrin told her. "There is nowhere safer."

"Good."

"Where is the little one?" Merrin asked.

"She's at home. She said to say hello, though."

He looked pleased when I said that.

"Very good. Now we need to get you to the city. The Queen has been anxious ever since you left us last time. She's not eating or sleeping well."

"I'm sure she's wondering if I would ever come back," I considered aloud.

"She knew you would come," he replied. "The

fruition of the prophecy is the only thing that matters. She did not doubt that you would return."

I bet she doesn't realise I'm bringing her best friend back to her though, I thought. Or maybe deep down she did, and that was why she was nervous. *She isn't the only anxious one*, I realised as I watched Mum wandering around and rubbing one hand against the other. It was her tell-tale sign that she was barely holding herself together.

"You're right," I agreed. "We need to go."

"How do we get to the city?" Mum asked. "Another tunnel?"

"It's the city in the sky, remember?" I said. "We go up."

"Up?"

"Up," I repeated and gestured to the corner where the cloud hovered, waiting.

Mum looked at me. "On that?"

"Yes." I smiled and hopped on; almost laughed out loud as she paused with one hand stretched out, just as Amber and I had done before. She hesitated a lot for someone who had said earlier that day that almost anything was possible. I guess it was harder to accept the impossible when you were all grown up.

To her credit, she soon stepped up and stood next to me, taking my hand in hers. It was the moment before the moment she would see her friend again. She squeezed my hand tight – really tight. More than anything, I knew she needed my support, so I didn't complain, just squeezed her hand in return. She seemed to realise how hard she held me and loosened her grip; mouthed "Sorry".

Standing quietly, I could feel her nervousness increasing as she shifted her weight from one foot to the other. She was much like Amber, who couldn't stand still when she was excited about a magic trick. Her grip grew tight on my hand again as we neared the top. If we didn't hurry up and get there soon, she might just crush my bones to dust.

Finally, the cloud slowed to a standstill, and Merrin stepped off. We were here.

Chapter 43

Courtney

For the first time in over thirty years, Courtney was going to see her friend again. All those years ago they had stupidly started a chain of events that resulted in losing one another, although not in the way she had initially thought. Courtney's heart pounded at the thought Tiana was still alive. While she felt overwhelmed that she would soon see her again, she couldn't help feeling nervous about their reunion. What if she didn't recognise her? What if Tiana hated her for leaving her behind? Tia wouldn't know that she'd done everything in her power to get back to her.

Tiana didn't know she was coming, which meant Courtney had no idea what sort of welcome she'd receive. It would be a massive shock for Tia to see her after all this time.

Courtney rubbed her hands together, squeezing them tight, and waited impatiently for Merrin to let them off the cloud. Despite her best attempts to check their surroundings, she couldn't see anyone wandering around out there, and disappointedly she followed Morgan and Merrin. She had half expected, half hoped, Tia to be standing there waiting to greet her.

"She's not here," Merrin said quietly to Courtney. How did he know who she was looking for? Neither she nor Morgan had mentioned her connection to Tia, nor the reason she was here. Regardless, they needed to keep moving. It wasn't all just about Courtney – there was a world to save.

"Let's go then," she replied.

Without another word Merrin turned and started walking, Morgan following close behind. Courtney stayed at the back, wanting to have that extra second to take in everything when she finally saw Tiana. Her mind was so focused she barely noticed the growing crowd following them on the path, hovering discreetly to the rear, just out of view, curious but hesitant to come too close. Their murmurs played around the edges of her thoughts.

"Stop that," Morgan whispered to her as she shot a stern look at Courtney's hands which she'd been subconsciously rubbing together. The habit had started during a stressful time back in her late teens – most of the time she didn't even realise she was doing it.

Courtney put her arms down by her sides. "Why are all these people following us?" she whispered back, now noticing fully the steadily growing crowd.

Morgan shrugged indifferently. "It's not far now," she said.

Eagerly, Courtney followed, ready for whatever came next. Up ahead, Merrin slowed down as he approached a building made of tree branches. When he knocked on the door, her heart felt ready to jump out of her chest.

The door slowly opened, and an elderly woman appeared. She squinted to see her guests more fully, her body leaning forward to get a better look.

"She's waiting for you," the lady said, bowing slightly to Merrin.

He nodded and entered, Morgan right behind him. Courtney breathed in deeply and mentally forced herself to put one foot in front of the other. Closing the door behind her, a rush of mixed emotions overcame her as she tightly held onto the handle to keep from fainting. Anxiety, fear, excitement, joy, all bombarded her senses like a city crowd trying to get on the last train of the day.

She was still trying to get her emotions under control when Tiana entered the room. She spotted Morgan immediately and gave her a huge smile. Moving forward with her arms open, she said warmly, "Morgan, you returned!"

She hadn't aged a day since Courtney had last seen her. Then Tia stopped a few short metres from Morgan. Her head turned as she noticed the person standing at the door. After a moment, she whispered, "Courtney…?"

Courtney picked the uncertainty in Tia's voice as time suddenly stood still. Her mind raced back that long thirty years. Courtney couldn't breathe. Her heart beat so loudly she could hear it in her ears, drowning out all sound, and she could feel it thumping through her entire body. A tingling feeling ran up and down her arms as she stood studying Tia, searching for any form of acceptance. Then her senses sharpened, and the air grew thicker as they stood there, joined at that moment by a past lived so long ago but never forgotten.

The bonds of their friendship rushed back to Courtney as memories of their best times together returned: when Courtney had rescued Tia from some bullies making fun of her because of her home situation, the time they first met at school – their first school dance, ignoring everyone else around as they danced the night away – with Tia and her crazy dance moves. Tiana had learned very fast not to care about what people thought of her. Then there were the sleepovers at Courtney's house; pillow fights and achingly beautiful honest conversations well into the hours of the morning. These memories and more welled up in her, reminding her again of the bond they had all those years ago.

"Court…ney…?" Tia's voice broke midway as she repeated herself.

Courtney nodded. It was all she could manage as she tried to regain control of her emotions, without much luck. Her eyes welled with tears that flowed freely down her cheeks. Her heart would break if Tia rejected her now. Looking at Tia, Courtney's eyes pleaded with her to understand without ever knowing what had happened. She tried to tell her without words how sorry she was that things had turned out the way they had but could only watch as a multitude of emotions ran across Tia's face. Which one would land first?

"Courtney!"

Happiness tore to the surface as Tiana raced to her and threw her arms around her. Courtney held her tightly, sobbing into her hair, all poise and self-control lost for the moment. They clung to each other, scared to let go in case they lost each other again. They stayed like that until the tears subsided, the room around them receding from their sight as only the other person mattered. Reluctantly pulling apart, they held hands and took a moment to look at the other in-depth.

"You look old," Tia said. Courtney burst out laughing which turned quickly into tears again. She brushed them from her face and smiled.

"You haven't aged a day," Courtney replied.

"Is it really you?"

"Yes."

Courtney shook her head slightly. Tia looked exactly as she remembered: her eyes sparkled with secrets and laughter; her smile reached the ends of the earth when she was delighted. Her hair was a little longer since she'd last seen her, but otherwise, she was the same Tiana.

Suddenly, Courtney felt self-conscious as she considered how she looked now. Gone was her youthful glow. Wrinkles had started to appear around her eyes and mouth, and while the years had been kind to her, there was no denying that she would never pass for a teenager again. Courtney's gaze lowered.

"You are as beautiful as ever," Tiana spoke to her softly and squeezed her hands.

Typical of the bond they held, she still knew Courtney's thoughts.

Tia then turned to Morgan and reached out a hand, still holding onto Courtney with the other. "I'm so glad you have returned."

Courtney still couldn't believe it: she was standing there with her lost friend, after all this time. She had somehow survived in this strange world by herself, unable to return to her own when all this time Courtney had thought she was dead. For the first time, Courtney began to wonder what Tia had been through.

"Tiana, I am so sorry, I never meant to leave you here," Courtney began. "I tried forever to get back into this world to find you, but the key disappeared."

Tia squeezed her friend's hand. "We can talk about that later. Right now, we have put things right again."

She turned to Morgan. "That's why you're here, isn't it? You found the other half of the stone."

Morgan nodded. And Tiana responded with a heartwarming smile. "Excellent! Oh, this is going to be a wonderful day!"

Chapter 44

I pulled the backpack off my shoulder and set it on the ground. Reaching in, I groped around the bottom for the rock.

"Is this it?" I asked, pulling it out.

Queen Tia held her breath as she reached for the stone. She held it gently in her hands, turning it over and over, studying the marks and the colours. The stone seemed different in this world, more alive somehow, the colours much brighter and appeared to run like a moving river through crevasses within the rock.

"Yes," the Queen replied dreamily, almost transfixed by the stone.

"Where is the other half?" I asked.

"Mardella!" Tia called out. Within moments the woman who'd answered the door appeared. "Bring me the stone."

Mardella turned immediately and left to get the other half. Queen Tia continued to roll our half over and over in her hands, Mum standing beside her. Merrin remained near the door, unofficially on guard. And me? I stood impatiently, wanting to see the stone halves back together.

I walked the room keeping an eye on the door, waiting for Mardella to return. Now that Mum and her friend were reunited, all we had to do was join the stone and fix this world.

For the first time, it occurred to me that the quest would end with bringing together not just this world and the stone, but Mum and Queen Tia as well. That didn't seem like a coincidence.

"How does it go back together?" Mum asked Tia. "Should I have brought some superglue?"

Tia smiled. "The prophecy says *'fusion of both halves will be made whole at its point of origin'*, so when the centres meet the two halves should meld together. No glue required."

Mum grinned sheepishly. "Oh. Well, I've never had to fix a rock before."

"It's a peace stone, Mum," I corrected her.

"Either way," Tia ignored us both, "we may just be able to correct this world and get it back to normal."

I noticed Merrin looking out the window, which reminded me of the crowd that had trailed us here. "What's with all the people that followed us outside?" I asked him.

"The prophecy, child," he said. "It's been handed down from generation to generation for hundreds of years. These people have grown up with stories of anticipation that one day the prophecy might be fulfilled. To see two strangers in our land is a sign that it may be coming true. Those people represent over 500 years of hope."

"Over 500 years?" I repeated. "Wow."

"Yes," Tia spoke softly. "Many of us were starting to lose faith that it would ever come true. It was fast becoming a fable, a fairytale to tell the children. Most people had lost hope by now, convinced it was just a bedtime story. But seeing your return has made them believers again."

"That's a lot of pressure for a thirteen-year-old girl," Mum said a little protectively.

"There's no pressure on Morgan," Tia replied. "It's all on me. I rule these people – it is up to me to restore this world, to bring peace back. It's my job to give them the best life I can. Even so, the prophecy is out of my hands – I have no control over it. At least I didn't until I saw your two beautiful girls in my vision cloud. That was when I dared to dream of the possibility. That's when the whispers started around the city. Now that you have returned, the people will be getting excited."

"Yes," Merrin continued for her. "Now the people may witness the prophecy coming true – something they never thought they would see. They watch and wait for a miracle now."

Mum and I looked at each other. I never realised just how important this was until now. Hearing about the people of the city who had listened to a story so many times, it had just become another tale, yet they had secretly held out hope that one day it might come true. Imagine living your whole life with a dream that was always just out of reach. It made me sad to think about it, but happy that I could help them achieve what they thought impossible. I had brought back hope in my backpack in the shape of a rock.

"Now we just need the other half," the Queen said, beginning to get impatient.

"Mardella!" she yelled as Mardella entered the room, holding a wooden box.

"I'm sorry, ma'am," Mardella replied but offered no excuse. She placed the box on the nearest table and retreated from the room.

Queen Tia passed the half she'd been holding to Mum and moved quickly to the chest. Once the lid was open, I could see the stone inside nestled in a bed of blue felt. She reached in, her eyes starting to sparkle as she looked up at us again; she lifted the stone out, and indeed, it looked the same as the half we had brought with us.

"This is it," she said softly. "The moment we've been waiting for."

She reached over and took the piece from Mum. Standing there with one half in each hand, she said, "Once these two pieces are whole again, we can return to the ground and rebuild our lives." She looked over to Merrin, who nodded.

"No more hiding in the clouds," he said.

"No more hiding in the clouds," Queen Tia agreed.

"Wait!" Mum said quickly. "What's supposed to happen when they join? How do we know it's worked?"

Great question, I thought.

"The city in the clouds will drop down to the ground. The elements will settle down. Did you feel the darkness when you entered this world? That feeling that something is not right?" Queen Tia said. "That will disappear. The world will feel light again."

"I felt strange every time I saw the ace of spades," I said, remembering my strange feelings. "I was afraid of it, even though I didn't know why. I just got this feeling in my stomach every time I saw that symbol."

"Yes," the Queen said, "That's what I'm talking about. We have all lived with that fear and doubt for so long; I don't even remember a time when it wasn't there. If this works, you'll feel the change."

"Well then," Mum said, "let's do this!"

Queen Tia nodded. The room fell so silent I couldn't hear anyone's breath. We all stood motionless in nervous anticipation. The butterflies returned to my stomach as the full gravity of the moment dawned on me. We were about to play a part in restoring the lives of millions of people, heroes in a story that was written just for us.

Queen Tia looked at both halves then gently brought them together. We waited as we watched the two halves join. They fit together perfectly, the protrusion on Tia's half fitting perfectly into the indentation on ours. She looked up expectantly. Four sets of eyes darted to one another, no one daring to move. We waited for the cloud to drop us down to the ground. Seconds became minutes as we stood like statues, not wanting to break whatever spell was woven.

"Maybe it takes a little time?" Mum queried softly.

"It doesn't feel any different," Merrin said sadly.

"He's right," I agreed. "It still feels the same."

Queen Tia's face fell. She sensed it too. Nothing had changed even though the Peace Stone was whole again. It was hard to watch her, knowing how much she had wanted this. *Imagine getting so close to your dream without being able to reach it. That would be devastating.*

Not knowing what to say, I watched as the Queen finally lowered her hands. And watched the stone come apart again.

Shocked, Merrin and the Queen looked at each other, a silent conversation going on between them. Queen Tia moved to the nearest lounge and plopped down into it, still holding a half in each hand. For the first time since I met her, she looked old for her age. Gone was the regal stance, the aura of time and wisdom she had radiated. Now she sat, a thirteen-year-old girl who no doubt felt like she had just destroyed everyone's chances – a thirteen-year-old with tears streaming down her face. I didn't know where to look.

"It didn't work," she sobbed. "I've let everyone down. It's my fault."

Mum rushed over and put her arms around her.

"Not at all!" Like second nature, Mum went straight into Mum-mode. "You haven't let anyone down, Tia. You've done everything you could; you got a lot closer than anyone else ever has. Don't you dare blame yourself."

"It's my fault," she repeated through her tears. "I've done something wrong. It should have worked."

"It's not your fault," Mum repeated. "Dry your tears. You're a Queen now, a leader, and you must lead your people. Good times or bad, you have a job to do."

"She's right," Merrin said. "This isn't the end. There's no deadline on a prophecy. It will happen when it's meant to."

Nothing they said consoled Queen Tia. She had placed the halves on the table and now held her head in her hands. Feeling useless, I kept coming back to the Queen's comment about doing something wrong. *Did we go wrong somewhere? Have we made a mistake?* It wasn't the rock: it was very clearly two halves of the same one. I ran through all the conversations I'd had with Merrin and Queen Tia. We were missing something.

Then a lightbulb went on in my head.

"Wait!" I said a little too loudly. They all looked at me. "What was it you said earlier about the prophecy? About the fusion? What were the exact words?" I asked, excited now.

"Fusion of both halves will be made whole at its point of origin," Merrin said.

"That's it!" I grinned. "That's where we went wrong."

"What do you mean?" Queen Tia asked, no longer crying.

"Its point of origin." I stopped to let that sink in, but they still looked at me blankly.

Now I couldn't stand still. I paced up and down the room, getting more animated by the second. "The stone doesn't belong here. This is obviously *not* its point of origin."

"We have to take it back to the Circle," Merrin finished for me, delight on his face. "That's where it needs to become whole again. Morgan, you're a genius!"

"That makes sense," Queen Tia said. She sat straighter. In front of me now was the Queen I had first met. "We must make plans to go straight away."

"We must get the Peace Stone back to the Circle immediately. I'll prepare what we need." Merrin left the room quickly.

Queen Tia stood up and approached me; cupped my face gently in her hands. "Thank you."

I smiled back. "You're welcome, Queen."

"Please," she replied, "call me Tia."

I nodded. "You're welcome, Tia. When do we go?"

"You're not going anywhere," Mum cut in firmly.

"What? That's not fair! I came all this way to help restore the world. I worked out what was wrong. It should be me going!"

"No, your mum is right."

Tia isn't going to let me go? "But I want to help!" I said. *It isn't fair to leave me out.*

"You have helped," Tia replied. "You've played your part. Now it's my turn. I need to do this for my people."

"I could come with you?" I pleaded.

"No, hon," Mum said gently. "This is for Tia and Merrin to finish."

Tia shook her head in disagreement.

"No," she said again, but this time it was to Mum. "This is for you and me to finish."

Mum stared at her for a moment, then spoke quietly. "Because we started this, we have to end it."

"Yes," Tia agreed.

"You understand, right?" Mum now looked at me for my understanding.

I didn't like it, but I knew why it had to be this way. I nodded. Satisfied, Mum turned back to Tia. "Okay. What do we need, and when do we go?"

"Packed and ready," Merrin said as he entered the room again, this time with two bags. He handed one to Tia and one to Mum.

"I guess we go now," Mum said, answering her own question.

Tia picked up the two halves and gave one to

Mum. "As it was at the start. You should carry one, and I the other."

They placed them in their bags and looked at me.

"You'll be safe here with Merrin," Tia told me.

Mum came over and hugged me. I held her tightly, knowing the sort of world she was walking out into. "Please be careful," I whispered.

"I will. I'll be back here with you in no time, I promise." She kissed me on top of my head.

"I love you," I told her.

"I love you too, hon," she replied. Turning to Tia, she said, "Let's go."

I watched as they walked out together, best friends reunited and ready to face the elements one last time.

Chapter 45

Courtney

The trip began in silence, as they both considered what they were about to do. The thought of returning to the world outside the tree constricted Courtney's chest a little, as memories of the fire they had just outrun kept flashing back to her. She also worried about Morgan up in the clouds and hoped she wasn't too upset about being left behind. It was the safest place for her, and despite only having just met Merrin, Courtney felt sure he would protect her with his life. She felt so proud of Morgan, making her way through this world and being brave enough to come back here again; proud she had put others before her discomfort. She was an amazing girl.

Now it was Courtney's turn. She needed to put on a brave face and help right the wrong she'd created all those years ago. Just as they had done thirty years ago, Tia and Courtney stood at a doorway, ready to step into the unknown.

"Do you know where we're going?" Courtney

asked her.

"Kind of."

Tia pulled something out of one of the pockets of the bag Merrin had given her and looked closely at it.

"What's that?" Courtney asked.

"It's sort of like this world's version of a compass, but different."

She opened her hand slightly to reveal a tiny cloud. "It's part of my vision cloud, the one that shows me the future."

"How is that going to help us?"

"We need to follow it." Tia opened her hand, and the cloud drifted up into the air. "This will show us the way. I've been in the city for many years now and have never been back to the Circle. I have no idea where it is."

"We're going to follow a cloud," Courtney said dubiously.

"Yes."

"Are you sure it will work?"

"I'm not sure of anything. What I do know is without it, we might wander out there forever. There's no Merrin out there to save us this time."

Courtney wondered what she meant by that. Was Merrin the one who had saved her the day they got separated? Before she could ask her to clarify, Tia looked at her and said, "Ready?"

"As ready as I'll ever be."

"Okay. We start with this tunnel," Tia pointed to

a door behind the hovering cloud. "After we enter though, we should be prepared to move. Earth likes to fill these tunnels in, usually while we're in them. If you see any of the walls or ceiling start to fall, start running. Fast."

"So how did you build them then?"

"With a lot of difficulty and some brave people creating diversions. We've worked out that while one element is at work, the rest of the place is peaceful."

Now Merrin's comment back at the cottage about having a small window of time made more sense to Courtney. An intense wave of sadness washed over her as she realised just how much her actions had affected these people.

"Not just you," Tia commented softly.

"Can you read minds too now?" Courtney asked suspiciously, wondering how Tia knew again what she was thinking.

"Something like that." She smiled. "But we have to get going. Put your bag over your shoulders; you'll need your arms free to run."

"What's at the end of this tunnel?" Courtney asked.

"According to the cloud, it's an old horse barn."

"Okay."

"There should be a torch in the side pocket — make sure you grab it before we go."

Courtney found the torch in the bag, then strapped the bag to her back. She was ready.

"How does Merrin know what to pack in the bags?" Courtney wondered aloud.

"We have what we call a 'Standard Survival pack' we take whenever someone leaves the city. It has enough in it to help us through most of the element outbreaks." Tia fished around in her own pack. "Now we have to get going." She opened the door and headed straight in.

Here we go, Courtney thought and stepped in behind her.

The tunnel was dark and cold, and Courtney immediately switched on her torch and flashed it around, checking out the walls and ceiling. Nothing seemed to be falling just yet. They walked quickly and silently, nervously waiting for the first signs of the destruction of the tunnel. Two torches continuously swung around in arcs, lighting up as a lighthouse might sweep across the seas. Their eyes swung just as quickly, and they stayed primed to run at a second's notice.

They reached the end of the tunnel faster than anticipated, the trip uneventful. Opening the door at the other end, they entered a stable, as predicted.

Tia frowned.

"What's wrong?" Courtney asked. "We made it through without a problem."

"That *is* the problem," Tia replied. "It's not normal. Something's not right here."

"Maybe we just got lucky."

"Maybe."

"The barn looks pretty quiet." Courtney peered over the stable door and slid the old bolt to open it.

"I know. Something's not right," she repeated.

"How about, instead of worrying about why something didn't happen, we try to stay positive and celebrate the fact that we came through it unscathed?" Courtney looked at Tiana. "We made it."

"It might mean something even worse is coming."

"Then we'll deal with it when it comes."

"Always the optimist." Tia smiled.

"Over the years, you realise there's no point in worrying about things that are out of your control."

"I've missed you," Tia said suddenly and hugged her.

"I've missed you too," Courtney said, hugging her back.

"Okay …" Tia stood tall. " … let's keep going."

Courtney followed her out of the barn and into the open. They were surrounded by rolling hills, dotted randomly with piles of rubble. The lack of living flora and fauna was evident. The sun shone down as they stood and waited for the cloud to show them the direction to move in. A light breeze blew past, reminding Courtney of a perfect spring day. It didn't feel threatening at all and she began to think they might make it to the Circle without any issues.

They trailed behind the cloud, still silent, lost again in their thoughts.

"What happened?" Tia asked suddenly, her gaze fixed to the way ahead.

Courtney's heart dropped. She had sensed this moment would come. How could she ever make it sound okay that she never came back to get her? That she *couldn't* come back to get her.

"I couldn't get back in," Courtney said, keeping it simple. "The key disappeared when I exited this world, and I couldn't get back in."

"How could it disappear?"

"I don't know. One minute it was there, the next it wasn't."

"Didn't you have it in your hand?"

"I had the rock in my hand, remember? We both took half and started running."

Tia remained silent for a moment.

"So," she hesitated, "you didn't just leave me here on purpose?"

Courtney looked at her, horrified. "No, of course not! Is that what you think I did? Robert and I tried for months to break down that door so we could get back in here. The key was gone, and nothing we did made the damn thing move a centimetre." She stopped and grabbed both Tia's hands in hers. "My heart broke that day, Tia. I was lost without you. I thought you were dead, gone forever."

Tia looked at Courtney, tears welling in her eyes. "But at some point, you stopped trying."

Courtney cast her gaze down. "Yes."

"You forgot about me."

"Never! I thought about you every single day. I still do."

"But you never came back."

"I couldn't. It wouldn't let me in."

"How long before you stopped trying?" She now sounded angry.

"Tia, we tried for over a year. We searched everywhere for the key. We tried to cut the door down. We tried to melt it. We tried to burn it. We tried everything a teenager could do."

"And then you gave up."

"I had to stop. I was driving myself crazy, trying to get back in. My parents started to notice the circles under my eyes, the restlessness. I was so focused on finding you that I didn't care about anything else. Including myself. I stopped eating, I got sick and eventually ended up bedridden for a month."

Tia looked at Courtney. "That's terrible."

"I know. As much as I missed you, I had to stop, or I would end up killing myself. I'd heard that grief could make you feel that way, but I never knew it to be true until the day we lost each other."

"Did you keep exploring?"

"No. It wasn't the same without you. I never came back again."

"Until now."

"Until now."

"So, Morgan found the door," Tia stated. She let go of one of Courtney's hands and started walking again, the other hand still clutched tightly.

"She did. Robert and I were mortified."

"You married Robert?" Tia asked, a genuine smile on her face.

Courtney nodded. "We watched Morgan closely to see if the door was going to appear for her. I didn't want her to come in and find this terrible world that had destroyed us. We thought we had got away with it until I heard the girls talking in the garden."

"She must've found the key then … if she was able to come in here?" Tia questioned.

"She must have. I wonder where she found it? I don't remember asking her."

"I guess it doesn't matter now. The important thing is that you're here." She looked up at the sky and shivered. "It's getting a bit cool."

Courtney looked around and noticed for the first time that the sun had disappeared. Clouds were moving fast and rapidly filling the sky. They walked a bit faster as the temperature plummeted, and huddled closer together with each step. In silent agreement, they stepped up the pace even further. A few seconds later, an angry wind picked up and started whipping them from all directions.

The temperature continued to fall and they lowered their heads, linked arms and pushed on. Talking became more challenging as the wind whipped their words away before they could reach their destination. And the temperature dropped further until their bodies shivered uncontrollably.

The wind surrounding them blew stronger by the minute, freezing them. Courtney rubbed her hands together to warm them up with little result and they looked at each other with unspoken worry.

Snow? Courtney looked around in disbelief as flakes started to swirl around them. Two minutes ago, it had been a beautiful spring day. Her fingers and nose started to prickle with pins and needles; redness flushed her pale skin; her ears ached from the wind, and her face felt numb. She wasn't dressed for this sort of weather, and her body protested the fact loudly.

Then snowflakes fell faster and harder, spinning through the air and plummeting to the ground. They walked on inches of snow that now covered grass that was visible only five minutes earlier. Before they knew it, it was up past their ankles. Courtney's shoes felt wet and cold, and she quietly added her toes to the list of body parts she could no longer feel. Her face tingled, her hands turned numb and both had gone pale. The wind produced unwanted tears that warmed her cheeks the moment they fell but then soon turned to ice.

"I think I'm getting frostbite," Courtney said, turning to Tia. Tia looked the same – red nose, pale face and more fear in her eyes than Courtney had expected. They needed to get out of the weather, and they needed to do it now. Courtney leaned in and stuttered in her ear. "Sh…sh…shelter!"

Tia nodded and steered her toward a group of

nearby trees. They huddled next to a large oak, using the canopy to hide under. Their arms wrapped around each other as they shivered, their teeth chattering.

"We won't … survive long if … we stay out here much longer," Courtney stammered. Already she could feel herself getting tired, her body using everything it had to stay warm. "Need … to … warm … up." Her breath turned to snow as the words passed her cold lips. And still the wind hammered around them, pushing snowflakes under the treetop to fall around their feet. They weren't going to warm up standing here. "Too … cold …"

Courtney didn't think Tia had heard her as she continued to hug her, staring out over her shoulder. Suddenly, Tia pulled back and grabbed Courtney's hand. She started walking in a different direction.

Where is she taking me? Courtney instantly wondered. *Is the Circle somewhere close? Maybe Tia has finally realised where we are and where we need to go. It's Tia's world, and she would know best.*

Courtney tucked her face in to keep as much of the snow and wind out of it as possible and followed without question.

Chapter 46

Courtney

Before long, they stood in front of a cluster of large boulders that looked like a natural formation. Several large boulders had fallen in such a way as to create a sizeable cave-like area beneath. A small flicker of hope fired up inside as Courtney recognised the possibility of shelter where they could wait out the storm. Tia pulled her straight in.

With the wind blocked, and the snow now unable to drift through the gap, they were finally out of the snowstorm. Courtney pulled the bag off her back and threw it to the ground. Shivering violently, she rubbed her hands together to create some heat.

"I can ... do ... b ... b ... better," Tia struggled to speak a clear sentence. Courtney watched as Tia's shaking hands reached into her bag and pulled out a matchbox. She lit one match and looked around. In the back far corner was the remains of an old tree. They pulled some of the branches to the middle of the cave and threw them in a rough pile. It was the best they could do. Luckily it didn't take long to light, and both Tia and Courtney eagerly sat around their little fire, slowly warming their hands and face. Neither spoke while they thawed out, and Courtney didn't know about Tiana, but she couldn't have spoken even if she'd wanted to. Gradually, she stopped shaking and was able to stand. Her hands still hurt, but she was oh-so grateful to be in front of a fire. Slowly able to move again, she pulled her shoes off, and sat down to rub her feet. Pins and needles returned as the heat and feeling came back.

"Oh my god," Courtney said, "I hate pins and needles, but that feels so good."

"I can't believe how quickly that changed."

"I know."

"We were just lucky to find shelter."

"How did you know this cave was here?" Courtney asked.

"I didn't. I just followed the vision cloud."

"You could see the cloud through all that snow?"

"Yeah, of course. It's my cloud. It's almost like it's a part of me."

"Do you have any idea where we are?"

"Not really. I don't think it's too far away now. But I'm not going back out in that," Tia said, nodding toward the entrance of the cave.

"Not a chance." Courtney agreed. "What's the plan when we get there?"

"I'm guessing we just get back to the middle, where we originally found the stone, and then we put it back together.”

Courtney sat silent for a moment. “Do you think it will be that easy?”

“I hope so. Haven’t we been through enough already?” Tiana replied.

“I know I have.”

They sat, legs crossed, watching each other across the fire.

“Tell me more about Robert,” Tia asked.

“No. Your turn. Tell me what happened to you that day.”

Tia sighed. “It’s a long story.”

“I’d like to know,” Courtney said softly. “Please.”

Tia stared at her through the flames and began her story, keeping her eyes locked on Courtney’s.

“How much do you remember?”

“All of it,” Courtney replied. “It plays over in my mind all the time.”

“Do you remember how we took the floating stone?”

“Yes. Then the ground started to shake, and I dropped the stone, and it broke in two.”

“We took half each and then the strong winds started so we ran.”

“It became a tornado and picked us both up. I got thrown out of this world through the gate and back into the corridor.”

“I didn’t know where you were. One minute it catapulted us into the tornado, the next minute it seemed to stop. I was dropped to the ground, no idea where I was. You were gone, had just disappeared. Everything was silent as I sat there alone. That's when I panicked. What was I going to do? Stuck in a world that I couldn't leave, my friend gone, no idea which direction to even travel in." Tia looked off into the distance as the memories flooded back.

"When I looked around, all I could see was brown grass. That tornado disappeared fast, but it left behind so much destruction. There were trees uprooted everywhere, and it had dug a huge path in the ground."

"That's where we came back in," Courtney said. "Right at the bottom of that valley."

Tia nodded. "I guess that makes sense. If I'm honest, I probably sat there for twenty minutes, crying my eyes out. Eventually, I had to do something, so I started walking along the valley's rim. It was nearly dark when I came across a little cottage in the middle of nowhere. A couple were out front. He was in the rocking chair on the porch, and she was watering the garden."

"Merrin and his wife?" Courtney asked.

Tia nodded. "They took me in, looked after me. It didn't take long for the elements to take control of everything after that. The earth destroyed all the vegetables in the gardens. Water flooded houses. Winds blew down most of the trees and those houses remaining. Blizzards killed a lot of the animals, and the following fires took the rest. These people had nowhere to go. Destruction only took about a month or two.”

“That’s terrible.” Courtney’s heart sank. They’d caused all of this.

“It really was.” She stopped, lost in her thoughts.

Courtney couldn’t imagine watching her world collapse around her, to see so much devastation. How quickly would you lose hope? How long before you gave in to despair and wanted to give up. Her heart ached with guilt.

“Do you feel guilty?” Courtney asked quietly. “I know I do.”

“Every day!” Tia said miserably. “Why do you think I became their Queen in the first place? I broke it; I needed to find a way to fix it.”

“How did that happen?”

“The wizard taught me everything. He handed it all to me.”

“Wizard? What wizard?”

“The Keeper of the Stone. He ruled this world and kept it together.”

“Okay, I’m confused. How did you go from Merrin and the cottage to being the Queen?”

Tia rose and looked through the gap at the front of the cave. “Still snowing,” she said under her breath. She turned to Courtney. “The Keeper lived near the Tree of Safety. When the elements took over, he cast a spell over the tree to protect it and everything in the clouds. People flocked to him for guidance when it happened. He sent them up to start a new life in the City of the Clouds."

"So Merrin and his wife took you there."

"Yes. The Keeper was Merrin's brother." She paused again. "He's been like a father to me."

"Why didn't Merrin take over then?" *Isn't that how it usually worked?*

"He never wanted it. He wanted a simple life with Maggie. That's why the Keeper taught me everything. Merrin said it was foretold in a prophecy that a stranger would come to rule the land. How was I supposed to argue with that?"

"Did you want it?" Courtney asked.

"Not really, but what else was I going to do? Where was I going to go? I'd created this mess. There was no going back for me."

"So, you became the Queen."

"The Keeper died a couple of years afterwards, and Merrin's wife not long after that. He's been loyal to me ever since. I trust him with my life."

Tia sat back down by the fire.

"The girls talk very fondly of him," Courtney said a few moments later. "Now that I've met him, I can see why."

"He's the dad I never had," Tia replied simply. "You know how many foster homes I went through. I hate to say it, but this was almost a blessing for me. Here I feel special. Here I feel important. Here I have a family."

"You had me," Courtney said quietly.

"Not the same." Tia smiled to soften her words.

"You were always there for me, but I needed more. I found it here."

Courtney couldn't stop looking at her. In front of her, she could see the thirteen-year-old girl left behind many years ago, yet the words she spoke gave away a different truth. The way Tia spoke, the way she conducted herself gave away her real age. It was the strangest feeling, to convince yourself that what you were seeing was not just a memory. Part of Courtney felt younger just looking at her, taking her back to the years when they would run to catch the bus to school together. If she were to close her eyes though, it would feel just like they were at home over a coffee.

"What?" Tia asked as she noticed Courtney's stare.

"Nothing," she replied. "It's just bizarre, seeing you as you are, still a teenager."

Tia grinned and then said, "Just think of me as the Childlike Empress in Neverending Story."

They both laughed.

"Any luck dragons in this world?" Courtney asked, still smiling.

"Haven't seen one yet," Tia replied as she stood and looked outside to check on the storm again. "Oh good. It's stopped."

"Good." Courtney heaved a sigh of relief and stood up, pulled on her shoes, and collected her bag. "Let's get out of here."

They gathered their things and put out the fire,

Courtney sorry to see it go.

"Do you know how much further we need to go?"

"I'm pretty sure it's not far," Tia replied as she stepped back into sunshine.

Courtney followed closely, looking around in amazement at the now perfect weather. Where had the storm gone? Any evidence of snow had also disappeared, the ground again an expanse of rolling meadows. The light breeze present was nothing like the howling winds they had battled only minutes ago.

"Let's go quickly," Tia suggested, "before anything else comes along."

Courtney wholeheartedly agreed.

Only minutes later, Courtney's thoughts were interrupted by Tia's fierce grip on her arm. The strength of it made her stop, luckily before she walked straight into her. Tia stood wordless, staring off in the distance.

"What is it?" Courtney asked quickly.

"The Circle," Tia breathed with quiet excitement.

Courtney's head snapped up. From where she stood, she could only just see the peak of a couple of stones. There was no doubt though; she knew it as surely as she knew her own name.

They had found the Circle.

Turning to each other, they grinned, and a weight Courtney didn't even know she was carrying lifted from her. For the first time since entering this world, she felt she could finally achieve something positive. It wasn't a fantasy or a wish. They had a chance at rebuilding this world again. The Circle of Stones stood in front of them, and they held the two pieces that could put it back together.

Not wanting to waste another minute, they moved forward immediately, Courtney clutching her bag a little tighter, not willing to get there and realise she'd dropped her half somewhere along the way.

As they drew closer to the Circle, Courtney saw the shape of the stones more clearly. They halted on top of the last hill, in awe of what was before them. Just as they had been all those years ago, four massive stones stood majestically, creating a perfect circle, guarding a treasure that was no longer there.

"This is it," Courtney whispered.

"Yes." Tia squeezed her hand. "This is where we destroyed the balance of this world, and it's where we will restore it."

"Let's go then." Courtney pushed on, not willing to wait one moment longer, her gaze fixed on the Circle of Stone ahead. So focused on what lay ahead, her other senses muted, she missed the first sounds of trouble. The second crack sifted through her thoughts, and she stopped instantly, spun around, grabbing Tia at the same time.

"Did you hear that?".

"Hear what?" Tia asked, reeling. She hadn't been listening either.

Courtney put a finger over her lips as she strained

to hear it again. "There," she said, "… off to the left.
Did you hear it?"

"Nope. What is it?"

"A crack, like a …"

A loud crack interrupted her sentence.

"… stockwhip," she finished. It wasn't the same
as thunder or even a gunshot. It was more like
something being ripped apart.

"I don't like the sound of that." Tia frowned.

"Me neither," Courtney agreed.

They stood motionless, waiting for whatever
would happen next. Frozen to the spot, fear shut
down all capacity for logical thought.

Another ear-splitting crack erupted, and with it,
the ground shook. Within seconds, a shrieking,
tearing sound followed. Courtney watched in horror
as the earth ripped apart as though invisible hands
were hell-bent on tearing the ground in two. A
crevasse appeared, growing wider as it came closer.
It headed straight for them.

Chapter 47

I sighed and sat down again. *What's taking them so long?*

It had been forever since Mum and Tia had left; they should have been back by now. Rising to my feet again, I walked the floor, the waiting torturous. Merrin came and went, staying busy with other errands, so I was by myself most of the time.

I'd explored the house from top to base, even though I probably shouldn't have. I knew it was rude to poke around in other people's houses, but I'd never been given advice on what to do when you're waiting around for hours for your Mum and her long-lost friend to save a world. *That* is what she should have taught me.

Back and forth I wandered from the fireplace to the door to the kitchen to the window. This house wasn't big enough to contain my energy, my frustration, or my worry. It made me think of zoo animals locked up in those enclosures, instead of out in the world where they had vast tracts of land to explore. Not that I was stuck here – I'm sure I could go outside the house if I wanted to. I just didn't want to. What if they came back and I wasn't here?

Merrin walked back in with some more wood for the fire. He placed it by the mantle, not paying me any attention. At least I thought he wasn't until he said, "Patience, child."

I turned to him. "They're taking forever."

"Not at all," he said. "It will take hours to get there, do what needs to be done and return home safely. They probably aren't even there yet."

I couldn't help it – I groaned out loud, causing Merrin to smile.

"Do you like to read?" he asked.

It seemed like an odd question to ask, but I replied with a "Yes."

"Follow me then." He turned and walked through the one door I hadn't explored, the door Merrin kept using as he went about his business, the one door I'd been afraid of being caught behind. He strode out of the room, and I quickly followed. The door led to a hallway, not unlike the one behind the magic door that had started all this. The house was deceptively large, with doors on both sides. We passed a couple before Merrin stopped and produced a key.

"This is the oldest library in this world," he explained as he swung the door fully open. "You will find many first editions in here, as well as hundreds of wonderful books you've likely never seen or will see again."

The smell hit me first – paper and leather, along with a slight odour of lemon. The walls were lined floor to ceiling with shelves, each shelf full to the brim. A wheeled ladder stood in the corner. This library looked like every grand library I had ever seen on TV, only bigger. I stepped into the room and turned in circles. Slowly, I made my way to one of the shelves, running my hands lightly across a number of spines.

It was indeed unlike anything I had ever seen before or would probably ever see again. When I reached the second corner, I noticed an open doorway, which led to another room, just as big as the first. This library, like the rest of the house, seemed so small from the outside yet inside it went on forever.

"Can I read anything in here?" I said, quietly excited, Mum and Tia temporarily forgotten.

"Of course," Merrin replied. "Be careful, though; some are very old. In the second room, there is a reading seat and table. Take your selection in there to read."

"Thank you," I said.

"You're very welcome. I'll leave you to it, but if you get bored, which I doubt you will, then you can always go back to the main room."

"Thanks, Merrin," I replied absently. I didn't even hear him close the door. How could I ever choose just one? I drifted into the second room, reading spines as I went. My eyes lit up as I spotted one of my favourites, The Wind in the Willows. I gasped as I opened the cover and saw the autograph of the author scrawled inside. Hurrying over to the seat, I settled into the corner and opened to the first page. If I could have chosen any way to pass the time, this would have been it. I sighed happily and began to read.

Chapter 48

Courtney

It would reach them in seconds. Courtney grabbed Tia and jerked her back so hard they both fell to the ground. The split in the earth raced past them, continuing to expand and effectively cutting them off from the Circle. They scrambled back further, not wanting to fall in.

"What the …?" Tia gasped as she pulled her foot back from the edge just as it stopped moving.

"Another attempt to stop us." Courtney shook her head.

The sounds that warned them of something coming now faded in the distance as it continued to tear through the land.

"What do we do now?" Tia despaired.

"We find a way to cross," Courtney replied. "Maybe we can climb in and climb out the other side."

"I'm not going anywhere near it."

"That's okay, I'll check." Lying flat on the

ground, Courtney wriggled closer to the edge until she lay close enough to peer over. Frowning, she studied the walls. Similar to the valley they had first arrived in, the walls of the crevasse were dark soil and not suitable for climbing. Small rivulets of dirt were already falling from its sides and therefore wouldn't hold their weight. Courtney couldn't see the bottom either, the walls melting into black nothingness. She wriggled backward until she felt safe again.

"Can't climb," she announced, sitting up. "We're going to have to go around or over."

"Well, that's better than climbing."

"True. Now, I wonder how far each way this goes?"

"What if we choose the wrong direction?"

"Then I guess we walk for longer."

"What if there's no end?"

"There has to be an end and a beginning," Courtney said.

"And if there's not?" Tia insisted. "We could be walking forever and still never find the end."

"Are you saying you don't want to go around it? Because going over it doesn't look like much of an option either. It must be at least five metres across."

"I don't know!" Tia heaved a breath of frustration. Then she stopped for a moment. "I'm saying that we have to think carefully here. We can't climb the sides. Walking around it might take twenty minutes or twenty days. That leaves going over."

"I can't see anywhere to cross over," Courtney said. "There doesn't seem to be any narrow sections either."

"So, if we can't go through, under, over or around, we've hit a dead end."

"There has to be a way," Courtney muttered under her breath, her brain ticking furiously.

Tia slumped. "It's hopeless."

"Never!" Courtney said firmly. For years she'd drummed into the girls how important it was to look for a silver lining. There was always an optimistic view. You just had to find it.

"Hopeless," Tia repeated.

"It can't be. Our only other option is to turn back and admit that we failed. Do you want to live the rest of your life in a tree? Really?"

"No. I don't want to fail my people either."

"Then we keep thinking until we come up with something. Failure is not an option!"

They sat in silence, staring at the great divide between where they were and where they needed to be. How were they going to make this happen? Courtney's frustration rose that they were so close, yet unable to reach their goal. The Circle was visible from where they sat and only a kilometre or so away.

"Okay," Courtney's logical brain kicked in. "We've ruled out climbing the walls of the crevasse. It's clear the soil won't hold us, besides which I can't see the bottom. So that's out."

Tia nodded. "Over doesn't look like an option

either. No narrow areas, no bridges. Nothing to help us get across."

"Unless Merrin put a bridge in that backpack …"

"Funny," Tia said dryly. "We don't know how far it goes, so it stands to reason it could take days trying to find the end. We don't have enough food with us to last that long."

"We don't have *any* food with us," Courtney corrected.

"Okay, no food," Tia repeated. She sat up suddenly. "But just because there's no bridge here, doesn't mean there's not one further down, right?"

"That's true." Courtney wondered what the chances were of finding a bridge around the corner. *Not very likely*, she thought.

"Maybe we can walk a little way and have a look?"

Courtney shrugged and pulled a face. "I guess it wouldn't hurt. We could leave a marker here, so we know where we were."

"We'll know. The Circle is right across from here."

"So, we go looking for a bridge, or something else we can use to get to the other side."

"It kind of kills two birds with one stone too, because we might find the end. You never know." This time Tia shrugged.

"Well," Courtney said, coming to her feet. "We have nothing to lose by trying, and nothing to gain by sitting here."

"When did you get so smart?" Tia asked.

Courtney laughed and replied, "Thirty years, marriage and two kids will do that to you."

"I'm just glad you're here with me." Tia hugged her.

"Me too," Courtney said, hugging her back. "Now we need to get moving."

And they did, both keeping their attention on the way ahead. Courtney had no expectations of finding a bridge unless the crevasse happened to go right under something as it ran. The conversation they'd had back in the cave ran through the back of her mind: Tia had told her how the elements destroyed the place; she'd said the wind had blown down and killed the trees. Courtney hoped to come across a dead tree or something big enough to bridge the gap. She'd seen smaller branches here and there; maybe they'd be lucky enough to find something a bit bigger up ahead.

They'd walked for about ten minutes when she saw the first tree trunk that might be usable.

"There!" Courtney ran towards it.

"What are you looking at?" Tia said, confused.

Courtney stopped in front of a large, long-dead tree trunk. Its bark had fallen off, leaving behind a smooth surface. It was about 30cm in diameter and attached to nothing at either end. No leaves, no roots.

"Do you think this is five metres long?" Courtney asked.

"Maybe a little more. What are you …?" Then it

dawned on Tia as she realised Courtney's plan. "Do you think we could move it?"

"Let's try." Courtney couldn't contain her excitement. "We need to loosen it from the ground first. Rock it back and forth until it starts to move."

With both hands close to the end of the trunk, they counted down to zero and pushed forward and back, unrelenting in their goal until they finally freed it from the earth. Wiping the sweat from her face, Courtney grinned at Tia.

"We may have just found our bridge."

Tia did one of her funny dances, making Courtney laugh out loud.

"Here's what I'm thinking … there's no way we can lift this and throw it across the gap and reach the other side. We're just not strong enough. BUT … if we can stand it upright, on the edge, we may be able to tip it over so that it lands on the other side."

"Yes! It just might be possible."

"First, we've got to get it to the edge of the crevasse. Let's roll it and move one end to the edge … not too close though. Then we can flip it over."

Without hesitation, they lifted and slid the tree trunk bit by bit. It was hard work, but they eventually reached the crevasse.

"Now to stand it up. We need to make sure it goes up straight so that it falls straight across. If it angles too much, we'll lose it to the bottomless pit."

"How are we going to do that?" Tia asked.

"We'll both lift the end to get it up high enough

for me to get under it, then I will keep moving forward pushing it up because I'm taller. When I have it up, you come in front of me and hold it while I get further under and push it up higher. Like that we should be able to get it standing on its end."

"Okay."

Courtney could feel her back strain as they started to lift the far end of the trunk. It was cumbersome but they pushed, pulled, and jostled it around until they finally had their hands around the trunk in a standing position. They looked at each other, tired but proud of what they had achieved.

"Now the important part," Courtney said. "You ready?"

Tia nodded, and they slowly pushed the trunk forward, making it lean towards the gap. Eventually, it tipped over the point of balance, and they let it go. It was now out of their control. Courtney watched, her fingers crossed, as it completed its fall, landing with a loud thud on the other side of the crevasse. They'd done it. They had built a bridge.

"Wow, it only just made it across," Tia said. "There's not much end on the other side." Indeed, it was only just big enough.

"That's all we need. You go first. You're lighter than me."

That was already apparent in Courtney's head.

"No, you should go first," Tia protested.

"No." Courtney stayed firm. "You're the Queen. If the bridge fails, it's more important that you fulfil this prophecy and restore things."

"But you're girls …"

It hurt Courtney to say it, but she knew this was how it had to be. "They have their father. You make sure Morgan gets back safely. It has to be this way."

Tia studied Courtney closely to see if she was sincere. "Okay," she said. "But it won't come to that."

"Just in case, you should have both stones in your bag." Before she could protest again, Courtney knelt and pulled her half out of the backpack, and handed her rock to Tia.

"What is that?" Tia said.

"What?" Courtney asked.

"I hear something. Do you hear it?"

Courtney paused to listen. It sounded like a train or a wind tunnel.

"What now?" she spat out in frustration.

Not even five seconds had passed when they saw a rush of water heading their way, inside the crevasse. It was moving fast toward them, filling the gap quickly. They wouldn't be climbing now. Courtney wasn't worried; they'd built a bridge that would get them across regardless of what was in the crevasse.

"How is that even possible?" Courtney muttered.

"What do you mean?" Tia asked.

"That crack was bottomless. How can water sit in it?" Courtney watched as the water gushed past them, under their natural bridge, flowing in the direction they'd come.

"I don't know. These elements play by their own rules. Did you find your half?" Tia said just as Courtney pulled it out of her bag.

"Here." She handed it to Tia. "Now go. This water is moving pretty fast. We need to get across and get going."

Tia put the second half of the stone in her bag and fastened the straps tightly.

Courtney followed the river to find the source of the water and found Tia was right. They didn't want to be crossing this if it got any faster.

"At least if we fall, we land in water, and not in a bottomless pit," Courtney tried to lighten the mood.

Tia shot her an evil look as she prepared to start the precarious creep across the log. At that moment, the sound of the water changed. Courtney looked up as a large wave came towards them. *A wave? Really? In a river?* She would not have believed it if she hadn't seen it for herself.

"No!!!!!" Courtney cried out as she realised what was about to happen.

They stood in disbelief as the wave swept away their only chance of getting across the gap. In seconds their bridge was gone.

Chapter 49

Courtney

Silenced once again by the enormity of what just happened, they watched as the tree they had worked so hard to put in place floated away. Despair washed over Courtney as she tried to deal with this latest setback. It had always been important to her to teach her girls to find something positive in everything that happened. Through the years as they had cried in her arms, she had helped them see the possibilities; to find a way through the sadness, the anger, or whatever had happened to bring them to tears.

But even Courtney struggled now. She sank heavily to the ground and lowered her head to her hands. She didn't want Tia to see her like this. Tia was relying on her to get them through, but Courtney didn't know if she had the strength anymore. The control she kept over her life now seemed like an illusion. They were so close, and the closer they got, the more determined the elements were to break them. It felt like something, or someone had been watching them and had moved quickly to put a stop to it.

The sound of rushing water kept intruding on her thoughts. *The damn river is laughing at me.* She knew that was crazy, but it was exactly how she felt. The gurgling rapids mocked her; shamed her for her failure. The sound of the water became almost angry as it raced past them, continual visions of the moment the tree was swept away and floated out of reach played over and over in her mind.

"Courtney," Tia interrupted her thoughts.

Courtney didn't respond.

"Courtney!" Tia said a little more insistently. This time Courtney looked up. "I have an idea, but we need to move fast."

Courtney now gave her full attention.

"Quick, get up!" Tia said, pulling on her arm.

Courtney got to her feet and followed quickly, wondering what Tia was up to.

"Here!" Tia's eyes sparkled with excitement as she pointed out another tree, close to where they'd found the last one. This one was only about three metres end to end.

"It's not long enough," Courtney said, disappointed. She thought Tia had an answer.

"Not to go across," she said impatiently. "They float! We get this to the edge of the water, jump in and hold onto the log. It will float us down the river, and we can swim out close to where we saw the Circle. But on the other side."

Could it work? The picture of their last bridge floating downstream popped into her mind. There was no reason why this one wouldn't do the same.

"We can do this!" Tia had mistaken Courtney's silence for hesitation. The more she thought about it, the more it seemed possible.

"Yes, we can." Courtney nodded.

"But we have to do it now before the water disappears, and we're back to square one." Tia sounded pleased with herself.

"Come on then; help me pull it across." Courtney grabbed one end and waited for Tia to pick up the other. Much lighter, they were able to carry this one to the edge.

"Make sure you hold on tight," Courtney warned her. "As we float down, we need to try to kick across to the other side. As soon as we're close enough, we need to grab hold on the other side and pull ourselves out."

"We should be on the same side then," Tia added.

"Good idea. Let's sit with our backs to the water and fall in backward."

They sat together, tree across their legs, arms wrapped around the trunk.

"Ready?" Courtney looked at her. Tia nodded. "Okay, on three. One, two, three."

They pushed back at the same time.

The cold water hit their backs instantly, almost taking their breath away. They held on tight, not wanting to get swept away, and together kicked their legs to influence the direction of travel. It didn't take them long to drift across the crevasse, and Courtney searched the edge of the bank downstream for an easy exit.

"Can you see the Circle yet?" she yelled at Tia. "Are we close?"

Tia craned her neck to look. "I don't think so," she yelled back. "Wait … hang on … yes! I think I see it!"

"Great!" Courtney retorted, her voice raised. "We need to get off this tree, and soon!" to which Tia nodded. Then Courtney noticed a jagged edge up ahead. It would give a perfect grip to hold onto the side. She nodded toward it with her head, and Tia understood and nodded in return.

It was time to let go, which proved harder than she thought. The water was moving fast; it would be easy to miss the jut and sweep past it with nothing left to hold onto to stay afloat. But they couldn't float along forever. They needed to get to the Circle of Stones, and out of the water before it disappeared. Courtney kept her eyes peeled on that piece of jagged edge, and finally let go.

The water took her much faster than she anticipated, and she almost missed it, barely grabbing hold with her left hand. Holding on with everything she had, she turned her head to see Tia continuing to float downriver.

"Tia!" she screamed as she watched her friend disappear.

Chapter 50

Courtney

Courtney wasn't sure that she'd been heard over the rush of water. She had to get out fast and find Tia. Both hands clutching land, Courtney dragged her body out of the water and rested on the ground for a second, exhausted. But there was no time to waste - she had to help Tia. Scrambling to her feet, she set out down the river, following its flow.

The water ran so fast Courtney couldn't keep up with it, even if she was a world-class sprinter. So she went at her own pace and dearly hoped Tia had managed to get out a little further along. Courtney's heart beat hard in her chest, and a stitch enveloped her side. Not only could she lose her dear friend again, but Tia also held both the stones. If they were gone, there was no hope for this world.

The thought made Courtney move faster.

Within seconds, the water started to slow down and recede. Courtney listened apprehensively as the water stopped as suddenly as it had started, and seemed to drop to the bottom of the fissure and disappear altogether. The emptiness returned. But where was Tia? If she hadn't made it to the edge in time, then she was dead. She would never survive a drop like that. Courtney felt a lump form in her throat. Had she just lost Tia again?

"Tia!" Courtney shouted, running along the edge. "Tia! Answer me!"

Nothing.

She ran faster.

"Tia!" she screamed.

Still nothing.

"Tia! Can you hear me?"

Full-blown panic set in. "Tia!"

A faint sound from up ahead made Courtney push on harder.

"Tia, is that you?"

Hope bloomed as the sound came louder. Someone was calling for help.

"Keep calling so I can find you."

As she went further, Courtney burst into laughter – somewhere Tia was singing the Neverending Story theme song, singing the same line over and over. Relief flooded over her and she kept looking. She came upon Tia sitting on a ledge a couple of metres down and clinging to the crevasse wall.

"What are you doing down there?" she asked, staring down at Tia, still laughing.

"Just hanging out," Tia replied. Her beautiful hair had fallen and had plastered against her face.

Courtney laughed again. "Neverending Story, huh?" She knelt on the edge above Tia.

"It was the only thing I could think of. I kept picturing the horse stuck in the mud. I feel kind of stuck myself."

"It shouldn't be too hard to get you out of there. Grab both my arms and I'll see if I can pull you out." For the first time, Courtney was grateful Tia was only thirteen years old. With their arms locked together, it took Courtney only a minute to haul Tia up. They sat for a moment catching their breath.

"Do you still have the stones?" Courtney asked.

Tia quickly checked and nodded.

"I'm glad that's over," Courtney said with a sigh.

"Me too," Tia agreed, "but we've still got to get to the centre of the stone circle. It's not over yet."

"True." Courtney stood up and reached out to help Tia. "Let's go then."

Determined to finish the quest, they linked arms, staring at the Circle in the distance. With one last check to make sure their backpacks were secured, they headed toward their destination. A strange sound only seconds later made them stop and look back.

The crevasse was gone.

Like it was never there.

They stared at each other for a moment, caught in the realisation that if it had disappeared two minutes earlier, Tia might not be standing here right now. Courtney held her a little tighter. "It's okay," her words sounded hollow even to her.

"I could have ..." Tia couldn't finish her sentence.

"But you didn't."

"No."

"Come on," Courtney dragged her forward. "Let's finish this."

In clear view now, the Circle of Stone lay straight ahead, flanked on both sides by imposing mountain ranges. Steep angles, combined with smooth rock faces forbade any chance of climbing. Courtney studied the path ahead. No matter where she looked, there seemed no way forward other than straight through. She stopped, bringing Tia to a halt with her. She needed more time to think this through. Tia looked at her, eyebrows raised.

"I don't like this. Where did these mountains come from?"

"It's right there!" Tia pointed ahead.

"I know but look at the path to get there."

The sheer size of the rock faces on either side looked overwhelming. "Once we start, there's no turning back. If something goes wrong, which no doubt it will, we can't escape easily. The only way will be back."

"Or forward, which is where we're going anyway," Tia countered.

"So, no matter what happens, we go forward then?"

"We go forward," Tia confirmed, "no matter

what."

"Forward," Courtney repeated. "We may have to move fast once we start."

"I think you're right. There have been too many blocks put in our path. It won't stop now."

"The question is, what is it going to throw at us this time?" Courtney wondered.

"Who knows?" Tia shrugged. "All I know is that we need to get the Peace Stone back to that Circle. My world depends on it."

"And we've gotten through everything so far. We can do this." Courtney nodded and looked at Tia, determination shining bright in her eyes. "Bring it on," she muttered under her breath and took the first step forward, Tia following close behind.

With each step, however, the knot in her chest tightened a little. It was easy to fake bravery; she'd been doing it for years. Those moments in life that make her hold her breath – those were the moments Courtney had taught the girls to swallow their fear and continue their journey. *Fear would only ever hold you back,* she used to tell them. *Take a deep breath and forge ahead,* she would say. *You'll regret it if you don't.*

Now she had to take her own advice. Everything up to this moment had felt possible, but now, she consciously had to make herself take each next step for the first time. With every fibre in her body, she felt something coming – same as the grand finale at a fireworks show, the electricity in the air was thick. Tia seemed oblivious to it as Courtney watched her stride forward, focused solely on reaching the Circle of Stone. She admired Tia for that, wanting badly to move confidently instead of feeling buried under a cloud of dread. *Be brave*, Courtney told herself.

They were now a quarter of the way through. The walls seemed to close in on them as they felt the wind pick up. Strangely, the breeze remained behind them, as if an invisible wall stopped it from going further. Courtney chanced a look back and stopped abruptly.

"Tia," she half-whispered as shock stole her voice.

The path behind them was now gone, replaced by a wall of snow. At least five metres high, it stood where they had been only minutes earlier. That wasn't the shocking part though; after all, they had already been through one ice storm.

"Is that ..." Tia trailed off.

"Fire?" they said simultaneously.

Like a cartoon cloud hovering in one area, the snowstorm was contained only to the entry of the route they were following. Each end slotted in neatly next to the mountains of rock, effectively closing off any retreat. Not only was it still snowing, adding to the height of the snow cap, but as the flakes hit the ground, they burst into flame. Each flame burned bright blue at its base, merging and creating a larger flame. The inside of the flame shimmered green, no doubt an effect from the snowflakes.

Continuing to grow, they watched as the snow

fell, burst into flame then combined with the nearest fire. It didn't take long for the whole mound to light up, hues of blue and green bouncing off the snow as they flourished upon reaching the ground.

"How …?" Tia's words fell silent.

"Notice the wind isn't reaching here either?" Courtney whispered.

"How does snow catch fire? It's impossible."

"Clearly not," Courtney responded, staring at the snowfire.

"I guess we really can't go back now," Tia noted.

"Forward no matter what, right?"

Tia interrupted. "No matter what … but what is that?"

"What?"

"That sound," she replied.

At first, Courtney heard nothing, but soon a deep rumble followed that intensified by the second.

"What *is* that?" Courtney questioned. "It sounds like thunder."

"Or a train."

"There are no tracks out here."

"Since when has anything made sense?"

"True," Courtney admitted. Looking around, she tried to find the source of the next attack. The snowfire continued to fall softly behind them; it wasn't coming from there. The rock walls on either side weren't moving, and neither was the ground. Whatever it was, it was sneaking up on them.

"We should keep moving," Courtney suggested,

worried they would again get stuck in an impossible situation. She tugged Tia's arm and started walking.

Moments later, they heard a large thud behind them and, turning, spotted a large rock where they had been only seconds before. A second rock fell from the sky and landed next to it. Frightened, Courtney looked again to the steep walls on either side. Quiet only seconds before, now a rainfall of rocks rather than water showered them. The stone that hit the ground behind them was tiny compared to some about to rain down.

"Run!" Courtney screamed as a large rock just missed her. Her cross-country training as a fifteen-year-old now came in handy as she dodged and weaved the rocks that continued to fall and land in inconvenient places. Tia stayed close to her, her younger legs keeping up easily. A stone ahead rolled onto the ground and bounced back off a mound of dirt that appeared from nowhere. As they watched horrified, the top of the pile opened, and a flame spurted straight up into the air.

After the first one, mounds popped up everywhere, each one throwing out a spout of flames only seconds after the bank itself formed. They emerged from everywhere, arrows of fire thrown vengefully into the air. Courtney forced her legs to push harder, desperation now controlling her. At least half the ground was littered with fire and boulders, rocks, stones and pebbles. Some even conveniently blocked fire spouts on impact. Where they didn't fall, fires kept erupting.

Her brain worked overtime as she tried to pick a path through the chaotic mess. If the rocks kept falling at this rate, they wouldn't be able to find any safe ground to stand on. Courtney's gaze darted around, not wanting to leave her footing to chance. The last thing she needed was a twisted ankle.

Scanning the earth as she continued to duck and weave, her glance fell to one of the walls, and a slight overhang. She tugged on Tia's shirt and pulled her across until they were safely under the overhang for the moment. Courtney paused to catch a breath while Tiana leaned against the wall next to her, their shallow breaths in sync.

"I haven't run like that in a long time," Tia gasped.

Courtney didn't reply, thinking of the fire she had outrun with Morgan when they'd first come into this world.

"Do you think it will stop?" Tia asked.

"Not … sure," Courtney gasped, her forty-three-year-old lungs trying to catch up with her. "But everything else … has. Eventually."

Finally, she drew a deep breath in.

"The fire," Courtney said with amazement.

"It's everywhere."

"It's the rocks I worry about. Did you see the size of some of those …" A boulder the size of a car dropped right in front of them. "… stones?" she finished.

Tia looked at her, eyes round as saucers. "That's the biggest one yet."

Courtney snuck a look past the boulder toward the Circle.

"We're so close!" She tried to keep the frustration out of her voice, but the constant attacks wore her down – she wasn't sure how much more she could take; she was fast losing hope of a happy ending.

Tia must have heard the resignation in her voice. "Don't give up," Tia urged her, her arms wrapping around Courtney's shoulders. "The world isn't all rainbows and sunshine. You and I know that better than anyone. Life is hard, really hard. We lost each other all those years ago, and to tell you the truth, I never thought I would see you again."

She looked straight into Courtney's eyes. "But guess what? We're here now. We can do this. Together. Life isn't about how hard you can hit. It's about how hard you can get hit and keep going. It's resilience, determination, and drive. That's what success is. Moving forward despite setbacks."

Courtney shook her head, defeated.

"Setbacks, that's all they are. These elements won't stop us. Not when we have each other, and all the determination in the world. There's nothing out there," Tia pointed, "that can stop us. Nothing."

Courtney again saw a Queen. She didn't see her friend in front of her. She saw the leader of this world, the person to keep hope alive for her people. Every outstanding quality she possessed shone out, strong and purposeful. Her difficult life in her younger years had prepared her for this. Bouncing in and out of foster homes, Tia had grown a fantastic resilience that served to motivate them now, and she was right.

"We just need to figure out how to get past this rockfall and then we're practically there." Tia half-smiled.

Courtney scanned the ground. Rocks were strewn everywhere, making a clear pathway impossible. Fire spouts still broke out in random places. Her neck craned, she looked up the rock-face above them to see if there was any pattern to the fall, looking for irregularities, anything that would give them an advantage.

The rocks that continued to fall closer to them were now broader than the rest, yet not quite as big as the one that had dropped right in front of them. The air around them was punctuated with the thuds of stones hitting the ground. She couldn't see a clear path through them.

"The wall?" Tia was studying the length of the wall.

Courtney watched for a minute. "I guess if we stayed up against it, it looks fairly safe. They seem to be bouncing off the wall and landing further out."

"That could work."

"Is there any fire along there though?" Courtney considered.

They watched a moment longer before agreeing

the fires didn't seem to be at the wall itself.

"Alright, let's do it."

Slowly they inched their way out from under the overhang. Tia had swung the backpack in front of her so she could keep her back tight against the rock-face. Courtney did the same. Sidling along, Courtney followed Tia, her hands splayed out feeling the wall behind her. Several rocks fell directly in front of them, at times so close air rushed past their face.

Hope bloomed inside Courtney as she began to think they may actually make it. They were now only a hundred metres from their target. Then the rockfall increased, came thicker and faster as they continued towards the outlet. Large boulders bounced off the walls and rolled into the middle of the valley, each one easily as tall as Courtney. Smaller, finer pebbles rained down, falling around the larger stones, seeming to accurately target them against the wall.

"We need to leave the wall," Tia said, turning her head.

"Why?"

"It's blocked up ahead."

"Where do we go?" Courtney asked, feeling hopeless. Pinned to the wall, she couldn't see the path anymore.

Tia scanned the area then said, "Follow me." She looked up briefly then stepped straight out into the clearing, Courtney having no choice but to follow.

Tia ran an invisible path, ducking between rolling boulders like it was a game of Crash Bandicoot.

Stopping and starting, she navigated the problematic track and they gained ground. Courtney now saw the four inner central stones standing proudly, drawing out the four points of the Circle. Just as she remembered, the four main towers were flanked by several smaller ones, creating four triangles pointing to the sky.

The last time they'd been there, not only had they seen this, they had entered the Circle and taken the stone that hovered above the centrepiece. Last time, they had knocked this world out of balance. This time would be different. It had to be. This world depended on them returning things to normal. There was no room for error. They had to succeed.

Chapter 51

Courtney

Before long, Courtney and Tia stood on the outside of the Circle of Stones, boulders still crashing behind them but no longer able to reach them. The wind began to whip up again, swirling around them with a ferocity that no longer surprised them. Between Courtney, Morgan and Tia, they'd seen almost every elemental storm, crater, waterway, and fire possible. What was a little more wind?

"We need to get the stones out," Courtney yelled loud enough to be heard.

Tia nodded.

"We do this together."

"That's the way it must be," Tia replied, sounding Queen-like again. "It's what the prophecy says."

The prophecy again. Courtney wished she knew the complete divination, but now wasn't the time to worry about it. Tia swung the backpack down and reached in pulled out one half, then the other.

"Ow!" she cried out, clutching her head.

"What?"

"Something hit me," she said, rubbing her head. "Ow!" she wailed again, looking around wildly.

At the same moment, Courtney felt a sharp sting on her arm and glanced down to see a red mark rising rapidly on her bicep. Another one followed only seconds later, hitting her in almost the same spot. This time, however, she saw what had hit her.

"It's hail!" Courtney shouted, and lifted her bag and put it over her head. "… the size of golf balls!"

"Tennis balls," Tia pointed to one that had just missed her. It was the biggest hailstone Courtney had ever seen. She shook her head in disbelief.

"We need to get the Peace Stone back in place. Now!" Courtney bellowed over the howling wind. The hailstones now came from all directions, making it nearly impossible to dodge them. The wind drove them sideways one moment then would suddenly drop so the next one could fall from above. Courtney's legs and arms felt beaten by a baseball bat as the hail bounced off her. Tia didn't fare any better. She desperately tried to protect her face and keep a grip on her half of the Peace Stone. Courtney had had enough! Determinedly, she strode ahead until she was able to slip between two of the triangles and into the Circle.

Inside the Circle, serenity dominated. Courtney turned slowly as the quietness filtered in. No sounds from outside penetrated the perimeter. Neither did the elements at work. She could see the boulders continuing to fall and roll, but she couldn't hear them. The fire spouts continued to splutter, but she couldn't hear those either.

Looking back, Courtney beckoned for Tia to follow her in as she let the bag fall from above her head. She placed it gently on the ground. Slowly, she walked to the nearest tower to take a closer look. A stillness overcame her as she reached out gently to place a hand on the centre tower. Almost immediately, hundreds of symbols started racing under her hand. The symbols glowed yellow against the grey stone tower. Without removing her hand, Courtney looked over her shoulder for Tia, who now stood there round-eyed.

"How is that possible?" she whispered.

"I don't know."

"What happens if you move your hand away?"

"Not sure," Courtney replied and moved her hand. The symbols continued to race.

"They're still there," Tia said in disbelief.

"Didn't the prophecy tell you about this?"

"No."

Courtney walked over to the next tower.

"What are you doing?" Tia questioned.

"I don't know. But something is telling me to touch them all."

"I'll try the next one," Tia said.

Not replying, Courtney reached out and touched the next tower. Symbols immediately began to race across the stone, left to right. The Peace Stone in

Courtney's hand started to warm slightly.

"It's not working!" came the cry from across the other side. *What does that mean?* Courtney wondered. *Why can I activate the symbols but not Tia?*

"Is anything happening to your Peace Stone?" Courtney asked.

"Not that I can tell."

"Mine's getting warmer."

"Can you hear that?" Tia asked as Courtney made her way to the third.

"What do you hear?" Courtney placed her hand on the next tower, watching the symbols again light up.

"A hum," Tiana said. "I can almost feel it go through my body. Can't you feel that?"

Courtney didn't feel anything except the warmth of her half of the Peace Stone. A sense of urgency came over her, and somehow, she knew she had to finish this quickly. She moved to the last tower and laid a hand on its surface.

"It's so loud," Tia complained, her hands clasped on either side of her head. Courtney barely heard her.

The air grew heavy as she slowly stepped back from the final tower. It was time to fix this. With some urgency, Courtney grabbed Tiana and pulled her into the centre.

"We have to do it now!" she said urgently.

"Where?"

"Where we undid it."

They both moved without delay to the altar-like stone in the centre of the Circle. Its surface was dish-shaped like it was meant to hold something. *A Peace Stone perhaps.*

They looked at each other.

"Ready?" Courtney asked.

"Ready."

Carefully bringing the two stones closer, the pieces seemed drawn to each other like a magnet. The nearer they came to the other, the harder it was to hold onto them. Something about this centrepiece drew them together, like puzzle pieces falling into place. The two halves met above the middle of the centre stone and Courtney let go and stepped back. So did Tia. Now complete, the Peace Stone hovered above like it had when they first saw it all those years ago.

The symbols on the four towers raced faster and faster, becoming a blur. The edges of the two pieces began to light up, like a weld sealing them again. They watched as the edges invisibly knitted together. Now complete, every colour of the rainbow replaced the light shining out of the now restored Peace Stone. The stone glowed brightly, letting out one final pulse of light that knocked them both off their feet.

Chapter 52

I sat engrossed in my book, already in by several chapters and wandering the forest with Mole, about to meet the wise Mr Badger. Merrin had been true to his word and had left me alone to read. Time meant nothing as I succumbed to the world of some of my all-time favourite characters. Now and then, my brain registered the ticking of the grandfather clock in the corner of the room. Beyond that, time could have been standing still.

It wasn't until an unfamiliar hum interrupted my thoughts that I chose to look up from the pages. I frowned, puzzled over its source. I felt sure it hadn't been there before I started reading, but then again, I'd been so excited about the library maybe I hadn't noticed it. Even in my distraction, I managed to place a bookmark into the valuable book before I closed it and put it on the table. Mum had taught us the importance of looking after things that weren't ours, and especially now seeing it was a limited edition, signed copy of my favourite tale.

Feet back on the floor, I stood, and despite enjoying my own company, I felt very alone. Unsure of what was happening, I decided to find Merrin again to find out what the hum was – I didn't want to be alone if and when it changed to something else. I'd been in this world long enough to know that nothing was ever what it seemed.

Retracing my steps to the first room, I hurried as the floor began to vibrate in sync with the sound. Before I reached the door, it flew open, Merrin on its other side.

"Something's happening," my voice squeaked.

"Come," he beckoned, holding out his hand.

Scared, I took it quickly and followed him out the door. The floor continued to tremble beneath us, taking away any security I had been feeling. *What's going on?*

Merrin escorted me to the main room and told me to sit, which I did. Then he rushed from the room and returned moments later with Mardella, and placed her on the lounge beside me.

The hum had become intense, drowning out our ability to communicate. I gripped the side of the lounge tightly as the floor shuddered beneath us, and for the first time, I remembered that we were up in the sky with a long way to fall.

Merrin sat across from us, in the chair Tia had occupied the first time I had come; he didn't seem too concerned about the strange things happening around us. I could have sworn the corners of his mouth had turned up in a small smile. *How could he be enjoying this? Doesn't the fact we could fall out of the sky mean anything to him? Maybe he's so old that he isn't afraid to die?* Whatever it was, I didn't share his ideas. I felt petrified.

Suddenly everything stopped. The humming ceased, along with the movement of the floor. I looked over at Merrin, confused.

"What was all that about?" I asked, unimpressed.

"Shhhh." He put a finger to his lips.

I watched Merrin as he watched the room, poised and ready to take action. I didn't know what he would do, but he reminded me of a cat about to pounce on a mouse it had been stalking. He definitely listened for something, almost like he knew what would come next. *Does he know what is happening? Is that why he doesn't seem worried?*

Clueless, I wasn't ready to release my grip on the couch. Before I could move, the room suddenly glowed brightly and let out a pulse of light, blinding me to the point I had to rely on my other senses. Then the floor began to move again, this time with a different sensation – almost a floating feeling. I surrendered and kept my eyes closed until the sense of weightlessness ended.

My vision stayed blurred; I could barely see Merrin standing at the window.

"They did it," he said softly, his voice catching.

My thoughts scrambled madly for a second as I tried to figure out what he meant. Then it clicked in my brain. *They did it. Mum and Queen Tia have put the Peace Stone back in place.*

"Are you sure?" I whispered.

"See for yourself."

At the window, I stared out at the grassy landscape that hadn't been visible previously. Gone were the fluffy clouds, the overgrown and far-reaching branches of the safety tree, these replaced now with rolling green hills, and sunshine – lots of it. I stared in delight as Mardella crowded in behind us to get a glimpse.

"They did it!" I laughed, then started jumping up and down. I leapt toward Merrin and gave him a big hug. "They did it!" I repeated in absolute wonder.

Mardella ran to the door of the house and threw it open. She took a step outside and turned back to face us, her face tilted to the sun. The look on her face, the rapture in her eyes told me all I needed to know. It was real.

Merrin and I followed her out of the house.

Standing outside the door, I took a moment to look around at the rest of the houses. Front doors were opening everywhere as families stood on the ground for the first time in thirty years. Hundreds of faces showed excitement, wonder, disbelief and even a little fear as they dared to step out into a world they had thought they would never see again. Some reached down to feel the grass while others soaked up the sun. Children ran and played and lit up the world with laughter. The whole place felt lighter and freer. It was a new start, a new life, a new world.

Chapter 53

Courtney

Shaking her head, Courtney propped herself up on her elbow and looked for Tia. She was only metres away, sitting up and brushing grass off her clothes and hair. She didn't look injured, and Courtney sighed with relief. Checking herself over and finding no damage, she rose to her feet.

"Do you hear that?" Courtney looked at Tia.

"Hear what? I can hear small sounds, but nothing unusual."

"I know," Courtney grinned.

Tia looked at her, confused.

"There was silence here before," Courtney explained.

"There was too!" Tia smiled back at her. "I got worried for a second. Every time one of us has said that the elements have attacked. I guess I was expecting something else to happen."

"It has." Pride welled up inside Courtney. "Tia, *everything* has happened. Look around. Listen. Feel."

For the first time, Queen Tia took in her surroundings, Courtney watching her face as it changed from confusion to disbelief, and finally to glee. She whipped her head back to Courtney. "It's over," she whispered, her eyes welling with tears.

Not trusting herself to speak, Courtney nodded in agreement.

"The Peace Stone. Look." Tia pointed.

The stone hovered a small distance above the altar, back in its rightful place, bouncing gently against invisible walls. Bright colours bled through the stone, occasionally catching the light and sending off a ray of pink, blue or green. In one piece again, the exterior looked smooth and round. It was indeed one of the most magical things Courtney had ever seen.

"No wonder we took it," she said. "No thirteen-year-old could have resisted that."

"I won't make that mistake again," Tia replied. "I think I'll put guards here just in case."

"Good idea," Courtney agreed. "What now?"

"We go home."

Home. For the first time, Courtney thought about Robert, Amber and Leah waiting patiently for their return. Home sounded like the perfect place to be.

"Sounds good."

They began to leave the Circle. "You know, I don't ever remember seeing those symbols when we were here the first time." Courtney stopped to get a better look.

The centre towers stood about three metres high each, and at least a metre wide. Not far from the top of each was a triangular symbol, each one slightly different. Courtney touched the tower again, this time only feeling cold stone at her fingers. No running languages, no glowing symbols. It was now merely a rock.

"I'm pretty sure that one over there is the alchemical element for fire. It's the only one I remember from school, because of the way the triangle points up." Courtney pointed across the Circle to the opposite side.

"That one you have your hand on," Tia said, "is the symbol of earth. I used to think the line showed the ground, and the triangle represented the tree and the roots growing in the earth. That's how I know it."

"I never looked at it that way," Courtney replied, looking closer. She was right, though. The upside-down triangle with the horizontal line just under halfway was just as Tia had described. If only Courtney had known that in school, she might have passed her tests!

"The others must be water and air, but I don't know which is which."

"Me either." Gazing around one more time, Courtney felt more than ready to leave, the edges of exhaustion creeping over her as the adrenaline began to wear off. "Let's go."

Silently, they left the Circle of Stone. Gone now

were the boulders and the fire mounds. Even the rock faces on either side had disappeared. Now they were surrounded by lush green pasture inundated with gently rolling hills, a land vastly different from what they'd endured on their way to the Circle. A soft breeze blew. Unlike the previous winds they had encountered, this one caressed their faces rather than battering them.

A small part of Courtney continued to search as they began their return journey, waiting for that next element to spring from nowhere and threaten them. But it never came, and each step slightly loosened the tightness in Courtney's chest. Without the elements to delay them, they made it back to the barn in a short amount of time. Courtney automatically veered off towards the barn to head back through the tunnel.

Tia's hand stopped her. "No need to hide now."

"Of course," Courtney said. "What will happen now to all the people up in the clouds?"

"Well," Tia considered for a moment as they walked, "I don't know to be honest. I guess we need to rebuild their homes on the ground. I can't believe anyone would want to stay up there."

"What about the animals?"

"I don't know. Hopefully, there are still some around, hiding."

"Well, either way, I'm happy we were able to fix it." Courtney linked her arm through Tia's.

Tia turned to Courtney and grabbed both her

hands. She stopped and stared straight into her eyes, more sincere than Courtney had seen her.

"No," she said firmly. "*You* did it. None of this would have happened without you. Or Morgan. This world is here now because of you."

"I disagree," Courtney said just as firmly. "We restored everything together. As a team."

"We do make a pretty awesome team," Tia agreed.

"We always did." Courtney hugged her briefly then started walking again.

Less than ten minutes later, they crested a small hill and stopped at the view before them. The Tree of Safety stood before them in the distance. Previously a monstrous tree whose sheer size overwhelmed at first sight, it now appeared dwarfed by its surroundings. An entire city seemed to have been built around its base, stretching out for miles in all directions.

"It's on the ground," Tia said in awe.

"Is that …?"

"Yes. That's our city."

She looked up to the tree's top branches. "Leaves," she breathed.

Courtney followed her line of sight. There were no clouds up there at all – just branches, like any other tree in any other place.

"This is amazing," Courtney exclaimed.

"Let's go!" Tia grabbed her friend's hand. It would be the last time Courtney would be with Tia,

her thirteen-year-old friend. Queen Tia was about to
return to her people.

Chapter 54

I'd been keeping an eye out for Mum and Tia to return since we'd stepped outside the house, and was amazed that they'd succeeded. I guess a part of me had doubted they would, but I was glad to be proven wrong.

People gathered around Merrin, asking questions for which he had no answers. He continued to gently but firmly put them off.

"Where are they?" I asked. "They should be back by now."

"Patience, child."

"I can't help it," I whined.

"They won't be far away."

At that moment, I saw them rounding the corner, a group of people following behind, most likely unnoticed as the two exhausted people stumbled in. The relief I felt at that moment was unmeasurable. They were back!

"Mum!" I shouted and bolted towards her. I slammed into her, engulfed her in a huge bear hug, which she happily returned. Holding her tight, I refused to let go.

"Are you okay?" she asked me, brushing my hair back gently from my face as she used to when I was little.

"Me?" I said in disbelief. "Are *you* okay?"

"You're crying," she pointed out.

"So are you," I replied.

"True, but they're happy tears. I'm fine."

"I'm so happy to see you!" I hugged her again. "Tell me everything!"

"There's plenty of time for that. Come on … I want to see Merrin and Tia."

Mum kept her arm around me and moved over to the crowd, who had gathered around the two of them.

"Please, everyone," she heard Tia saying. "We will celebrate tonight, I promise. Right now, I need to talk to Merrin."

She opened the door to her house and ushered him in, indicating for us to follow.

Before the door was even closed, Queen Tia spoke rapidly. "We have much to do. We need to build roads; better transport now that we are on the ground. We need a Keeper back at the Circle so this does not happen again. The tunnels can stay, as a backup. I hope we never need to use them, but you never know. Did everything drop from above? It all looks like it's still in one piece."

Merrin looked a little overwhelmed as Tia continued. "We need to form a development council. We need to make sure we move forward in the best interests of everyone out there. It will take months, even years, to get back to where we need to be. I'll oversee the council of course. I need to address the people about the prophecy and what has happened. Let them know that it's finally over. I'll do that during celebrations tonight."

She looked around. "Mardella!"

The woman appeared from nowhere.

"Mardella, can you please put together a celebration for everyone in the common area tonight? Get some of the ladies to help. I'll be addressing everyone as the Queen so make sure it's somewhere where I can see everyone."

Mardella nodded and left the room just as fast as she'd entered.

"Have I forgotten anything? I'm sure I have." Tia's energy suddenly disappeared.

"We can brainstorm later. You must be tired." Merrin took her elbow and led her to the lounge. "Sit. I'll go get you some tea – you rest awhile."

She smiled at him wearily and watched him leave the room before she turned to Mum and me.

"You will stay for the celebrations?"

Mum ignored Tia's question. "What did you mean when you said you would oversee the council?"

"I can't leave it to others to run; it needs to be right ... for the future of my people."

"But ... I thought ..." Mum didn't finish her sentence.

"Thought what?" Queen Tia replied.

"Well … that you might come home. With me. With us."

I stayed very still and tried to sink into the cushions and make myself invisible.

"It's been thirty years. Don't you want to come home?" Mum asked her.

Tia sat silent for a moment, unwilling to upset her old friend, then she said, "You're right. It's been thirty years. But in that time I've had to come to terms with the fact that I would never see you or your family again. It took me a long time to make peace with that."

"And now you can come back; you don't need to stay here anymore. I found you."

"No." Tia shook her head sadly. "What about my people? Who will lead them if not me?"

"Merrin will." Mum grasped at straws.

"He doesn't want to. I'm happy here, Courtney, I am."

"But the life you left behind … you could pick it up again. You could come and stay with me – with us. Don't you want that?" The pain in Mum's voice was hard to bear.

"How would that work, Court? I'm still thirteen there. How would I explain that? How can I get identification when my true age is not how I appear? I wouldn't be able to go anywhere or do anything. It just doesn't work." She sighed. "My place is here."

"What …" Mum hesitated. "What … about me?"

This was the real question she had wanted to ask.

"You," Tia started as she moved closer to Mum, "are the most beautiful person I know. You just put your life on the line for thousands of people you don't even know. We were inseparable as kids, and we had a bond that no one could ever break. That will never change, just as it didn't change now, after thirty years. Being in different worlds won't stop us."

The emotion in Mum's face tore at my heart. Usually such a proud person, she now struggled to hold herself together. Her chin trembled to stem the flow of tears that threatened to fall. Her eyes shone with unshed tears and her face had fallen with each word Tia had spoken, somewhere inside knowing it was the truth.

"And while I can't leave here, there's nothing to stop you from returning, right? So, this isn't goodbye – it's see you later."

I saw the moment Mum accepted Tia's decision. She stood taller and squared her shoulders to pull herself together; she lifted her chin a little in defiance. "You're right," she admitted. "I'm sorry. I just can't bear the thought of losing you again."

"You haven't lost me," Tia replied. "You found me. I'm right here. Anytime you need me."

"Can we stay for tonight?" I asked after they had hugged it out.

"You should," Tia said. "After all, you two are the heroes of this story. You should stay and bask in the glory."

"Okay but not for too long. It's been a long day, and our family is waiting for us."

"Yeah, but they'll only be waiting for five minutes," I said.

"True, but it's been a long day, and I'd like to go home," Mum replied.

"Then come to the party, and I will get Merrin to sneak you out and take you back to the gateway," Tia added.

"Deal," Mum said, smiling.

A few hours later, we walked silently under the cold night sky, following Merrin back to the gateway. The party had been fantastic, with plenty of food and a lot of adoration from the guests. Queen Tia had made a big speech about how the prophecy had been fulfilled and made sure we gained recognition for it. She also kept her word and had Merrin sneak us out without attracting attention. Mum had made it very clear that she didn't want another goodbye with Tia and was very happy to melt into the background.

Merrin walked in silence on the trip back, busy with his memories and hopeful plans for the future. As we approached the gate, he turned to us and took a hand in his.

"Thank you," he said simply.

No more words were required. Merrin kissed us each on the cheek, turned and walked away.

Mum looked at me. "You ready to go home?"

"I am."

"Do you still have the key to this door?"

I reached into my pocket and pulled it out, showing her.

"Good," Mum smiled. "I want to come back again."

"I'll bring you back whenever you want, Mum," I said, putting it back in my pocket.

Smiling, I took a step through the gateway, my foot landing back in the dark corridor with Mum right behind me. At the far end, I could already see the glow of my bedroom through the opening and pictured Amber waiting with Dad and Aunt Leah, Amber probably driving the other two crazy. While I felt a little sad to be leaving this world, at least I knew I could come back at any time. I also knew deep down that the world was no longer scary. To be sure, I looked back at the ace of spades on the door and felt nothing.

Chapter 55

Amber

"Honey, sit down," Robert told Amber, although she barely heard him. "You're making me dizzy."

She couldn't help it. Amber had to keep moving, keep busy or her brain would do dumb things like imagine all sorts of horrible things happening to her mother and Morgan. She still felt left out, and it wasn't fair that she was always left behind. *Well, okay, not always*, she admitted inwardly. *But this time, yes.*

Absently, she flipped a coin in her right hand, not even conscious of how smoothly it transitioned between fingers. She'd been working for ages with the coin, and it had finally paid off. She didn't have to think about it moving now. Which was good, because all Amber could think about was that time was almost up and they would be back any second.

"They'll be back soon," she told her dad.

"Pacing won't bring them back any faster," he replied.

"Leave her alone, Rob. She's anxious. Kind of

how I feel right now," Aunt Leah piped up. She was always on the girls' side.

"It's been nearly five minutes." Amber moved past the door for what felt like the hundredth time, peering down the corridor as she passed. Still nothing.

"It has, so they'll be back any minute now," Aunt Leah said, trying to be brave for Amber. Just because Amber was a kid didn't mean she couldn't see the extra wrinkles in her aunt's face or the way she kept looking at the magic door every few seconds. Aunt Leah may have been sitting on Morgan's chair, one elbow back on the desk like she did when relaxing around a pool, but everything else about her showed concern. Just like Amber, she feared the worst. The only thing that was going to fix that was seeing them both step into this room.

"They're coming!" Amber yelled excitedly. She could now see the silhouettes of two people slowly getting larger. Standing just before the doorway, Amber wasn't stupid enough to try to go through, as much as she wanted to. She still remembered what had happened the first time. Robert and Aunt Leah stood up quickly and rushed over to stand behind her.

Robert put a hand on Amber's shoulder, most likely to stop her from jumping up and down. His face appeared over Amber's left shoulder, and she felt his breath near her ear as he released a sigh.

"That's them," he smiled.

"Thank God," Aunt Leah added, wondering who else would be coming down the corridor. Satisfied, she stepped back again.

"Who else would it be?" Amber mirrored her thoughts but she got no answer.

Gradually the shapes increased: black silhouettes became the outlines of her sister and mother as they drew nearer. Eventually, Amber could see their faces, both happy and sad, excited, and exhausted. Finally, they stepped through the doorway and back home again.

Amber threw her arms around Morgan, who was the first to step back into the room; she squeezed her tight. Robert quickly stepped around Amber to wrap Courtney up in his arms. Amber, so glad to see them both again even though they'd only been gone five minutes, was thrilled they were okay.

"Welcome back …" Aunt Leah hugged Mum and squeezed Morgan's shoulder at the same time.

Mum returned the hug and smiled tiredly.

"What happened?" Amber couldn't wait to hear the news.

"Hon, I'm exhausted. It's been a long day. Can we talk in the morning?"

"No way!" Amber cried out as her dad said, "You can't do that to us!"

"I'll make you a coffee." Amber pleaded. "I'll make you two. Please don't make us wait." Not that she knew how to make a coffee, but she was ready to get down on her knees and beg if she had to.

"Okay, okay!" Mum laughed. "Someone make me a coffee, and we'll sit down in the lounge. But then it's off to bed."

"Deal!" Amber shouted and raced off to the lounge to get her favourite seat. This was going to be a remarkable story.

Chapter 56

Even though Amber wanted to hear about our adventures, once we arrived home my body succumbed to fatigue. The adrenaline that had kept us going throughout the day instantly fled. For the first time, I was tempted to accept a coffee just to stay awake, but instead settled for the hot chocolate Aunt Leah made me. Grateful, I wrapped my hands around the mug and sank into the corner of the lounge. It was the most comfortable I had been all day, and if we hadn't just defeated the odds in a strange world while our family waited behind to see if we succeeded or not, I would have fallen straight to sleep.

"Did you do it?" Amber squealed. "You did, didn't you? Did you save them? Was it your friend?"

"Yes, and yes," Mum answered.

"It was her?" Dad looked shocked.

"It was. Tia was just as I remembered her."

Amber fidgeted as she tried to find a place to get comfortable. She fidgeted and watched Mum intently so she didn't miss a thing. I looked around the room, thinking how lucky I was.

"Did you fix the stone?" Amber asked. "How is Merrin? Did he help? Who else did you meet?"

"Slow down!" Mum laughed.

"Start from the beginning," Dad suggested.

"Yes," Aunt Leah agreed. "Don't leave anything out. I want to hear it all."

My mind drifted off as Mum began our tale.

I looked back on everything that had happened since my dreams had started. What a wild ride! So many amazing things had happened. So many friends I'd made along the way, Merrin being the best of all. Despite his age, he had looked after all of us, and never once complained. Merrin had made me feel special. He was like a grandfather to me, and already I couldn't wait until I could go back and see him again.

During the celebrations, he had pulled me aside when Mum was busy with Tia. She hadn't noticed as we slipped around the side of one of the nearby buildings.

"I knew you would come. I never gave up hope." he had said. "You know she was never lost, right? She was exactly where she was meant to be."

Never lost? That reminded me of something I had heard somewhere before.

"Who?"

"Tia. She was not lost."

"Okaaaaay…" Puzzled, it had finally clicked. *All is not lost; she is not lost.* That's the clue I was given in the first two doors I'd gone through. They were talking about Tia!

"*Two must become one,*" I then recited: that had referred to the Peace Stone. I'd been given hints all along. It was meant to happen this way.

Merrin had then reached into his pocket and pulled something out; he had held out a closed fist.

"Take this. Your help is needed here too," he had said, and quickly followed it with, "it's time to go. Wait here; I'll get your mother."

I'd been confused at the time, but now, sitting here in the lounge, surrounded by family and love, it had never been more apparent. I reached into my pocket and felt for the key he had given me – the black key, with its strange symbol at the top, a symbol I hadn't yet seen on any other door. I knew I'd have to tell everyone eventually, but right now I just wanted to relax and enjoy the story we had to tell. That would be my secret for another day.

THE END